PETAWAWA

G.A. SCIBETTA

Petawawa

Copyright © 2024 G.A. Scibetta

Registration number 1213235
Canadian Intellectual Property Office
Category: Literary/Dramatic

All rights reserved. No part of this book may be reproduced or used in any manner without the written permission of the copyright owner except for the use of quotations in review purposes.

This novel is historical fiction. Any names, characters, or incidents are the product of the author's imagination based on historical events. Any reference to real persons or business entities is entirely coincidental as this work is fictional.

Cover Artists
Giustino Scibetta-Lawson
Angelika Promny-Tavares

Book Designer
Alexandra Asada

Editor
Maryssa Gordon

Library and Archives Canada Cataloguing in Publication

Scibetta-Lawson, Giustino
Petawawa
Published: 2024
ISBN: 978-1-7389975-7-2 (Paperback)
ISBN: 978-1-7389975-9-6 (Hardcover)
ISBN: 978-1-7389975-8-9 (E-book)
1. Title
Further data is available upon request.

00 01 11 25

Golden Mile Press

First edition published 2024.
Toronto, Ontario

www.gascibetta.com

To the families separated by accusations.

ACKNOWLEDGMENTS

I would like to extend my heartfelt gratitude to **Dr Michael O'Hagan**. Your extensive published research has been instrumental in filling crucial gaps in historical information, greatly enriching this project. To my editor, **Maryssa Gordon**, your meticulous attention to detail and insightful feedback have been essential to refining this work. I am also grateful to **Library and Archives Canada** for providing the digital versions of the original blueprints of Petawawa. Your resources have been invaluable to the progress of this research. A special thanks to **Joe Baiardo** and **Sam Cino** for everything you do. Your tireless dedication to the Italian-Canadian community is deeply appreciated and has made a significant impact in many lives. Thank you to **Emma Campbell, Megan MacDonald,** and **Sierra Lawson** for being my first beta readers. Your suggestions helped bring the Bucci family to life, and your insights were truly invaluable. I am deeply grateful to **Angelika Promny-Tavares** for putting up with my many annoying voice notes and text messages with plot alterations. Your patience and support have been my lifeline during the writing process. Finally, to my Nonno, **Raffaele Scibetta,** your endless stories of life moving from Sicily to Canada, though after the war, were invaluable in painting an era gone by. Your memories have brought a richness and authenticity to this work that words cannot fully capture.

"Have a heart that never hardens, and a temper that never tires, and a touch that never hurts."

– Charles Dickens

REGNO D'ITALIA

PASSAPORTO

PER L'ESTERO

Il Ministro per gli Affari Esteri rilascia il presente passaporto al Signor __Salvatore Bucci__

accompagnat da __Leonarda Bucci, Emilio Bucci, Raffaele Bucci__

QUESTURA DI AGRIGENTO

COMUNE DI AGRIGENTO

GOVERNMENT OF CANADA INSPECTION

PORT OF ENTRY...... HALIFAX

INSPECTOR......

LANDED IMMIGRANT

DOMINION GOVERNMENT
ONTARIO
IMMIGRATION OFFICE

PETAWAWA

PART ONE

1

1920

The dry air and scorching sun assaulted the town's landscape almost daily—today was no different. Leonarda closed the barn wood door to the Bucci family home behind her as she returned from her daily mother-recommended stroll. The wood, almost as rugged and ancient as Agrigento itself, scratched her delicate fingertips as she touched it. The stairs that led to the main family room were too much for Leonarda to handle, with a nearly developed fetus bursting from her womb. Her body ached with non-existent stab wounds—wounds she swore were real.

Salvatore had moved an old cot and an end table to the ground floor, a set he used when their family came to visit from Racalmuto. He refused to sleep downstairs with his wife despite her many pleas. The upstairs bedroom was much too comfortable for Salvatore, a sacrifice that he did not see fit. In his mind, he believed that Agrigento was safe, that his wife did not need a man to stand guard over her, something Leonarda was indifferent about. Every time the ever-so-slight creak of the wind hit the ground floor shutters, Leonarda's muscles clenched, and her mind raced to the darkest of conclusions. Many women had been attacked in the town, mostly by men who didn't understand the meaning of 'no.'

Leonarda sat on the bed, its springs screaming as her body put pressure on the cold metal. The mattress was archaic, filled with handfuls of dusty feathers that balled up under her back. As she lay down each night, a large crack in the plaster was about the only thing she could focus on. Cold water from a busted pipe in the kitchen dripped onto her face each time Salvatore turned on the faucet. Salvatore swore he would fix the pipe nearly fifty times, but it never got done. Like many things in Agrigento, the Bucci house was exhausted.

The light re-entered Leonarda's eyes in a sudden burst. It was still the afternoon as she glanced out the broken shutter across the poorly lit room. The sparse sunlight bounced off her husband's tools that lay scattered across the floor. The stab wounds felt just as sore as when she had laid down, only this time, a sharp, acute pain began deep inside of her.

As Leonarda's legs drifted inwards, her hamstrings slid across damp bed sheets. The water had soaked into the lumps of feathers beneath her, which, for a moment, made Leonarda believe her husband had been washing dishes upstairs. A sharp internal contraction squeezed her insides, making her grab the iron bed frame for support.

"Salva!" Leonarda yelled.

Salvatore was fixing a broken chair leg that had given out when Fabrizio had been over for drinks. The chair almost sent Fabrizio to God at age twenty-five, something Fabrizio cursed the saints for as his skull collided with the terracotta tiles.

As Salvatore raced down the stairs, his wife's screaming grew exponentially. The bed appeared redder than the Battle of Calatafimi he had read about in history books as Leonarda ripped back the sheets. Her naked body disturbed him, appearing like a corpse on the battlefield. Salvatore had not tried to be intimate with his wife since they found out that she was pregnant, as the thought of a human consuming her from the inside made his stomach churn. Her blood-soaked silhouette was that of an Austrian soldier he blasted at the Piave. He could still see the soldier's face each time he lay in bed at night—gasping for air as the death pooled into his oesophagus. Salvatore remembered the split second between the soldier's arms going up and his own rifle firing, realising now that he didn't have to pull the trigger.

The only thing absent from his memory was the soldier's rifle. Rather, in its place were the cries of Fabrizio as he realised the soldier never possessed one. Instead, his arm had a red cross on a white band—a secret they both swore to take to the grave.

Salvatore paced down the streets like a madman, a pace he hadn't used since his time in the army. The townsfolk gathered around him as he shouted for Dr Massini, the only doctor who serviced their neighbourhood. The blood smeared across Salvatore's shirt made the people of Agrigento wonder if he had been shot—his cries supported their theories, whispering to each other as Salvatore stood helpless in the streets.

Dr Massini had been at the bar drinking his fourth liquid cigarette that he swore he would cut down on. Hearing his name from Salvatore's lips made his head spin across the bar and sent his gaze onto the street as Salvatore was slightly more than a stranger to him. The last time he spoke to Salvatore was at the bedside of Salvatore's dying bisnonna ten years ago.

"Doctor! Please!"

"What's the matter?" Dr Massini asked, approaching the distraught man.

"It's. It's. My wi—" Salvatore said, gasping for oxygen.

"Your wife, Leonarda?"

"Yes!"

Dr Massini's arm was dragged by Salvatore then the two began in a synchronised march towards the Bucci house. The wood door, still propped open, pulled the fabric on the back of Dr Massini's Oxford shirt as the two men entered.

Looking across the room, Dr. Massini met the image of Leonarda with her legs propped vertically up the plaster wall with her back across the bed. Her screaming startled the doctor as he frantically searched for tools of opportunity. Time did not favour Leonarda. The top of a head emerged as she screamed. Her hands gripped the bottom of the bed frame while Dr Massini rushed to her side. Salvatore could not bear the sight and buried his pointy face into the backside of his arm. Blinded, the sounds grew louder, more defined in his mind.

With one final push, the baby's full silhouette slid onto the bed between the wall and Leonarda, the doctor's hand cradling the child from contacting the plaster.

As the soft twilight filled the room, Leonarda sank into the tired embrace of the bed, worn but welcoming. With each painful contraction, her resolve only sharpened like steel tempered in fire. She embraced her role as a mother, surrendering to all the pain that ensued.

Meanwhile, Salvatore stood by her side, his face etched with worry and anticipation. His clenched fists betrayed his sense of helplessness as his heart churned with conflicting emotions, threatening to engulf him in doubt and fear.

The room was shattered by the raw cry of new life—a sound that seemed to bounce off every wall of the house. With the practised precision of a seasoned sailor navigating treacherous waters, Dr Massini delicately sliced the umbilical cord with his pocket knife, setting Leonarda and her baby free. As the newborn's cries pierced the stillness, filling the room with life, Salvatore summoned the courage to meet his child's gaze, his heart fluttering within his chest like a trapped bird seeking escape.

As Salvatore inspected the delicate contours of the newborn's face, he found himself engulfed in a tempest of emotions—a turbulent sea of relief mingled with fear, pride entwined with uncertainty, each emotion vying for dominance within the depths of his soul. The boy had the same mark of evil upon his left cheek—a small birthmark that mimicked Salvatore's Uncle Aldo.

Losing both his parents young, Salvatore bore the scars of his childhood, where his uncle's fists were the only language he understood. It was a vicious cycle that only ended with his uncle's last breath. The most prominent memory was off the mark on Aldo's face being the last thing on Salvatore's mind before crashing down the basement stairs of his uncle's house and then his world going dark. One time was an accident. Once a month, not so much.

Despite the weariness that weighed heavily upon her, Leonarda extended a trembling hand, her fingers brushing against the soft, downy skin of their son. Tears of uncontrolled joy sparkled in her eyes as she whispered his name —Emilio—a name steeped in the richness of Agrigento, Leonarda's Agrigento rather. Emilio was the name of Leonarda's true love, a boy who kissed her behind the duomo in her school years. A boy who left for New York on a floating iron city. A boy unknown to her husband.

As Salvatore stood vigil by their side, his heart a crucible of emotions, he found himself grappling with the weight of Aldo's legacy—a legacy marred by the scars of betrayal and obscured by the shadows of secrets long buried. The uncanny resemblance between Emilio and Salvatore's late uncle, a man whose looming presence cast a long shadow over his past, stirred within him a pot of resentment—a resentment born of wounds left to fester, of scars that refused to heal.

Yet, amidst the tumult of his emotions, Salvatore could not deny the stirrings of paternal instinct that welled within him—a primal longing to protect and provide for the fragile life that lay cradled in Leonarda's arms.

*

Weeks rolled on, and Salvatore found his resentment began to wane—a wrestling match of sorts in his own mind. He knew he wanted to look at Emilio and feel love, to let his paternal instincts kick in, but he couldn't yet. Salvatore noticed that Emilio even had the same eyes as Aldo, piercing and cold.

*

Meanwhile, in a neighbouring villa, the Savoia family celebrated the birth of their own child—a daughter named Floria. Giovanni and Maria Savoia, revered figures in the community, ruled over their expansive estate with a regal air. Their affluence bled through their pores. Their residence, an opulent farmhouse nestled amidst sprawling vineyards and rolling hills, was a testament to their extravagant lifestyle.

With its sprawling gardens, marble fountains, and meticulously manicured shrubs, the Savoia estate stood as a beacon of wealth and sophistication. Every corner of their lavish abode exuded luxury, from the grandiose chandeliers that adorned the ceilings to the intricately carved furniture that filled the rooms. Guests marvelled at the exquisite artwork that adorned the walls, each telling a story of the family's illustrious lineage. Rumours circulated that the Savoia's history was of common linage, that Giovanni fabricated each intricate story that he told about every painting that adorned his hallways.

Giovanni, a savvy olive oil merchant, commanded respect and envy in equal measure for his business expertise. His energy drew people towards him, even those who rather despised him. Maria, his seemingly committed wife, exuded warmth, her presence a soothing balm for all who crossed her path. Her hair, always neatly held up by a golden clip, exposed her dainty neckline—a stark contrast to her brute of a husband.

Giovanni was the tallest man in the town, built like a field ox. His black wavy hair was always combed and gelled, not a single hair out of place. Unlike Salvatore, Giovanni avoided the war. Whispers among townsfolk circulated that Giovanni had a bad leg, but to Salvatore, Giovanni's legs worked just fine.

In the tight-knit community of Agrigento, disdain for the Savoia family ran deep—except for the Buccis. Giovanni had thrown Salvatore a lifeline after the war, providing him with work as a picker that ensured Leonarda was fed. For nine hot hours in the Sicilian sun, Salvatore picked olives until his fingers went numb. When he was picking, Salvatore was given odd jobs to complete by himself around the property that filled his days. All his time alone surfaced vivid pictures of the war, mostly the bloody Austrian medic. He tried for months to draw a rifle in his mind but without any success.

One day, Salvatore swore he saw the medic standing on a ladder over three trees, which was only disproven once he blinked three times. The only thing Salvatore enjoyed about being alone in the grove was the fragrant lemon blossoms from a neighbouring farm that wafted across the hill, the scent reminding him of his life before Uncle Aldo, a life with his mother and their many lemon trees. Salvatore knew that without Giovanni, the Bucci family would be extinct. It was a debt Salvatore knew he could never fully repay.

2

1930

Emilio's curiosity was rather a burden for his father.

In Emilio's eyes, rules were more suggestions than concrete laws by which he was to follow within their house. As Emilio grew, so did the tension between Salvatore and Leonarda. The birth of their second son Raffaele, a couple years following Emilio, had not mended the fractures in their marriage; if anything, it had widened them. Raffaele was a carbon copy of his brother in terms of their looks, each a bearer of the mark of the beast.

Salvatore buried himself in his work, spending long hours in the olive groves of the Savoia estate as much as he could while Leonarda tended to their children. Each day, Salvatore returned home weary and worn, his hands covered in soil and face dripping in sweat. He was made the manager of the estate, looking after all affairs in place of Giovanni, who took up a new hobby of gambling across Europe, only coming home every few months to check in.

In the dimly lit kitchen of the Bucci house, Leonarda sat at the worn wooden table, her hands trembling as she cradled Raffaele in her arms. Salvatore hated that she coddled their almost eight-year-old. Rather, it disgusted him. The flickering flame of an old oil lamp cast eerie shadows on the walls, illuminating the worn faces of Jesus in the faded paintings that adorned the room.

Leonarda's heart yearned for her Emilio, but her oldest son was the closest she knew she would ever come to him.

Salvatore would never be her Emilio; Salvatore would always wear a silver medal. She longed for the warmth of a man's embrace, the reassurance of his presence, but they remained distant, elusive figures shrouded in shadows.

The second he broke through the front door, Salvatore pushed past both of his boys and locked himself in his bedroom, only acknowledging his wife with a simple nod. Leonarda considered herself lucky if her nod was followed by a brisk greeting on some days.

As Emilio grew older, he became increasingly restless, his boundless energy driving him to explore the world beyond the confines of their home. Leonarda watched with a mixture of pride and apprehension as her son ventured further and further afield, his curious gaze fixed on the horizon. In some twisted way, Emilio had the same prideful aura as her Emilio. She knew that Emilio possessed a spirit as wild and untamed as the Sicilian countryside itself, a spirit that could not be contained within the walls of their home.

Outside, the scorching sun beat down mercilessly upon the parched earth, casting a hazy veil over the landscape. The lemon groves shimmered in the heat; their twisted branches were laden with ripe fruit that glistened like drops of gold in the midday sun. It was in these groves that Emilio allowed his untamed nature to flourish, well known to the farmer who owned them. Mr Girgenti had a face as sour as the lemons he grew—eyebrows permanently arched with beady eyes of resentment.

His wife had died thirty years ago of a heart attack, something he blamed Agrigento's rumours for causing. Emilio liked to pick on Mr Girgenti, not maliciously.

Rather, he believed it brought a secret smile to the old man's face behind closed doors. Mr Girgenti would curse at Emilio with every Sicilian swear word that existed, some of them so ancient that even Emilio struggled to understand them.

*

One sweltering afternoon, as the sun dipped low on the horizon, Emilio raced down the streets, nearly knocking over Sister Maria, who had been carrying a stack of pamphlets for Sunday's mass. Racing up the hills towards the city limits with a mischievous twinkle in his eye and a skip in his step, he disappeared into the lemon groves, his laughter echoing through the stillness of the afternoon air. Noticing that Mr Girgenti had been airing out his house, Emilio crawled back onto the road, which led back to the spot his friends usually hung out at.

Unbeknownst to Leonarda, Emilio had befriended a group of local children who roamed the countryside like a pack of wild animals. Together, they embarked on daring escapades, exploring abandoned farmhouses, climbing the rolling hills, and dodging the watchful eyes of their elders. Emilio relished the freedom of their adventures, his heart pounding with each adventure that the gang partook in.

Encouraged by his friends, most of whom were older than him by two to four years, with Floria being the exception, he started participating in mischief and mayhem more frequently. He delighted in tormenting the unsuspecting townsfolk with his reckless antics. From stealing fruit from the market stalls to playing cruel pranks on the local farmers, mostly Mr Girgenti, Emilio and his gang revelled in the chaos he created. Mr Girgenti was one of their favourite amusements.

Under the cover of the unkempt shrubs, the children crossed different rows of lemon trees, intersecting paths as they made their blitz. Today was different. Today, the open windows presented an opportunity like no other.

"Toss it, Emilio!" whispered one of the boys.

Emilio reached his hand into the basket of decomposed tomatoes they had stolen from the bin out back of the fruit market. His fingers let out a wet squishing sound as they pierced the furry red fruits. Winding his hand back, he tossed the first tomato, which splattered across the back door of the house, spraying the wood with seeds, mould, and tomato skin.

"Another!" said Floria, giggling with her request.

This time, Emilio managed to fit two tomatoes in his hand, jamming each in its own respective place. As his arm sprung back, all of the boys began to laugh uncontrollably. The tomatoes' velocity increased as they followed a near-perfect parabolic path, flying through the ground floor window of Mr Girgenti's kitchen.

"My God—Emilio!" a man's voice screeched from inside.

The children, with faces of panic, each began to sprint across the lemon grove like soldiers in retreat. Floria looked back at Emilio but knew she couldn't save him. Emilio, still frozen with his arm in the air, tried to make his legs start, but they didn't cooperate. Collapsing into a ball, Emilio braced for impact, waiting for the old man to burst out with a rifle in hand.

As the tomato-stained door to the farmhouse slammed shut, a violent marching sound approached Emilio, hearing each step grow closer to his body. A slight pinch of his earlobe caused Emilio to ascend by force. Mr Girgenti's sour face scanned the boy's, but Emilio refused to open his eyes.

Despite Emilio's expectations, the old man said nothing at first, shaking his head in disapproval while still gripping Emilio's ear like a vice grip. Guiding Emilio by the ear, Mr Girgenti dragged the boy like a sack of potatoes while townsfolk watched with probing glances.

Reaching the Bucci house, Mr Girgenti had yet to break his silence. Leonarda answered the violent pounds on the door, shrieking when she laid eyes upon her son.

"Tell your husband to come see me after work. I need a word."

"W-What happened?" said Leonarda.

"This is between men," Mr. Girgenti said as he pushed Emilio into Leonarda's arms.

*

Salvatore broke through the door later that afternoon, his stride more aggressive than usual.

"How did you know?" asked Leonarda.

"Where's the boy!"

"Who told you?" she said, disregarding her husband's demand.

"Emilio Bucci! Here! Now!" said Salvatore then he turned to his wife, "This town speaks, does it not?"

Leonarda hung her head, hyper-focusing on her husband's dirty work boots. "He's just a boy, I'm sure he didn't mean it."

Emilio began to shuffle down the stairs, dragging his left foot behind his right at a leisurely pace. He couldn't bear to look at his father.

"I have no words, no words!" said Salvatore. "It's bad enough your mother lets you run wild—"

"Salva, stop!"

"Silence! Both of you!" Salvatore shouted. "This boy has the devil inside of him."

Emilio's face temperature rose twenty degrees, and tears began to bud in the corner of his eyes as he looked up at his father. The glance made Salvatore shudder then his blood began to boil, staring into the eyes of the beast.

"Let's go!" said Salvatore as he slammed his left hand onto his son's shoulders, causing Emilio to flinch.

Dragging Emilio, Salvatore led the sobbing boy out the front door and down the alleyway behind their house. Emilio knew exactly where they were headed and attempted to dig his heels into the hard, dry soil beneath them.

"No, please, no," Emilio said while forcing his legs to stiffen.

"Enough!"

"Please!" said Emilio.

The cellar door swung open, and the rusted hinges made a violent screech that violated the ears of anyone within its proximity. Emilio reached for his father's arm as a last resort, but Salvatore swatted them away.

With one hard shove, Emilio tumbled down the four short steps that led to the cellar, scraping his knees on the last step as he fell. The cellar door slammed behind him, and then Emilio heard the metallic sound of the latch clicking in place as the sunlight vanished. Among him were old wine bottles, a crate of empty jars, and a rusty hammer that had been tossed and forgotten about. Laying in a ball on the floor, Emilio rubbed his bloody knee and then smeared the blood down his leg. His father's footsteps disappeared, yet his mother's cries were faint but still distinguishable.

*

Emilio woke to the slight brush of his non-bloody knee, feeling the sensation of fur. Now adjusted to the light, he glanced down to see a set of beady black eyes and whiskers staring directly at him.

"Rat! Mamma, please! Rat!" Emilio screamed.

The rat, terrified of Emilio's cries, sprinted up the stairs and through the crack in the cellar door. Emilio's calls went unanswered, the outside world silent so he began to hyperventilate. His heavy breathing eventually placed him in a trance, drifting into another dimension.

*

Night fell upon Agrigento, which made Leonarda restless, but Salvatore refused to negotiate with his wife. Despite her pleas to free her son, Salvatore declined to listen.

"Please, he's just a boy!" said Leonarda.

Salvatore shook his head in disgust, then stepped past his wife and walked towards Raffaele's bedroom. He slammed his son's door shut as Raffaele had been awake, trying to eavesdrop on his parents' conversation. The sudden collision of the wood door on its frame started Raffaele, making him jump under the covers. Although sleeping in total darkness freighted him, he knew it was nothing compared to his brother's arrangements.

Peeking out from the covers, Raffaele looked up at the virgin's portrait hung above his headboard and thanked her that he was the one inside. After thanking her, Raffaele sunk into his mattress and began sobbing for his brother. Afraid of alerting his father, he quickly shoved the other pillow over his face to dampen the sound, soaking the feathers inside.

Leonarda waited about twenty minutes until the upstairs level was completely silent. Her husband's door had clicked shut in their bedroom about ten minutes ago, and she knew it took him about five to disappear into the abyss. Silently, she grabbed a loaf of yesterday's bread that was drying out in Salvatore's workshop, which she had planned to turn into breadcrumbs. She thought about going upstairs to the kitchen, but their bedroom was barely divided by a wall thinner than the eucharist. She knew any sudden movement would send the soldier back to the front lines, jumping up to defend his domain.

Closing the front door behind her, Leonarda carried the crusty bread under her arm, the outside scraping her skin like a jagged rock. The door made a slight squeak as the frame met the panel, which made her pause. She waited, pressing her ear against its coarse surface, but inside the house remained still. As she hurried down the alleyway, the scandalous eyes of Mrs Rossi stalked her every movement.

Mrs Rossi was the town's self-elected security guard—the night watch.

The latch to the cellar was stuck as Leonarda tried shoving her index fingernail under the flap to pry it loose. Finally, the latch screamed as it opened, startling her son inside. Leonarda called Emilio's name, but no sounds returned. His eyes reflected the moonlight, staring miles beyond his mother as a single tear fell down his face.

Suddenly, Emilio shot up the stairs and then jumped into his mother's arms, which knocked the loaf onto the first step. Hungry, Emilio descended violently to the loaf, tearing it before Leonarda could speak.

"Thank y—"

"Quiet!" Leonarda said, then placed her index finger on her lips. "Between us, understand?"

Emilio shook his head in agreement, swallowing the bread in unchewed chunks.

"I love you," said Leonarda, bending down to caress her boy's head.

Emilio stopped ravaging the loaf for a moment, then looked up to his mother. "Am I. Am I. Am I."

Leonarda's eyes filled with tears as her son choked on his words.

"Is it true?" asked Emilio. "Am I from th-the devil?"

Leonarda used all her strength and picked up her son, his feet only a few inches off the ground. Without saying a word, she wrapped her arms around him, his tears soaking her shirt. She kissed the top of his head and carried him back to the bottom of the cellar. The urge to defy Salvatore burned like a coal locomotive being fed. Having to place him gently on the ground made her stomach churn.

PETAWAWA

As she left in a hurry, the latch was not shut properly. The moonlight broke through, giving Emilio the nightlight he always needed to sleep—information his gang was forbidden from knowing.

3

Leonarda awoke to the sound of her chatter coming from the room over, her consciousness gradually emerging from the depths of sleep. The morning light filtered through the sheer curtains, casting a soft glow on the room. Stretching languidly, she felt the warmth of the cosy comforter enveloping her. Her gaze drifted to the empty space beside her on the bed, where the sheets were ruffled from her husband's earlier departure.

As Leonarda pushed herself up with her legs still under the covers, her eyes wandered around the room, taking in the familiar sights that surrounded her. A bookshelf stood against one wall, filled with worn paperbacks and cherished trinkets collected over the years. Most of them were Salvatore's books from his childhood. Leonarda opened them occasionally but struggled to put together the meanings and sounds of words aligned in tightly knit lines. Some words she knew, but most were foreign.

Her attention was drawn to the large window that overlooked the rugged backyard garden. It hadn't rained in a month, which made her plants cling on for dear life. A gentle breeze stirred the sheer curtains, allowing the unpleasant fragrance of dry, dusty air to waft into the room.

Leonarda's gaze lingered on the antique vanity nestled in the corner, its ornate mirror reflecting the morning light. It had been a gift from Salvatore's great aunt in Milan from when they got married. The surface was adorned with an array of cosmetics and perfumes, each item meticulously arranged.

Beside the vanity stood a vintage jewellery box, its polished wood gleaming in the sunlight. The only piece that lived inside was her great-grandmother's necklace—a single pearl suspended on a silver chain. Leonarda thought the necklace was quite foul, but she still wore it to please her family when they visited.

With a soft sigh, Leonarda swung her legs over the side of the bed and padded across the terracotta floor to the wardrobe. She pulled open the doors, revealing rows of neatly hung clothing and neatly stacked shoes. Although she had a sufficient wardrobe, Leonarda lived in her apron.

As she made her way towards the bedroom door, Leonarda couldn't help but notice the faint sound of multiple children, which sent her into a panic. The realization that Emilio had, in fact, been imprisoned and that she didn't have a nightmare hit her at once. Leonarda opened the bedroom door and looked into the kitchen, meeting the image of both of her boys sitting at the dining table. Shocked, she called out to her husband for an explanation. Instead, Salvatore was missing. She called down the stairs, yet the ground floor remained silent.

"He's at work," said Raffaele.

"Work?" asked Leonarda, still staring down Emilio, who was averting his eyes from hers. "Emilio—what—how—"

Emilio looked up at the ceiling, still refusing to look at his mother. "He let me out."

Leonarda nodded her head up and down.

"Mamma, he went to work," said Raffaele.

"Did he say why? He doesn't work Saturday," Leonarda asked.

Emilio turned to his brother. "He's not working, stupid, he's—"

"Don't call your brother stupid, Emilio!"

Emilio shrugged then turned to his mother. "He went to the Savoia house after speaking with Mrs Rossi. He looked surprised after she whispered something to him."

Leonarda's face reddened, and her hairline moistened. "Did he say anything?"

"No, nothing!" said Emilio, shrugging.

"Nothing?" Leonarda pressed.

Both Emilio and Raffaele shook their heads in uniform.

Leonarda sat down at the table and hung her head in defeat. Hyper-focusing on the clay tiles, her eyes began to blur as tears formed in the corner of her eyes. Unable to control herself, her sobs began to escape despite her efforts to contain them. Suddenly, the sensation of a small hand rocking on her shoulder in a gentle tap.

"Mamma is everything—" Emilio said but was interrupted.

"Everything is good, Lio."

Emilio hated when his mother called him that as he felt it was a name fit for a baby. Swallowing his pride for his mother's sake, he ignored her comment and wrapped his arms around her back. The embrace made Leonarda's sobs more defined, her head falling onto the tabletop.

The front door swung open, which made Leonarda ascend her chair violently. She quickly rubbed the tears from her eyes and braced herself.

"Salva?"

Salvatore stomped his feet, using his full body weight. "Shit!"

"Wh-What's the matter?" said Leonarda, then she took a deep inhale.

"It's Maria and Floria, they—"

"Maria and Floria?" asked Leonarda as her face regained colour.

"Yes, Maria. She's going. On a boat. To America. Well, to Canada. She's going. She's taking Floria with her," said Salvatore while panting between each sentence.

Emilio collapsed at the top of the stairs and buried his head in the floor.

"Canada?" Leonarda said as her eyes widened. "But what about the olive grove?"

"She isn't telling anybody. I don't think Giovanni knows! She had a signed letter from her uncle and her papers. She's ready to leave. I just—I just don't understand."

"What about your job?" asked Leonarda. "What's going to happen to—"

"I don't know. I'm going to write to Giovanni. He needs to know," said Salvatore.

"What about poor Floria? Emilio will be devastated!"

Emilio ran to his bedroom, leaving a trail of tears in his path. Raffaele began to chase his brother, but the bedroom door shut forcefully in his path. Raffaele knocked hard, but Emilio refused to let his brother witness his tears. Emilio knew that if Raffaele saw him cry, the gang would never let it go.

Leonarda was consumed by a mixture of emotions swirling inside her as she processed the news. Shock, disbelief, worry, and a hint of anger danced within her heart.

She couldn't fathom why Maria would leave so abruptly, taking Floria with her. It felt like a betrayal, not just to Salvatore and herself but to the entire town.

As Salvatore paced back and forth in the living room, muttering to himself, Leonarda felt the weight of responsibility settling on her shoulders. She knew she had to be strong for her family to keep them together. But her mind raced with questions and worries about what the future held.

"Salva, we'll figure this out," Leonarda said, her voice trembling slightly. "We'll talk to Giovanni, see if there's anything we can do to stop Maria from leaving."

Salvatore nodded, though his expression remained tense. "I'll write to him tonight. He needs to know what's happening."

Leonarda placed a hand on his arm, offering what little comfort she could. "And what about Emilio? He's going to take this hard."

Salvatore sighed heavily, running a hand through his hair. "I don't know, Leonarda. I don't know how to help him."

"We'll give him some time," she said softly.

Salvatore nodded, his shoulders sagging with exhaustion. Leonarda could see the worry etched into every line of his face, and she knew she mirrored his expression.

"I'm sorry," Salvatore mumbled.

"Sorry?"

"It didn't have to be just bread," Salvatore said, then pouted.

Leonarda scanned his face as her heart sank.

"I promise I won't be like him. I will try to do better. But that boy needs to stay out of trouble. He needs to stay home until he learns how to act," said Salvatore.

Leonarda nodded her head and then exited the room. On the way to bed, her eyes rolled each time she mocked her husband's voice under her breath.

*

With each passing day, Leonarda watched as Emilio withdrew further into himself. He spent hours holed up in his room, refusing to speak to anyone except Raffaele. She sent Raffaele into Emilio's bedroom with a tray of cookies each day, practising the different recipes that her mother had taught her.

In turbulence, Leonarda always tied her hair back and began baking. Mixing flour in a bowl silenced her thoughts, forcing them to retreat into the deep chambers of her mind. Even though it was only a temporary relief, Leonarda accepted that an hour of silence was better than an hour of chaos.

Meanwhile, Salvatore threw himself into his work at the olive grove, trying to maintain a sense of normalcy in the face of disorder, a refuge from the storm that brewed within. Every day, he returned slightly angrier than the previous, his resentment towards Maria growing parabolic as her departure date neared. His letter to Giovanni's Parisian hotel was returned unopened and covered in dirt. Salvatore had only assumed that Giovanni had been staying there; in fact, he wasn't certain that Giovanni was in Paris at all.

One afternoon, as Salvatore had left to clean out his tools from the Savoia house, Leonarda was hanging laundry out to dry in the warm spring sun. She heard the sound of footsteps approaching from behind and turned to see the silhouette of a woman standing behind a bedsheet, the sight frightening her. Leonarda pulled back the sheets and gasped at the shell of a woman she once knew, her eyes red-rimmed and puffy, a stack of papers clutched tightly in her hand.

"Maria?" Leonarda said, her voice catching in her throat.

Maria rushed forward, wrapping her arms around Leonarda in a tight embrace. "I'm so sorry, Leonarda. I never meant to hurt anyone."

Leonarda felt a surge of anger and confusion rise within her, but she pushed it aside, focusing instead on the woman standing before her, her friend and confidante for so many years.

"Why are you leaving, Maria?" Leonarda asked, her voice barely above a whisper.

Maria pulled away, and her eyes were filled with tears. "I have to, Leonarda. I have no choice. My husband is God knows where, and the money I have, my family has, is drying out. You may think I'm some aristocrat, but that's not the case. I have to look out for my family."

Leonarda searched her friend's face for answers, but all she saw was a throbbing pain. She wanted to understand, to offer her comfort, but the wounds were still too fresh, the betrayal too raw.

"I don't understand, Maria," she said finally, her voice trembling with emotion. "How will my family eat?"

Maria shook her head then her shoulders slumped in defeat. "I understand. But please, Leonarda, know that I never wanted to hurt you or Salvatore or the boys. I had to do what was best for Floria, for both of us."

"So that's it then?"

"There's no money in this country!" Maria shouted. "We can't rely on these damn olives to provide for us all. There's a whole other world out there, America, with lots of opportunity."

Leonarda said nothing. She squinted at Maria in disgust.

"You should come to America, well, Canada. Salvatore can find work, and the boys can go to school in Canada. Emilio could learn to read and write in English. We could live together in the same neighbourhood, start a community out there," Maria said then smiled.

"We have a community here!"

"It's dying, and you know that," Maria said, then pouted.

Leonarda, growing increasingly angry, turned her back on Maria. She folded the last of the sheets and stormed back to the house in a haste stride.

"Think about it," said Maria as Leonarda closed the door behind her.

Maria stumbled away as the dry soil crunched beneath her feet. As she exited the yard, a pile of dust trailed her.

As she put down the laundry basket, Leonarda looked up at the stairs to see Emilio sitting on the third step.

"When are they going, Mamma?" asked Emilio then rested his head in his palm.

"Tonight, Lio. Tonight."

"Will I ever see Floria again?"

Leonarda shoved her front teeth into her lips and swallowed her saliva.

"Will I?" repeated Emilio as he bit down on his fingernails.

"I-I don't. It's possible. Life works in ways we can't understand," Leonarda said.

"Can I go? I know I'm not supposed to be leaving the house because of the—you know."

Leonarda shook her head from side to side. "I'm sorry, but—"

"Mamma, please!" said Emilio as he sprung up from the steps.

Leonarda stared into her son's soul through the passage of his hazelnut eyes. Emerging from the passage was a darkness he was too young to possess.

"I will be right back!"

"Emilio, I know this is hard, but your father—"

"Please!"

Leonarda covered her face with her hand, concealing the tears underneath.

"Please, Mamma," whispered Emilio.

"Come right back, Lio. Right back."

Emilio closed the rugged door behind him, looking left and right to ensure his path was clear. Following the alleyway to the next street over, Emilio's palms filled with sweat, and his shoulders tightened. The scent of bread baking wafted down the alley as saliva pooled in his mouth. As Emilio reached the end of the alley, he began to sprint down the road that led to the Savoia house. The charge made necks turn as he dodged every person in his path.

Reaching the Savoia house, Emilio heard the faint sound of his father's voice coming from across the courtyard. He crouched down beside the stone wall that bordered the house and picked up a pebble from the dry, sandy dirt he lay in. Aiming for Floria's bedroom window, the stone missed, bounced off the wall, but was dampened by landing in an aloe shrub. Emilio reached for another stone, this time nailing Floria's windowpane. The glass vibrated and nearly shattered, causing Floria to rush to the noise. Emilio looked to Floria's window, which began to open.

"Floria," whispered Emilio.

Floria, caught off guard, scanned the courtyard for the noise.

"Floria," repeated Emilio as he waved with his head poked over the wall, catching her eyes.

"What are you doing?"

"Come!"

"Now?" asked Floria, her eyebrows raised.

"Come!"

The back door of the Savoia estate closed gently as Floria emerged. Her white linen dress drifted in the slight breeze—the same breeze that moved her chestnut brown locks. As she crossed the courtyard to the wall that Emilio was hiding behind, Salvatore's voice startled her.

"Where are you going?" asked Salvatore.

"Oh, Mr Bucci, my mother wanted me to go to the market. She needs me to get some more bread."

"Bread?" repeated Salvatore. "Aren't you leaving this evening?"

"My mother said her cousins in Canada don't have good bread. It's not the same she tells me," Floria said, then chuckled.

"I see. Well, if I don't see you tonight, I wish you a safe journey," said Salvatore as he approached to hug her.

"Thank you, Mr Bucci. I'm going to miss you."

Salvatore unwrapped his arms from Floria, and she smiled. As he turned around to return to the tool shed, Floria walked out of the compound and passed Emilio as if he were a ghost. When she reached the next house, Floria motioned for Emilio to follow.

Carefully, Emilio crawled on his arms across the dry soil, the jagged pebbles below him scraping his pasty arms.

Floria grabbed Emilio's hand, dragging him down an alley behind the bakery.

"Where are we going?" said Emilio.

"You tell me!"

"I can't believe you lied to my father like that!"

"Did I lie?" Floria smiled, which repeated on Emilio's face. "The bread in Canada is bad. That is true."

"How do you know?" asked Emilio with a grin.

"I know a lot of things. Don't you ever read your parents' letters?"

"I can't—can't—"

"Spit it out!" Floria said, then smiled.

"I can't read. Well, I can a little bit, but not fast enough," Emilio said, then looked down.

Floria let out a chuckle, which snowballed into a full-blown laugh. The sound made Emilio's cheeks turn a shade of crimson she had never seen before.

"Shut up!"

"I was only teasing. But how can you not read? We read in school all the time," Floria said, then grinned.

"Will you come back to visit me?" Emilio said abruptly.

Floria's smile dropped, her gaze narrowed, and her shoulders wilted.

"Will you?" Emilio repeated.

"Of course. When I'm all grown up, I'm going to travel the globe like Christopher Columbus, going from place to place," Floria said as she motioned her arms around the invisible globe in front of them.

"Who's that?"

"You can't be serious, Emilio?" Floria giggled.

"Shush!" Emilio replied, then lightly shoved Floria into the wall of the alley.

"You should read more," Floria said, then laughed.

Emilio mocked her voice, repeating her with added bass and slowness. "I'm going to miss you, Floria."

"Are you sure? I can be mean."

"I'm going to miss you being mean," Emilio asserted.

Floria leaned over to hug Emilio and then planted a swift kiss on his right cheek. As her lips made contact, Emilio's body was constricted, and his hairline was filled with sweat. As Floria pulled away, Emilio grabbed her to extend the embrace. As he finally pulled away, Floria whispered something he couldn't make out. Crying, Emilio wiped his tears onto his dusty shirt.

Floria began running, but Emilio couldn't catch her. He screamed her name, but her stride didn't lessen. As she turned the corner, Emilio called out one last time.

"Until next time!" Floria yelled, her eyes red and puffy.

4

1933

It had been nearly three years since Salvatore had made contact with Giovanni Savoia. Secretly, Leonarda had been writing to Maria after nine months of silence since her departure. The olive grove had become one with nature; the grasses were almost half the height of the olive trees themselves.

As for the Savoia residence, the charred remains of a once-regal estate were all that was left. Last year, vandals threw alcohol-soaked linen rags that they had ignited through a hole in the boards. The rugged stone walls remained but the interior was destroyed. Mrs Rossi watched the entire scene play out, yet her weathered legs prevented her from getting help in time. In the ashes, Salvatore's last fibre of hope turned to dust. The Agrigento he knew was no more.

Jobless, Salvatore had no choice but to beg for small jobs around the town. Fortunately, the town's butcher, Massimo, offered Salvatore a job packaging meat. While this didn't provide the life they once had under the tenure of the Savoias, Salvatore did everything he could to ensure his family was fed. To Emilio and Raffaele, he ensured they remained ignorant of their finances. Leonarda did not share the same sentiment; rather, she talked about money openly with her sons.

Despite the hardships, Salvatore found comfort in the routine of his work at the butcher shop. Each morning, he'd rise before dawn, the cool air biting at his skin as he made his way through the narrow streets of Agrigento. The aroma of freshly baked bread mingled with the scent of fish from the nearby sea, a reminder of the simplicity and beauty that still existed amidst the ruins.

At the butcher shop, Salvatore threw himself into his tasks with pride, his hands swiftly moving to package the cuts of meat with practised efficiency. When he first started, he lacked speed but realised speed was the only thing preventing starvation. Massimo, the butcher, took notice of Salvatore's work ethic, often praising him for his reliability. Though the pay was low, Salvatore was grateful for the opportunity to provide for his family once again, even if it meant sacrifice.

Meanwhile, Leonarda's letters to Maria remained a source of both comfort and longing. In her correspondence, she painted vivid pictures of their lives in Agrigento, sparing no detail of the challenges they faced or the memories they cherished. She contemplated lying, hoping that she could convince Maria to return to some fairy tale she had fabricated, but Leonarda shredded each draft that contained falsity.

Maria, thousands of miles away in Hamilton, held onto each letter as a lifeline connecting her to her childhood friend and the life they once shared. She kept each letter in an old biscuit tin on her desk. The letter informing her about her old house being set ablaze was the only one she didn't keep; rather, she ignited it after wiping away the single tear drop that formed in her eye.

Maria kept Floria ignorant of the fire, thinking that telling her would do unnecessary harm. In her letters, Maria informed Leonarda of the fact she had not heard from Giovanni, with Leonarda confirming the same. They crafted outlandish theories; among those were that he had blown his money in some casino and taken a new wife. Another theory Maria had was that Giovanni had ripped off some powerful people, and they collected their gambling debts from him. In truth, neither cared.

Emilio and Raffaele, unaware of the true extent of their family's struggles, carried on with the innocence of childhood. Although they knew there had been some changes due to their mother's rants, they didn't grasp the entire picture. Together, the Bucci brothers roamed the streets of Agrigento, their laughter echoing through the stone alleys as they played games of football and explored hidden corners of the ancient city. As time progressed, more houses became abandoned, offering exploration expeditions for the boys. Salvatore, watching his sons with a mixture of pride and sorrow, hoped to shield them from the harsh realities of their new life for as long as he could.

As the days turned into weeks and the weeks into months, Salvatore clung to the hope that someday, somehow, they would find a way to rebuild what they had lost. He had asked Massimo many times for a raise, yet despite Massimo's wishes to provide one, there was a lack of money. In place of a raise, Massimo, a well-connected man, made promises to Salvatore that he would eventually lend him a hand. The butcher shop could barely afford the staff they had, as Massimo often lived on less income than his workers, so Salvatore took his promise with a grain of salt.

*

One evening, Salvatore came through the front door with a smile for the first time in years. His feet lightly bounced off of the floors as his body ascended the stairs. Leonarda had been frying fish in a shallow pan of rancid olive oil. Years ago, the oil would have been discarded, but wasting food became impossible. The scent filled the air with a slightly sour aroma, causing Emilio to pinch his nose each time he entered the kitchen.

The scent of reused, old oil was so foul that Emilio hid in his bedroom when his mother was cooking. Sitting at the table was Raffaele, who had been drawing a picture of an olive tree in his sketchbook. His sketchbook consisted of twenty loose pieces of paper glued between a flap of leather from his mother's old, torn handbag. The pages often fell out, which Raffaele had to fix with a half-dried-out bottle of glue from his father's workshop downstairs.

As Raffaele looked up, he caught his father's giddy stare. Raffaele, caught off guard by the sight, closed his book and waited for his father to speak.

"Salva?" Leonarda said with a look of confusion. "You don't usually come home for another hour."

"Today is a different day. Today is different," Salvatore replied.

"Did you lose your job again?" asked Raffaele, then smirked.

Salvatore lifted his hand in the air to smack his son from across the room, swiping at the air while clenching his teeth from afar.

"Sorry, I was only joking."

"Raffaele, that's not funny!" added Leonarda.

Salvatore rushed to the table, slamming down a brown paper folder that nearly knocked over Raffaele's water glass. Hastily opening the folder, Salvatore pulled out a green booklet, the cover making a scraping sound as it rubbed against the paper.

"What's this?" asked Raffaele. "Passport, for what?"

Leonarda rushed to the table, her eyebrows raised, and her pupils widened. Her eyes scanned the document, but her brain could not comprehend it.

"There's more!" said Salvatore as he reached into his trouser pockets and then tossed a smaller envelope onto the table.

"S-S," Leonarda said as she read out loud but stopped on the rest of the name.

"Yes, that's right, the SS Serenità Blu," said Salvatore. "We're going to Canada!"

Leonarda's complexion went ghostly pale, and her eyes unfocused.

"To Canada?" asked Raffaele. "Why Canada?"

Hearing the commotion from his bedroom, Emilio burst through the door like a child on Christmas morning.

"How did you get these?" Leonarda said, managing to string words together.

"Massimo's cousin from Palermo bought them for us and sent them here. I have to pay him back eventually."

"How—what—why—" Leonarda stuttered.

"Are we really going to Canada?" Emilio asked, then grinned. "Are we leaving forever?"

"I found work in Hamilton. Massimo has a cousin who moved to Canada a few years ago, and he owns a butcher shop there, Giuseppe. He's going to make me a manager."

"I'm not leaving!" said Raffaele as he slammed his fists on the table. "My friends are here. My life is here. I'm staying here!"

Salvatore let out a laugh and then turned to Raffaele. "Good luck to you."

Leonarda pulled Salvatore aside while the boys remained dumbfounded, both analysing the tickets. Salvatore dodged every question she had, disregarding her concerns in a snarky tone. Despite her reasons to remain, Salvatore considered none of them.

*

The week after, Salvatore began saying his farewells, making his rounds around Agrigento. Fabrizio took the news the hardest, as he cried in front of Salvatore for the first time since the Alps. He had followed Salvatore to Sicily as nothing remained of Fabrizio's family at home. As a parting gift, Fabrizio tried to give Salvatore his standard-issue pocketknife that he had carved his first initial into.

On the battlefield, Salvatore had lost his knife when an Austrian soldier knocked it from his hand, the mud consuming it instantly. As Salvatore placed his hand on the knife, a thousand memories surfaced, causing him to break down in the middle of the street. Accepting the gift with a mixture of gratitude and reluctance, Salvatore felt a flood of memories wash over him once again as he felt the knife weigh down his trousers. Each notch and scratch on the knife's surface seemed to tell a story, a reminder of the moments they had shared—the triumphs, the losses, the unspoken. Yet, amidst the rush of emotions, Salvatore couldn't shake the feeling of unworthiness that gnawed at his conscience.

Sensing his friend's unrest, Fabrizio insisted, gently placing the knife back into its sheath and slipping it into Salvatore's trouser pocket.

With a red face, Salvatore embraced Fabrizio one last time, vowing to carry the memory of their bond with him wherever he went.

As Salvatore turned the corner, the weight of the knife in his pocket seemed to anchor him to the ground, each step forward a struggle. The streets he had tracked countless times now felt unfamiliar, with every corner whispering echoes of memories past. He looked at the cathedral, its steps covered in family members. Some departed. He saw baby Emilio dressed in white, followed by Leonarda and Father Gianni. Father's hair was brown again, and he didn't walk with a limp.

Salvatore shook his head, and they all disintegrated; the stairs were vacant once again. Looking to the left, Salvatore's eyes met the image of a toddler-sized Raffaele, Leonarda, chasing after him as he sprinted. Her cries were followed by laughter as she caught up to their son. As Salvatore called out to his family, their images vanished. Looking again, the only person in the square was Mr Caruso, sitting against a building with a cigarette hanging from his mouth. Salvatore waved, yet Mr Caruso's weathered eyes couldn't make out shapes past his own arms.

As he passed by the fruit market, where they shopped every week, he noticed his wife had been arguing with one of the vendors about the price increase of cucuzza. Leonarda was dressed in a sundress she hadn't worn in years. Behind her was a small Emilio who had been on the ground, picking through the rotten fruits. Salvatore cursed Emilio's name, but as he did, the vendor looked up, and his family was gone. He shook his head once again, and the vendor stared until he turned the corner. Salvatore couldn't help but feel he had made the wrong decision, contemplating terminating the move.

He reached his hands into his pockets, but they sank deeper than he remembered, only feeling a few loose coins. Startled by their vacancy, Salvatore's heart rate increased, and his stomach tied into a knot. The life he once knew died years ago, and he knew it, yet a part of his brain did not wish to accept such a reality.

As Salvatore walked, the hours passed by almost unnoticed. He felt the sea breeze get closer; the aroma of fish infiltrated his nostrils, one of his favourite scents. As he reached the beach, Salvatore sat in the sand, his sweat-soaked clothing bonded with the sand below him. The view was the first thing he was sold on when making the move to Sicily from Milan. Leonarda's beauty aided in his decision to move, yet the tranquil blue sea sealed the deal.

He remembered the first time she brought him here—two children untainted by the world. His family had been travelling to the island when they met in the piazza, Leonarda's chestnut hair blowing in the breeze. The lightning strike of love captivated Salvatore as he and Leonarda stayed in touch after he had returned to Milan. His uncle called him mad, constantly pointing out that a pure Milanese woman would suit him better and that Salvatore was degrading their blood.

After the war, Salvatore didn't believe in such an idea; everyone bled the same; he saw it firsthand. The second the war ended, instead of returning to Milan, he fled to Leonarda, his vacation sweetheart. His uncle never returned the letter he sent, yet Salvatore felt it in his bones that he had received it. Leonarda's family was not impressed with him being a soldier, yet they knew he was her only chance at marriage. The strings had been pulled to place Leonarda in a convent had she not taken a husband despite her wishes.

Reflecting on the past, Salvatore turned his gaze towards the horizon, where the sky met the sea in a blaze of fiery colours. The uncharted sea before him filled his heart with anxiety and comfort simultaneously. He grabbed the knife from his pocket, his hand trembling as he did, and removed it from the sheath. Aiming his hand back, his gaze was directed at the sea in front.

As Salvatore began his throw, his arm stopped before he could release the knife, death gripping the handle, preventing its flight. Salvatore placed the knife back in its sheath and collapsed to the sand beneath him, sobbing as he lay on his back.

5

Neither Emilio nor Raffaele had seen the big city in their lives. Palermo's bustling streets of thousands brought more anxiety than excitement. In Agrigento, life moved at a slower pace, where everyone knew everyone else's business. But here, in the heart of the capital, they were just two faces lost among a sea of strangers.

The air was thick with the aroma of horse excrement baking in the streets, mingling with the pungent scent of fish from the nearby markets. Narrow alleys twisted like tangled yarn, each corner revealing a new spectacle: merchants haggling over prices, children playing games with makeshift toys, and women gossiping over laundry hung out to dry.

Despite the vibrant chaos, Emilio and Raffaele couldn't shake the feeling of displacement, of being adrift in a city that swallowed them whole. They longed for the familiar comfort of home, where the sun dipped below the horizon, painting the sky in hues of orange and pink and the sound of silence.

But here, in Palermo, amidst the towering buildings and harshness of voices, they were confronted with the harsh reality of urban life, where they couldn't trust anyone, something Salvatore reminded them of constantly. And as they wandered the intricate streets, their hearts heavy with longing, they clung to each other. While Emilio blended in with the other children, Raffaele hid in their room most days, terrified of the world outside.

As Leonarda walked past the innkeeper, he motioned for her to come to his desk. His glare appeared irate, yet she knew he had been paid.

"That boy, the one who was with you before, do you know what he did?" asked the innkeeper.

"Boy?" Leonarda repeated, her head tilted to the left.

"Don't play games with me. The boy, the one who came in with you?"

"Surely, you are mistaken!" Leonarda said as she raised her eyebrows.

Emilio came running down the stairs into the lobby, shocked to see his mother.

"That boy!" yelled the innkeeper.

Leonarda's face went red, her eyes shifting to the ground.

"Mamma! I was just about to go play with some boys down the street. They invited me to play a game of—" said Emilio as Leonarda cut him off.

"What did you do to this poor man?"

"He knocked over a vase with his ball. It shattered into a thousand pieces. He never bothered to even acknowledge me; rather, he shrugged his shoulders and ran into the streets with the other boys. A boy like him is too old to not apologise. This is going to cost you greatly!"

Emilio hung his head and closed his eyes.

"Please, sir, whatever you do, let's keep this between us. I will settle this, but my husband cannot know," said Leonarda, placing her hands gently down on the desk.

"Do you understand how much that vase was worth?"

Leonarda leaned in as the innkeeper motioned for her to. As he told her, Leonarda's complexion was drained of colour.

"I didn't mean to. It was an accident," Emilio whispered to himself.

"I will settle this; please, give me a day. We don't leave for two days."

"Alright, one day, no more."

Leonarda sent Emilio back to the room. As Emilio walked past the desk, the innkeeper stared at him and shook his head, causing Emilio to choke.

As she walked down the street, Leonarda took in the sights of Palermo. She couldn't help but feel overwhelmed by the chaotic energy of the city. The air was muggy, causing her hair to become wiry like that of a stray.

A boy selling newspapers handed her one, then demanded money, its headlines an open Mussolini love letter, yet was of no interest to her. Leonarda handed the paper back, the boy looking defeated as she did.

"Please, just buy one. My boss told me I can't leave until I get rid of this stack," said the boy, sadly looking at his pile.

Leonarda looked into his soul, his eyes not much older than Raffaele. "Alright, just one."

As she turned the corner, Leonarda ditched the paper in a bin, not bothering to look at a single picture. As she walked past the Massimo Theatre, she was alarmed to see a group of protestors waving signs she could not make out. They appeared angry but excited at the same time, their faces red and puffy from their continuous screaming.

Leonarda's gaze fell upon a jewellery store nestled down an alleyway. The façade was daunting, with iron bars covering the windows. If it hadn't been for the sign out front, it could easily be mistaken for a small prison. The front door had a brass frame, yet the metal had a patina that matched the weathered aesthetic.

With a sense of resolve, she stepped inside, the screaming brass rubbing on itself and announcing her arrival. Inside, she found herself surrounded by glittering displays of gold and precious stones, each piece from years gone by.

As she inspected the offerings, her mind raced with memories. A ring stood out to her, as she had seen it on her grandmother, who had long been gone. The entire store was her grandmother's style, stuck in an era she wished she could forget. The only person inside was a man, about seventy, sitting behind a glass display case. His bald head pointed downward, and Leonarda realised he was asleep.

Placing her grandmother's necklace down on the counter with force, the man awoke instantly.

"Good morning," Leonarda said, then looked at the necklace.

The old man, still half asleep, stumbled out of his seat and walked a few steps towards the counter.

"That's incredible! The necklace is a very fine piece you have," said the man.

"How much?" Leonarda said hastily.

"Hold on a minute. We can talk about that in a moment, but first, I must introduce myself."

"How much?"

"My name is Mr Tabone, but please call me Claudio."

"Leonarda. Leonarda Bucci," she said rashly. "Now, how much would you buy this for?"

"Well, that depends. I would need to grade the pearl and determine the type of silver used in this piece. If it's what I think it is, we could have a whole other—"

"If you won't give me a price, I will have to go down the street. A man offered me fifty thousand lire."

Claudio chuckled, then placed his hand on the pearl, rubbing it between his index finger and thumb. "Well, fifty thousand lire is a fair price, but I wouldn't take such a low offer if I were you."

Leonarda's pupils dilated, and she swallowed the saliva in her throat.

"Do you understand what this is?" asked Claudio.

"Yes, it was my grandmother's necklace. Quite honestly, I find it rather dated. I never wear it," Leonarda said while pushing her hair back behind her ear. "Gold is my colour," she said while exposing her earrings.

"Gold is your colour; that is true," said Claudio with a smile. "But you must understand what you have here. This necklace, and I don't know if it's her necklace for certain, may have belonged to Queen Maria Carolina of Naples and Sicily or somebody in her court."

Leonarda looked at Claudio, expecting a laugh, but he didn't give her one.

"I don't understand, that's not possible. My grandmother was poor all of her life."

"I can tell because of the clasp; see how it closes. She preferred this clasp so that it didn't catch on her—"

"That's not possible!" Leonarda shouted.

"Leonarda, I have been in the business for fifty years, and I am very serious when it comes to jewellery. Now, I can't verify the authenticity without having my partner here. He won't be here for another three days, but—"

"I can't wait three days; I need to get rid of it today!"

"Well, in that case, I'm prepared to offer you slightly less than you would like. I can do half a million lire, nothing more."

Leonarda, still in shock, shook Claudio's hand.

"Does your husband know you are selling this? I better get his permission first."

"I'm afraid he's dead. His soul departed years ago at the Piave River."

Claudio hung his head, and a single tear formed in his eye.

"I'm fine by myself, truly," Leonarda said as her stomach tied in a knot.

"M-My son, Roberto. He also died while fighting. I told him many times that war is not a game and that he could be hurt, but he refused to listen. Yet, here we are, both without our loved ones."

Leonarda felt dizzy, her neck tightening as she grabbed onto the counter for support.

"I'm very sorry. Now, where were we?" Claudio said as he wiped his eyes.

Leonarda placed her hands on the necklace yet felt nothing.

"Ah, yes, I will be back in just a moment."

A minute later, Claudio returned with a stack of money—more than Leonarda had seen at once. As he counted it, she felt, for the first time, shameful. In the corner of her eye was her grandmother's ghost, shaking her head as Claudio handed her the money. When Leonarda turned around, her grandmother vanished into oblivion.

As she exited the store and walked down the street, her ounce of guilt vanished. In its place, excitement flourished. Leonarda quickly shoved the money into her bag, burying it below her paperwork.

Leonarda hurried back to the inn, her steps light with the weight of newfound possibilities. The weight of the money in her bag seemed to anchor her to reality, a tangible reminder that things did not matter; only her sons did. Yet, with each step, she felt a surge of liberation, shedding the shackles of her grandmother's judgement.

Pushing open the heavy wooden door of the inn, Leonarda was greeted by the newly familiar scent of cooking and the low murmur of voices. The innkeeper was gone, yet his energy lingered. She made her way to their room, eager to share the news with Emilio. But as she climbed the creaky stairs, her excitement waned, replaced by a sense of apprehension.

Emilio was sitting on the edge of the bed, his back hunched and his head tilted down. Emilio's eyes were fixed on the floor, and his expression was like that of a soldier who had returned from battle. Leonarda's heart clenched at the sight of him, and she hurried to his side, kneeling down to meet his gaze.

"Mamma," Emilio mumbled.

"Emilio, what's wrong?" Leonarda asked, her voice soft and concerned.

Emilio looked up, his eyes glistening with unshed tears. "Mamma, I'm sorry," he whispered, his voice barely audible.

Leonarda's heart broke at the sight of her son's distress. She reached out and gently lifted his chin, forcing him to meet her gaze. "What happened, Emilio? You can tell me."

Emilio took a shaky breath, his words tumbling out in a rush. He recounted the incident with the innkeeper, his voice trembling with emotion as he described the vase shattering into a thousand pieces. Leonarda listened in silence, her heart aching for her son's anguish.

"Lio, it's just a vase. There will be many more vases displayed in that lobby and many more children like you who accidentally break it," Leonarda said, then grinned.

"Yes, but when does it stop?"

"Stop?" Leonarda repeated.

"I'm a bad person. I have the devil inside of me," Emilio said, then pouted.

"That's not true, Lio. You—"

"He tells me all the time!"

"Your father? What does your father know about the devil? Did you know that when your father was a boy, he used to get into all kinds of trouble? He used to tell me stories about his days as a boy when—I better not tell you; please disregard that."

Emilio smiled, then looked into his mother's eyes. "Tell me what?"

"You're a good boy, Lio. Don't ever forget that," said Leonarda while stroking her son's hair.

Emilio wrapped his arms around his mother, inhaling the scent of her rose-scented perfume.

PETAWAWA

*

In the evening, Salvatore had returned to the room with Raffaele, both of them laughing and well-fed. They brought back a bag with two loaves of bread, with Salvatore explaining that the bread in Canada was going to be different and that this would be the last chance they had to eat what they knew. Reluctant, Leonarda tore a piece of the loaf off for Emilio, then fed herself. She hated the way bread sat in her stomach, yet the fear of the unknown made her eat some.

Later, Salvatore fell asleep with Raffaele in his arms. Emilio had fallen asleep beside Leonarda, yet she couldn't commit to it yet. Her eyes remained open, and her thoughts remained persistent.

Quietly, Leonarda moved the paper-thin bed sheet from her body and placed it on her son's. The room was ancient, the floor creaking as she placed her feet down. The stale air seemed to suffocate her. In her nightwear, Leonarda slipped into the hallway, closing their room door behind her. She reached into her bag and counted a few bills. Still in disbelief, she pulled the money out and held it up to her face. The smell of crusty paper bills hit her nose with a peculiar smell, yet the smell loosened her muscles.

As she made her way into the lobby, she noticed the innkeeper had been doing paperwork at this desk. Leonarda tapped on its surface, and the innkeeper looked up at her. His ocean eyes and the slight shadow of a beard softened his rather unpleasant face.

"Here, the money; count it if you must," Leonarda said with her eyebrows raised.

"I'm surprised. To tell you the truth, I never expected to see the money. Thank you, thank you very much."

"I'm a woman that keeps her promises," Leonarda said, then smiled.

"Very well."

As Leonarda shuffled back to the room, a shadow began trailing her from a dark spot in the stairwell. Tired, she shook her head, expecting the shadow to vanish.

As she ascended the stairs and into her hallway, the shadow moved closer, sending a chill down Leonarda's spine. Suddenly, a hand, unknown to Leonarda, wrapped around her mouth while an arm wrapped around her waist. Leonarda attempted to scream, but the sound was muffled by the thickness of the fingers, suffocating her. The arm around her waist tightened, and then the two tumbled to the ground.

"Silence," whispered a man's voice.

Leonarda thrashed, making the man spread his legs on her to hold Leonarda down.

"It will only be a second, I promise," whispered the man.

Leonarda heard his trousers slide down his legs, and then his penis touched her legs. She bit down with force on his fingers, and he growled. As he pulled his hand from her mouth to inspect the damage, Leonarda took a deep breath.

"Salva! Salva!"

"Silence, you whore!" yelled the man while wiping his bloody fingers on his shirt.

"Salva!"

Salvatore, alarmed by her screaming, awoke to see Leonarda's space disturbed and her body missing. He quickly shot up and ruptured through the door into the hallway.

"Salva, here!"

Salvatore looked down the hallway to find his wife underneath a man with long black hair and no trousers. His pale bottom reflected the moonlight from the window in the hall.

Salvatore began sprinting fiercely, faster than he did when being shot at by the Austrians. His hands made contact with the back of the man's shirt, lifting him vertically like a corpse on the battlefield.

Leonarda shuffled away and curled into a ball, yet her clothing remained intact and untainted.

Salvatore dropped the man on his face, then kicked his groin with his dominant foot. The man let out a scream that caused the rooms along the hallway to awaken. The shuffling of footsteps echoed in each room, and a few doors began to open.

Once again, Salvatore kicked the man again, yet this time, his foot became stuck between the man's legs with his testicles underneath Salvatore's toes. Pressing his weight down, the man was neutered instantly. As Salvatore lifted his toes, the man's head dropped, and he fell into the abyss.

Hearing the commotion, the innkeeper rushed up the stairs and gasped. Salvatore, along with a woman who had heard the entire scene unfold, explained everything. The innkeeper, wide-eyed with shock, quickly apologised to Leonarda and Salvatore for the horrific incident that occurred under his roof. He expressed deep regret and assured them that such a thing had never happened before and would never happen again. Salvatore, still seething with rage, demanded that the man be taken to the authorities immediately. The innkeeper nodded vigorously, apologising again.

Meanwhile, Leonarda sat trembling on the floor, her mind reeling from the experience. Salvatore rushed to her side, kissing her head and holding her in his hands, his anger momentarily replaced.

Salvatore helped Leonarda to her feet and led her back to their room. Once inside, he insisted that they leave Palermo immediately, not wanting to spend another moment in a place tainted by such horror.

"One more day, one more day, and we are gone," said Leonarda while looking at the ship tickets.

"It couldn't come soon enough," Salvatore said, wiping the sweat from his forehead.

Raffaele and Emilio sat up, awoken by the commotion, both with faces of distress.

"Mamma, what happened?" asked Emilio.

"There was—" Salvatore began before being cut short.

"I fell and hit my head, that's all," said Leonarda while holding her head in her hand.

"Fell?" repeated Raffaele.

"Yes, now get back to bed, you two. We have a busy week ahead of us. Take all the rest you can now."

6

The SS Serenità Blu rested elegantly in the energetic harbour of Palermo; its grand silhouette captured the attention of all who passed by. Echoing the luxury and grandeur of its sister ships, the majestic vessel boasted an impressive length, longer than any ship to ever leave the city. Her hull was painted a pristine white with a striking navy blue stripe running along its length.

The decks towered above the hull and had been adorned with intricate details, including gold filigree accents around the windows and doors, reminiscent of the elegance seen in postcards from England, but never Sicily, not the Sicily known to the Bucci family. Four tall, black-topped funnels, each with a distinctive red and gold band around their bases, towered above the decks.

Along the decks, polished mahogany railings gleamed under the Mediterranean sun. The lifeboats, painted in matching white with navy trim, had been neatly arranged along the sides, each bearing SS Serenità Blu in ornate gold lettering. Large, decorative portholes had lined the hull, their brass fittings shining brightly. The grand promenade deck was only open to those of first-class status, a spectacle that hid the horridness of the third class below. In contrast, the third-class areas lacked everything seen from the shore; nothing shined where the light did not reach.

Salvatore handed his tickets over to the officer responsible, and then he called each family member listed on the travel documents. Stamping the pages, the officer wished the Bucci family a safe journey, smiling at Emilio as he had been staring at the office intensely during the entire interaction.

Leonarda carried both her sons' bags, their entire lives contained inside. Her mind was still so fixated on the man with long black hair that she failed to realise where she was and the significance of it all. She looked down at Raffaele, who had been pouting the entire day leading up to their departure. The pain he felt transferred to her, travelling between their bodies through magnetic forces.

As Salvatore led his family down a narrow, dark corridor, he read out the stateroom number that had been punched on their tickets. Second deck, room seventeen. The door to the room was a plain cream colour, lacking any ornate features from the decks above. As the door swung open, Salvatore looked left to see two cots stacked on top of each other, smaller than he slept on during basic training. To the right, a small closet contained a sink basin, but missing was a toilet. This, he had been told by a crew member, was down the corridor to the left, a shared space for their entire deck. To the right of the sink was his wife's bed, and on top was his.

Emilio's eyes fluttered as he took in the room, standing behind his father timidly.

"It will be cosy, but this is home for the next couple of weeks," Salvatore said, then smiled.

"Cosy? Our washroom is larger than this," Emilio said with widened eyes.

"Take me home! Take me home," Raffaele demanded.

Salvatore smiled again, then said to his son, "You're looking at home. This is it."

"No, take me home!" repeated Raffaele.

Leonarda slid her hand on Raffaele's back, then patted his head. "Now, Raffaele, I understand this may not be ideal, but when we get off this boat, we will have a new home in Canada. There's going to be plenty of space in our new home, and you will learn to love it. I promise."

"Come unpack your things and choose a bed," Salvatore said, then took a deep breath. "We will make the best of this; I know we will."

After unpacking their belongings, Leonarda took both of her boys up to the top decks to wave farewell to the ancient island they had always called home. She wanted to see her beauty for the last time and marvel at the sights she had known for her entire life. Deep down, her feelings were those of Raffaele's, but she knew that she had to do what was best for Salvatore. The weight of her homeland being ripped from her heartstrings was immense, but she hid it well with her motherly smile.

As they approached Deck Nine, Emilio led the way, following the signs posted on the walls. Attempting to step onto the promenade, a man dressed in uniform stepped in front of Emilio, blocking his path.

"I'm sorry, son, but this area is off limits, I'm afraid," said the man, scanning Emilio's loose white button-down shirt and beige trousers with disgust.

"Oh, but we were just going to step outside to see—" explained Emilio as the man chimed in.

"Son, this area is not for you."

"Excuse me, is there a problem?" asked Leonarda as she caught up.

"Madam, this area is strictly for our passengers in first class. I'm truly sorry, but you and your family will not be able to come through this way, unfortunately," said the man while adjusting his crimson cap.

"I don't understand; we are paying passengers. Why not?" returned Leonarda, her face scrunching and her eyebrows pointing down. "How do you know we are not in first class?"

The man attempted to contain his giggle, shoving his teeth into his bottom lip.

"I just want to say goodbye," said Raffaele, his eyes beginning to turn red.

Leonarda reached her hand into her bag and flashed a few bills at the man, saying, "Can't you look the other way? Just this once, and I will never disturb you again."

"Madam, if you try to go through this way, you will leave me no choice but to fetch the ship's master-at-arms. I do not wish to do that, Madam, so please leave at once."

"Bastard!" shouted Emilio, then panicked, anticipating that his mother would smack him.

"Bastard!" repeated Leonarda, then smiled at her boys.

"Bastard! You're a bastard!" said Raffaele, then giggled.

The man shook his head and then said, "Please, take these feral sons of yours back down to cargo amongst the other—Sicilians." He scoffed. "I do not want to see you anywhere here!"

"Sicilians? I will have you know that my sons are half Milanese. Their father is practically royalty," said Leonarda angrily. "Are there no Sicilians in first class then?"

"There are a few, but those ones are—how should I say it, civilised."

Leonarda spit on the ground beside the man, purposely missing his decorative leather shoes. He looked up at her and shook his head once again.

The three of them mocked the man on the way down to deck seven, laughing hysterically together. Leonarda knew that had her husband heard her boys speak in such a manner that she would be in trouble, but her worries dissolved, knowing her sons needed the release. Emilio questioned her comments about them being royalty, but Leonarda just chuckled, explaining that it was justifiable to lie in the face of fools.

Deck Seven's darkness contrasted with its affluent counterpart. The lights were sparse, and the furnishings, or lack thereof, consisted of a few hard wooden benches and white, sterile walls. The corridor that led to the outside smelled of mildew and fresh paint, the combination of the two assaulting those who strolled for too long. The exterior portion of the floor was bare—not even a place to rest and take in the view.

The deck informed those who used it that they were not welcome in every way possible. Iron bars, painted white, covered the only part that allowed third-class passengers to look out. As Raffaele had not begun puberty, his boyish figure could not see over the rail, so Leonarda lifted him for a brief minute to wish his farewell, all that she could take physically.

"I don't want to leave," said Raffaele, stomping his feet.

"Oh, will you shut up? Do you think that I want to leave? Do you think that our parents want to leave?" Emilio shouted while shaking his head. "What don't you understand in that thick head of yours? There's nothing for us here. Nothing. So please, if for the next couple of weeks while we sail the seven seas on this stupid boat, would you at least do me a favour and shut your mouth?"

"Lio!"

"What! You know it's true, Mamma; you know it's what you want to say, but you won't!" Emilio said, then collapsed into a ball on the wooden deck below him, tears streaming down his face as he buried his head into his knees tightly.

Leonarda jumped down to comfort her son, but he wouldn't release his form.

"You're a bastard. You really are," said Raffaele, his shoulders tightening as he took a deep breath.

"Enough, both of you! Now, we are going back to the room, and you both are going to not say a word to each other. Do you understand?" Leonarda declared.

"I will not go back to that dungeon," said Raffaele.

Emilio's face changed, letting out a slight smirk as he lay on the deck.

"You will because I am your mother and I—"

Emilio cut his mother short with an ill-mannered laugh, unable to control himself. "It is a dungeon, isn't it, Raf?"

Raffaele smiled at his brother in agreement, causing Leonarda to exhale the tension built in her shoulders.

"Let's go; dinner will be soon. We must not keep your father waiting," said Leonarda with a defeated tone.

*

Later in the night, the entire family, with stomachs full of inexpensive starches, lay asleep in their cots. Emilio could not sleep as he lay on his back, staring at the bunk above him. He could make out the initials of the passengers before him, each scraped into the paint in a chaotic handwritten mess. He scraped his fingernail across the paint, which flaked as soon as he touched it, and began carving his own. After he marked his domain, the urge to urinate grew exponentially inside. As he looked over at his father, Emilio could tell he was in a deep state of sleep and that waking him was not something he considered a good idea.

Slipping on a pair of shoes, Emilio quietly opened the door to the long corridor and clicked the door shut behind him gently. His nightwear, a pair of blue and white striped pyjamas, the only set he owned, appeared grey in the dim lighting, concealing the tattered fabric.

The hallway was eerily silent, the only sounds being the distant rumble of the ship's engines and the soft creaking of the wooden floor beneath his feet. Emilio moved cautiously, his eyes scanning the dimly lit corridor for any signs of life.

As he turned a corner, he froze. A pair of tiny, glinting eyes stared back at him from the shadows. It was a rat, its whiskers twitching as it assessed him with the same level of curiosity.

Startled, Emilio took a step back, nearly stumbling over his own feet. The rat, equally spooked, scampered away into a small gap in the wall. Emilio's heart pounded in his chest as he tried to steady his breathing. He continued down the hall, more aware of every creak and groan of the ship around him.

A few doors down, Emilio spotted a figure about his height. The boy was leaning against the wall, his face partially obscured by the shadows. Emilio's initial fear was replaced by curiosity as he approached.

"Hello?" he called out softly.

The boy turned, revealing a face that was both familiar and foreign. He had the same look of weariness that Emilio saw in his own reflection, the kind that came from travel. The boy nodded in response.

"I'm Emilio," he said, offering a small smile to ease the tension. "I was just on my way to the washroom."

The boy hesitated before replying, "I'm Giacomo." His voice had a noticeable stutter, which made the simple introduction seem like a monumental effort.

"Nice to meet you, Giacomo," Emilio said kindly, hoping to make him feel at ease. "Are you from Sicily too?"

Giacomo nodded. "Yes, Racalmuto, w-we're going to H-Halifax. My f-family and I."

"How do you feel about that?" asked Emilio.

Giacomo's eyes shifted away, avoiding the question. He shrugged, a gesture that spoke volumes. Emilio understood the unspoken words; they all had mixed feelings about this journey.

To break the uncomfortable silence, Giacomo began to share stories he'd heard about Canada. "D-Did you know," he started, his voice a little stronger now, "that Canadians l-live in houses m-made of ice?"

Emilio's eyes widened. "Really? Ice houses?"

Giacomo nodded solemnly. "And that it n-never stops snowing," he continued, his tone so sincere that Emilio couldn't help but begin to believe him.

"Wow," Emilio said, imagining a land of endless snow and ice.

Giacomo seemed pleased that Emilio was taking his stories seriously. "Y-Yes, and the w-wolves there are as b-big as horses. They eat people wh-whole," he added.

Emilio listened intently, captivated by the fantastical image of Canada that Giacomo was painting. In the back of his mind, he knew some of these things couldn't be true, but the sheer wonder of it all made him want to believe.

After a while, Giacomo excused himself and continued on his way, leaving Emilio to finish his original mission. The washroom was as bleak and uninviting as he expected, but the urgency of his need outweighed his discomfort. Once relieved, he quickly made his way back to the cabin, his mind still buzzing with the myths Giacomo had shared.

Emilio lay in bed and imagined himself in Canada, braving the harsh winters and living in an icehouse. The idea seemed absurd, but it was a distraction from the uncertainty of his real future.

The ship rocked gently, and Emilio could hear the soft snores of his father nearby. He turned to his side, trying to find a comfortable position. Despite the late hour and the exhaustion that clung to him, sleep remained impossible. His mind was a whirlpool of images and possibilities, each more fantastical than the last. In the dark, with the low hum of the ship filling his ears, he let his imagination take over. For a while, he wasn't a boy on a crowded ship heading to an unknown land; he was an explorer.

7

The dining hall was crammed; people packed shoulder to shoulder under the dim, flickering lights. Leonarda hated eating in the windowless room, making Salvatore bring her back a piece or two of stale bread for her to eat in the room. The scene reminded her of her childhood, with her grandmother feeding her cousins around her large wood table, all twenty of them bouncing elbows as they ate. The difference was that the food her grandmother made had soul, filled with flavour and love. The dining hall food was bland, cold, and past its prime.

Emilio passed a crusty roll to his father after knocking it on the table to show its age. Salvatore shook his head, promising the boys that this was only temporary. Raffaele refused to eat more than a few bites each meal, his figure beginning to disappear with each day at sea.

"I want to go home," said Raffaele while poking his bowl of slop with the end of his spoon.

Emilio looked at his brother's discontented face and said, "Me too."

The slop was unrecognisable; its grey-brownish appearance and lack of scent confused everyone. Salvatore assured his sons that in Canada, food was abundant.

"Meats, cheeses, fruits, anything you could ever dream of," said Salvatore, motioning his arms as he described the foods.

"What about the bread?" Emilio said with a smile.

"Well, there is bread, but it's not the same as what we know."

Raffaele looked down into his slop and noticed a long, thick, black hair. Its curled appearance made him gag.

Salvatore stuck his fingers into the slop and picked up the hair. The hair was half-coated, sticking to his fingers by itself.

"Can we not be fed a decent meal?" said Salvatore as he rose from his seat, triggering a few passengers to look up at him. "Would you believe the shit they call food? A hair in my son's food! Is this what we paid for?" he yelled as his face turned bright red.

A crew member rushed from behind a corner, investigating the commotion.

"Sir, please sit down. We don't want any trouble," the crew member said, his voice calm but firm.

Salvatore, still fuming, glared at the crew member. "No trouble? My sons are being fed rubbish! Do you call this food?" He held up the bowl, the hair dangling from his fingers, drawing gasps and disgusted murmurs from the passengers nearby.

"Sir, I understand your frustration," the crew member replied, taking a cautious step closer. "But causing a stir won't help. We are doing our best with the supplies we have."

Salvatore sighed, lowering the bowl. "Your best isn't good enough," he muttered, sitting back down. The crew member gave a small nod and retreated, leaving the family with their inadequate meal

*

Later in the day, Emilio started feeling uneasy. The gentle rocking of the ship that lulled him to sleep now churned his stomach. He tried to ignore it, thinking it was just the bad food, but as the hours passed, the queasiness grew worse.

By evening, Emilio was pale and clammy, lying on his bunk in their small cabin. Leonarda noticed his discomfort and quickly moved to his side, placing a cool hand on his forehead. "Lio, what's wrong?" she asked as she rubbed his head.

"I don't feel well, Mamma," Emilio mumbled, closing his eyes tightly as another wave of nausea hit him. "I think —I think—" Emilio dry-heaved, nothing exiting his mouth.

Leonarda shook her head, thinking of the animal festering in his stomach. The confines of their room seemed to close in on her as she realised there was little she could do to make him comfortable.

Salvatore entered the stateroom, his face still flushed. "What's happening?" he asked, noticing Emilio's condition.

"He's seasick," Leonarda explained, gently stroking Emilio's hair. "Can you find something, anything that might help?"

Salvatore nodded and left the room, determined to find something to ease his son's suffering. Meanwhile, Raffaele sat on his bunk, watching his brother with a mix of worry and helplessness.

Leonarda continued to comfort Emilio, whispering soothing words and holding his hand. The ship's movements felt more pronounced in their windowless confines;

every creak and groan of the vessel seemed to echo Emilio's discomfort.

As Salvatore followed the corridor to the dining hall, he noticed a queue had formed. Seven people stood motionless in front of him, each ordering their drinks at a leisurely pace.

"May I?" said Salvatore, stepping in front of the group.

"Sir, you have been causing quite an issue today with us. Now, as you can see, there is a queue of people waiting to be served, so please return to the back," said the same crewmember from breakfast while shaking his head.

"Please, it's my son!" Salvatore said with panic in his voice. "He's sick; your food makes him sick!"

"Sir, if you would be so kind as to keep your voice down, that would be most appreciated," said the crewmember while fixing his hair. "Now, please, return to the end."

"No, let him order," said the old woman behind Salvatore with a soft, motherly voice.

"Thank you," mumbled Salvatore, then turned back around to face the crew member. "Please, just a cup of tea, something to ease his stomach."

"Tea? What kind of tea?"

Salvatore had never been asked that question before, catching him off guard.

"Tea, any tea you have."

The cook behind the counter reached for a plain white teacup, different from the ones on the upper decks in their ornate gold and florals, then placed it on the counter. Salvatore took the cup, carefully trying to balance the saucer as he carried it back to the room.

Bursting through the door, Salvatore quickly handed the cup to Emilio, who appeared three shades lighter than before.

Emilio put the cup up to his lips, took a sip, then spit across the entire room, soaking Leonarda in tea. As he began to dry heave once again, Leonarda handed him a bowl she made Raffaele steal from the dining hall, and Emilio expelled three days' worth of slop into the bowl, rancid air filling the room. The scent made Raffaele gag while Salvatore groaned.

"Th-There was an onion in th-the tea," cried Emilio.

"An onion?" inquired Salvatore, his body filling with heat.

Salvatore snatched the cup that had been thrown on Emilio's bed, confirming that there was, in fact, a slice of onion leaking its pungent flavours into his son's tea. He then grabbed the cup and saucer and stormed out of the room into the hallway.

"Salva, please, don't do anything to get you—" Leonarda said as the door shut, cutting her short.

Raffaele descended his bunk, Leonarda missing his arm as he raced after his father. By the time Raffaele reached the dining hall, he had heard the commotion before he saw it.

"Do you think this is acceptable!" Salvatore growled.

"Sir, I can assure you, this was not on purpose. I am truly sorry that this has happened. I can get your son anything else he may need," said the crewmember with an ingenuine face.

Seeing red, Salvatore leapt over the counter as onlookers gasped. Raffaele stood in the corner, watching his father in horror. The crewmember braced, looking Salvatore in his brown, squinted eyes.

Salvatore grabbed the man's shirt, threw his nimble body against the wall, and then held his left fist high in the air. Before he could swing, the burly cook grabbed Salvatore's arm, pinning both men. As the cook held Salvatore against the wall, the crewmember slid away, then ran out of the room, pushing past each passenger in his path.

A few moments later, the crewmember returned with the master-at-arms, who slapped a pair of handcuffs on Salvatore and then led him away from the dining hall. On his way out of the room, Salvatore caught the glance of his son, which made Salvatore's face turn bright red. He thought about fighting back with the officer, feeling the boyish grip he possessed, but Salvatore knew that would land him more issues than he could handle.

"Mamma! Mamma!" shouted Raffaele as he opened the door. "They took him! They took him!"

"Who took him?" said Leonarda with enlarged eyes.

"The police! The police took him," explained Raffaele while jumping up and down.

"The police? What happened?"

Emilio sat up, his eyebrows scrunched down and his gaze intense on his brother. "What do you mean? There's no police out here in the middle of the ocean."

"It was a man in a blue jacket and a cap!"

Leonarda sighed, then collapsed her head into her hands, the weight of the situation sinking in. After a long moment, she lifted her head and took a deep breath.

"Is he going to prison?" asked Raffaele with fear in his face.

"Raffaele, stay here with Emilio. I'll go find out what's happening with your father," Leonarda instructed, her voice steady.

She left the room, her footsteps echoing down the narrow corridor. It didn't take long for her to find the master-at-arms' office, a small, windowless room at the end of the passageway. Inside, Salvatore was already locked up in an iron-holding cell, his face a mixture of anger and shame, appearing like a caged animal.

"May I help you?" asked the officer as he stood up from his chair.

"Yes, you have my husband," Leonarda snapped. "He's the one in th-that cage," she said as she pointed over the officer's shoulder.

"Leonarda! Everything is going to be alright!" affirmed Salvatore, holding on to the bars and smiling.

Leonarda shook her head, silencing him, then looked at the officer as if her husband were absent. "What happened?"

"Madam, your husband has some temper. I caught him behind the counter, attempting to assault one of my men," the officer expressed as Leonarda shook her head. "Your husband tells me that your son's drink was tampered with, but my men would not do such a thing. Now, I would suggest, once I release him after he has the night to reflect, that he stay away from the dining hall," said the officer as he flipped through his notes, stroking his beard. "Am I clear?"

"It was that onion. They put it in Emilio's tea on purpose!"

"That's enough," the officer scolded.

"Until tomorrow, then?" asked Leonarda. "How will we eat if my family cannot go to the dining hall?"

"Not your family, just your husband."

"The thing is, the food they serve there is not food. My boy, with assistance from the waves, has been ill all day," explained Leonarda. "Please, there must be something we can do."

"These are not matters that I oversee, madam," explained the officer while shrugging. "In this part of the ship, this is what you people are fed."

Leonarda stared at the officer, then said, "You people? What exactly does that mean?"

"Well—what I meant to say was—"

"Sicilians, right?"

"No, not at all; I was—"

"Sir, I know what you meant," asserted Leonarda as she exited the room.

*

Later in the evening, Emilio's nausea subsided, and his colour returned. He filled his stomach with packages of crackers that Leonarda found in the dining hall, the only thing he vowed to eat until they reached Halifax. Although they had over a week and a half remaining, Emilio knew that survival meant sacrifice, they all did. For three meals a day, the Bucci family planned to eat crackers and drink ale, even the children. The water was murky, festering with creatures the eye could not see. Leonarda hated the aftertaste of the ale, yet she treated it as the elixir of life, savouring each drop in her mouth.

As Leonarda drifted into a deep sleep, Emilio lay motionless, waiting for his brother to do the same above. After thirty minutes, Raffaele began to snore, vibrating the bunk. Emilio's curiosity began to gnaw at his mind, consuming his thoughts.

Emilio slid the covers off, stood up, and buttoned his shirt. He spritzed himself with his father's perfume, filling the room with bergamot and replacing the acidic stench of vomit. He slipped on a pair of trousers, then slid on his shoes, taking extra care not to wake his family.

Closing the door behind him gently, Emilio crept down the corridor, searching for his father.

"Emilio," whispered a soft voice behind him.

Emilio turned around, and Giacomo smiled at him.

"What are you do-doing? It's late," said Giacomo with a grin.

"I'm looking for my father. He was arrested," Emilio said as Giacomo's eyes opened fully.

"Arrested? Oh, my father s-said he saw a man get arrested."

"My brother told me he got into a fight. Well, kind of," Emilio explained as he shrugged his shoulders.

"A fight?" Giacomo said as he approached Emilio. "Well, I would he-help you, but I h-have to go to bed."

"Why do you talk like that?" asked Emilio while tilting his head. "I have never heard anybody talk like that before in my life."

Giacomo hung his head and took a deep breath, then said, "I-I was born w-with it, that's all. W-when people point it out, it g-gets worse."

"I'm sorry, I was just curious. I didn't mean to upset you!" explained Emilio.

"No, it's o-okay. I know I'm strange."

"No, you're not strange!" Emilio proclaimed with a red face. "I'm so sorry."

Giacomo smiled, then pointed to the end of the corridor. "M-My father said that a m-man was taken in handcuffs down there."

"Thank you," Emilio said as he began walking down the corridor. "I hope you're right."

Once he reached the end, Emilio looked left, then right, but none of the doors were labelled. The first door on the right was a supply room filled with cleaning products and crates. As he looked back, Giacomo was gone. The room on the right was locked but appeared to be a stateroom by the sound of snoring that echoed inside.

Emilio tried a third door, which led to a staircase—a staircase he had never taken before. A red velvet rope separated their worlds with iron railings meeting marble and wood. Emilio's heart pounded as he took his first hesitant step, ducking under the rope and onto the staircase, the marble slippery and smooth beneath his feet. The lavish interior was a world away from the corridors he knew. The polished bannister gleamed under the soft glow of the lighting. Curiosity thrummed in his veins, urging him upwards despite the soft warnings of his mother's voice echoing in his mind.

Each step brought Emilio closer to the heart of a world he had only glimpsed from afar. His eyes darted around, taking in the elaborate details—the intricate carvings on the wooden panels and the subtle, intoxicating scent of roses.

He could hear the buzz of conversations, the clink of glasses, and the distant strains of a piano playing a gentle waltz. He reached the top of the staircase, his breath catching in his throat as he took in the grandness of the first-class gentlemen's club. Emilio, drawn by his own curiosity, edged closer, his small frame slipping easily into the shadows cast by the furniture around him.

The room was full of leather and mahogany, bursting with the aroma of cigars and the faint hint of brandy. Emilio had smelled brandy once in his life when his great-uncle visited from Milan. A large fireplace crackled invitingly, its flames dancing. Several elderly gentlemen were seated in plush armchairs, their voices a low hum of conversation interrupted by the occasional laugh. Emilio's eyes flicked to the grand table in the centre, covered with newspapers and half-empty glasses, the air above it hazy with smoke.

Emilio crouched beneath a table, his heart pounding in his chest. He was close enough to hear the men's conversations clearly, their voices a blend of regional accents. They spoke of politics, and their discussions weaved complex opinions that both intrigued and confused him. Emilio couldn't understand why adults cared so much about people who didn't know they existed.

"Mr Rossini, what is your take on Mussolini's latest decree?" one of the men asked, his voice carrying a note of scepticism.

Mr Rossini appeared to be a stocky man with a moustache who puffed on his cigar thoughtfully. "Mussolini is a master of rhetoric, but his policies are a different matter.

The economy struggles, yet he insists on grand projects and military posturing. It is the people who suffer most."

Another gentleman, slender and sharp-eyed, leaned forward. "But you must admit, Mr Rossini, that his vision for Italy is ambitious. The Pontine Marshes, the modernization of the railways—these are no small jobs."

Mr Rossini sighed, his expression exhausted. "Ambition, yes. But at what cost? The censorship, the repression of dissent. Italy is being shaped into something unrecognisable."

Emilio listened, enchanted by the gravity of their conversation. He barely noticed the servant approaching until a shadow fell over him. The man's eyes widened in surprise, then narrowed in disapproval. "What are you doing here, boy?"

Before Emilio could scramble away, a firm but gentle hand rested on his shoulder. He looked up to see one of the gentlemen peering down at him with a curious smile. "Leave him be. The boy is only curious."

The servant hesitated, then nodded curtly and stepped back. The gentleman, a tall man with silver hair and piercing blue eyes, gestured for Emilio to stand. "Come, sit with us. We could use some fresh perspective, even if it is from young ears."

Emilio's heart pounded as he rose, his eyes wide with a mix of fear and excitement. He took a seat on the edge of an armchair, feeling very small amidst the serious faces around him. The gentleman who had invited him in leaned back, a cigar held delicately between his fingers.

"What is your name, son?" he asked, exhaling a cloud of fragrant smoke.

"Emilio, sir," he whispered.

"Emilio," the man repeated, nodding thoughtfully. "I am Mr Conti. Tell me, Emilio, what do you know of politics?"

Emilio hesitated, then shrugged. "Not much, sir. My father talks about Mussolini sometimes. He says things were different before. My mother hates him, if I'm being honest."

Mr Conti chuckled softly, his eyes appearing amused. "Indeed, things were different. These days, everyone talks of Mussolini and his grand plans for Italy. But it is important to understand the past to make sense of the present."

As the men resumed their discussion, they occasionally turned to Emilio, explaining terms and historical references he didn't understand. They spoke of the rise of fascism, the impact of the Great War, and the social and economic changes sweeping through Europe. Emilio listened intently, absorbing their words like a sponge.

"Remember this, Emilio," Mr Conti said, his tone serious. "Politics is not just about people like Mussolini. It is about us people, our prospects, our uncertainties, and our visions. It is about how those in power, like Mussolini, shape the lives of everyone else."

*

The evening wore on, the men's voices rising and falling in a rhythm that was almost hypnotic. Emilio felt a strange sense of belonging as if he had stumbled into a secret world where the future was being shaped by the conversations held within these walls. The servants moved quietly around them, refilling glasses and tending to the fire.

Eventually, the conversations began to wind down, with the gentlemen exchanging tired but satisfied nods. Mr Conti looked at Emilio, then smiled. "You have been a most attentive listener, Emilio. Perhaps one day, you will be the one shaping the future of Europe."

Emilio flushed with pride, unable to suppress a small smile. "Thank you, sir. But I don't think I will. I enjoyed listening, though."

Mr Conti patted him on the shoulder. "Good boy. Now, off with you. It is late, and I am sure your family is wondering where you are."

Emilio nodded, slipping out from under the table and making his way to the door. As he stepped back into the corridor, the sounds of the gentlemen's club faded behind him, replaced by the quiet hum of the ship at night. He hurried back down the staircase, his mind racing.

As he slid back into his stateroom, Leonarda had been sitting up, staring at the door.

"Where were you, Lio?"

"I met some friends. I was safe, Mamma." Emilio smiled.

"Friends?"

"Well, kind of," Emilio said with a grin.

PART TWO

8

Halifax emerged on the horizon as Emilio and Raffaele watched from a porthole. The dense, foggy morning air gave the city an ethereal, ghostly appearance. The outline of the city was barely visible through the mist, and the waters of Halifax Harbour shimmered with a silvery glow, reflecting the muted light of the early sun.

The SS Serenità Blu chugged steadily towards the port. As the ship drew closer to the docks, the sounds of the busy harbour began to cut through the fog: the distant cries of dockworkers, the clanking of metal, and the low hum of engines preparing for the day's work.

Emilio placed a reassuring hand on Raffaele's shoulder. "We've made it, Raf. Canada is not as icy as I would have thought. Although, it still looks very cold."

Raffaele nodded, his eyes wide. "It's bigger than I imagined," he muttered, taking in the sight of numerous ships anchored at the docks.

The ship docked smoothly, and the passengers began to disembark. Emilio and Raffaele gathered their belongings from the stateroom as their parents had just finished packing. The four of them strolled down the corridor, Salvatore nodding at the crew member he nearly struck, then joined the queue of third-class immigrants headed towards customs.

The port authorities, with their stern faces and sharp uniforms, moved efficiently, checking papers and directing the newcomers. As they stepped onto Canadian soil for the first time, the reality of their situation hit them. The air was brisk, carrying a hint of salt from the sea, and the city drummed with activity.

Navigating their way through the crowded dock, they finally emerged into an area with hordes of people, all speaking different languages. Salvatore had been the only Bucci with the ability to understand and speak English, as he learned from his Charles Dickens books as a schoolboy. During the war, a few British officers taught him the basics of conversation, enough to get by.

As they reached the front, Salvatore handed the immigration officer a stack of papers. The officer flipped through the passport violently.

"Names?" the officer demanded, pressing a stamp into the passport.

"Salvatore Bucci. This is my wife, Leonarda, and my sons, Emilio and Raffale."

"Country of origin?" said the officer briskly.

Salvatore stared at him in confusion as the passport told him.

The officer's round glasses slid from his nose, and his stare became more intense. "Do you understand English?"

"Yes, well, I do," said Salvatore proudly. "My family only speaks Italian."

"Then Italy is the answer I'm looking for. You are all Italian citizens?"

"Yes."

"Great, please sign this document. It verifies you are not coming here with illnesses and that you agree to an examination."

"An examination?" repeated Salvatore.

"Yes, we must verify your health and the health of your family."

"Oh, well, my family is all healthy; look at them," said Salvatore with a smile.

Leonarda and the boys stared in confusion, trying to make out the interaction.

"I understand, but this is not optional," said the officer as he signed the papers in front of them. "And how is it that you plan to support yourself in Canada? Also, what is your final destination city? Do you plan on remaining here in Halifax or venturing west?"

Salvatore handed the officer a letter from Massimo's cousin, Giuseppe. It explained his ventures and his job offer was described in detail. The officer nodded and stamped the letter.

Salvatore glanced at Leonarda and the boys, offering a reassuring smile despite his own nerves.

The doctor, a middle-aged man with spectacles perched on the bridge of his nose, began with basic health inquiries. "Any history of illness?" he asked in hesitant Italian.

Salvatore shook his head firmly. "No, we are all healthy," he replied in English.

The doctor nodded, then methodically proceeded with the examination. Leonarda was first, stepping forward with hesitation. The doctor measured her height and weight, checked her eyes and throat, and listened to her heart and lungs with a stethoscope. She glanced back at Salvatore, who gave an encouraging nod. The boys, wide-eyed with curiosity, watched closely, their hands gripping their father's shirt.

Next, the boys were examined. Each stood still as the doctor inspected them, checking for signs of disease. They squirmed slightly but remained mostly cooperative under the doctor's gentle but firm instructions.

Finally, it was Salvatore's turn. He removed his cap and stepped forward confidently. The doctor repeated the same procedures, occasionally making notes on a clipboard. Throughout the process, Salvatore tried to communicate his family's good health with his English abilities, hoping to expedite the process, which surprised the doctor.

After what felt like an eternity, the doctor finally smiled and nodded, indicating they had passed the examination. Another officer stamped their documents.

"Welcome to Canada," he said as he closed the passport in his hand.

Salvatore breathed a sigh of relief, sharing a moment of silent gratitude with Leonarda.

*

The train journey from Halifax to Hamilton was too long for Emilio. He detested being crammed like cattle into the frigid train car, each kilometre the cold intensifying. He considered himself lucky as his seat wasn't below the open window, but it wasn't much help. His only coat was not nearly thick enough, providing only a small amount of heat. The only thing he enjoyed about the journey was the view —the Canadian countryside was vast and filled with small touches of beauty in Emilio's eyes.

Although most of it was grey and snow-covered, it reminded him of what his father described the countryside of

Milan to be like, exactly the same as he pictured in his head as his father told stories of snow-capped hills. The only difference was that Canada lacked the rocky peaks—at least in this part of Canada. His father told him that further west, there were mountains just as tall as the ones he grew up around, but Emilio didn't believe him now. He needed to see it to believe it.

Across the aisle, a family of four sat huddled together. The father, a burly man with a thick moustache, was engaged in a spirited conversation with his wife. Their two children, a boy and a girl, sat quietly, bundled in layers of clothing. Emilio had been chatting with Raffaele, which alerted the family across from them.

"Those Italians," the father grumbled, his voice carrying over the rattle of the train. "They're everywhere now. Can't escape them, even here."

The mother nodded, her face pinched with disapproval. "I heard they're all coming here in droves. The newspapers are full of stories about their homeland being taken over by that man," she said as she ran her hands through her golden curls.

Salvatore, listening in, began taking deep breaths. He had heard these kinds of comments before, but they never failed to bite. He wanted to stand up to defend his family, but he knew better than to draw attention to himself. Instead, he directed his gaze outward and tried to focus on the passing landscape.

"They all wanted that Benito fellow there, and they will want him here," the father continued, "and they will want to take away our Canadian way of life. Mark me. In three to five years' time, there will be so many of those people here that King George will lose his grip. You watch. Victor Emmanuel will come here and claim this place as his own, and those people will let him. They will outnumber us!"

"Francis, keep your voice down," whispered the wife.

"Why? They can't understand us anyway. Dagos don't learn English. They group together in their little neighbourhoods and never have to learn a word of our language. These ones are probably headed to one of those slums as we speak," Francis said as he shook his head in disgust.

The boy, who looked about Raffaele's age, blurted, "Pa, are they really that bad?"

"Yes, William," the father said, his voice certain. "When you try to get a job one day as a grown man, the whole country will be run by dagos. If you don't speak their language, they won't hire you. Simple as that, son."

Salvatore's knuckles whitened as he gripped the edge of his seat. The idea that they were seen as unwanted, as intruders, was a bitter pill to swallow. He tried to tell himself that these were the opinions of this small family, yet he considered the idea that there were more who thought these things about his family.

The mother added, "I just hope the government does something about it. We can't have our country overrun by foreigners who refuse to integrate," while flipping through her newspaper.

Just then, the train wobbled, and Salvatore was jolted from his thoughts. William dropped his book, and it slid across the floor, stopping at Emilio's feet. He picked it up and handed it back with a polite smile.

"Thank you," William said, looking a bit surprised.

Emilio nodded and smiled.

For a moment, his son's eyes met William, but Salvatore saw a flicker of curiosity and confusion in William's stare, as if he only, for a split second, realised his parents knew alternative truths.

As the train continued its journey, Salvatore leaned back in his seat and closed his eyes, trying to block out the conversation still buzzing across the aisle. His family's ignorance was the only thing keeping him silent despite the urge to put on a show.

*

As Emilio peered out the window, tall smokestacks pierced the sky, belching thick plumes of smoke that mingled with the overcast clouds, casting a greyish hue over the city. The sun was a dim, hazy orb struggling to enter the thick atmosphere. Emilio's gaze followed the dark trails of smoke as they snaked upward, dissipating into the murky expanse above.

The factories themselves were colossal, hulking masses of metal, concrete, and brick. Massive chimneys, some reaching skyward, each contributing to the oppressive shroud that encased the city. Occasionally, a burst of steam or a flare of fire would punctuate the scene, momentarily illuminating the grim landscape with a flicker of harsh, industrial light. Emilio felt a deep sense of isolation as he took in the scene. The natural world seemed distant and unreal, replaced by this stark display of industrialisation.

The train finally pulled into the station, and the Bucci family gathered their things, eager to leave the cramped car behind. As he stepped onto the platform, Emilio took a deep breath of the cold, crisp air. He noticed a scent he had never smelled before—a mixture of sulphur and the slight aroma of decay. Pinching his nose, he turned to his mother, who began to laugh.

Salvatore explained that they would get used to it and that the nearby factories caused the smell. "There's lots of money being made in the factories here. Something you wouldn't see back home. Well, this is your home now."

Raffaele appeared horrified and said, "This is not my home."

Emilio looked around in disbelief that his father had chosen this foul, cold, grey city to call home. No matter how he tried to justify it, he couldn't.

As the Bucci family made their way through the train station, the collection of voices filled Emilio's ears, adding to his sense of disorientation. The flickering lights, the walls decorated with faded posters advertising goods he had never seen in a language he didn't understand, made Emilio overwhelmed. Salvatore led them through the crowd with the confidence of someone who had done this many times before, his grip firm on his battered leather suitcase.

As they stepped outside, the city emerged before them in all its industrial majesty, a stark contrast to the hills and clear skies of Agrigento. Leonarda clutched Raffaele's hand tightly, her fingers cold and trembling despite her attempts to appear brave.

The landlord, an older gentleman with a grey beard dressed in a pressed white dress shirt and charcoal jacket, met Salvatore in front of their new building. The four-storey apartment appeared weathered, with the light-grey bricks soot-covered and decrepit. The windows were stained a hue of amber, yet they were not supposed to be. The concrete steps leading to the front door were disintegrating in places, exposing the dark gaps below them.

"Welcome. I'm sure you have come far," said the landlord while adjusting his cap.

"Very far, yes," said Salvatore, then slightly grinned.

"I have a few Italians in this building. Good people they are. They keep it quiet and don't cause any fuss. Now, I intend to keep it that way."

Salvatore nodded, appearing slightly annoyed.

"Oh, and one more thing. Should you need me for any reason at all, I left my telephone number on a piece of paper in the kitchen," said the landlord.

"Thank you," Salvatore said as the landlord began to leave.

While they climbed the stairs to their new apartment, the weight of their new reality settled heavily on Emilio's shoulders, and he wondered if they would ever truly feel at home here. His father again spoke of opportunities and prosperity, but to Emilio, it felt like they had been consumed by an idea.

Leonarda picked up an envelope that had been half wedged under their front door. As she opened it, Salvatore stepped behind her, reading the letter out loud in Italian.

Welcome! When you are all settled, come see us. 3434 Dundurn Street. – Maria & Floria

Emilio smiled, feeling warm for the first time since arriving in Canada.

9

1936

Giuseppe's Butcher Shop did not survive the winter like many businesses around the country. Boarding the windows of his dream gutted Giuseppe as he constantly repeated to his staff that people had to make sacrifices in these times—meat being one of them. Salvatore helped clear the space, but they were in no rush. They both knew no tenant could ever afford such a location, not now. The emptiness of the shop was too much for Giuseppe to handle most days, so he often left Salvatore to his own devices to finish the job. Once the last of the boxes had been cleared and the last meat scale had been sold, Salvatore locked the door for the last time.

While working for Giuseppe, Salvatore made quite a name for himself in the neighbourhood. Every person within a five-kilometre radius knew the Sicilian man who could slice steaks faster than any crank machine ever could. Many were impressed by his English, as most of the employees that Giuseppe had could not speak it. Alberto, the man who ran the cash register, knew ten English words, using his gestures and nods to confirm customers' questions. It worked most of the time, as the neighbourhood was about 80% Italian. If an anglophone happened to stumble in, Salvatore would jump in with his blood-soaked apron in Alberto's place.

Outside of work, surrounded by mostly Canadians, Salvatore's native tongue remained dormant. He often thought to himself that if it hadn't been for his job and Leonarda, who refused to learn more than 'hello,' he may have forgotten Italian entirely.

Leonarda never grew to love Hamilton the way her husband did. She spent most of her days cleaning their apartment, then cleaning the same spot the next day despite the need. When she could, Leonarda visited Maria in the afternoons and then left in time to make dinner each day. The Savoia house on Dundurn was small, yet each room reminded Leonarda of home. Maria had smuggled a few of the décor pieces from the olive grove, adding a touch of Agrigento in places one would least expect.

The painting above the fireplace was the same painting Leonarda and Maria admired as young girls, as it had once hung above Maria's dining room table in her childhood home. When her father died, Maria inherited the painting—its scene was set in 1850s Palermo. They only knew it was set then by the date on the back, as Palermo had looked the same for generations—the city stuck in time.

Emilio spent most of his evenings at the Savoia residence, which made his father furious as he came home for dinner about once a week. 'Mrs Savoia is going to start billing us for the food you eat,' is what Salvatore said to Emilio each day that he came home late from seeing Floria. Emilio didn't care about his father's opinions. Floria was his only tie to his home. She made him feel things nobody else did—things he could not explain.

One afternoon after school, Floria and Emilio lay on her bedroom floor, Emilio running his fingers through Floria's doll's hair. She had received the doll from her great-aunt, as her aunt still saw her as a little girl in her senescent mind. Floria was under strict orders to send her a thank-you letter every time she received one.

"Do you ever miss it?" asked Emilio pensively.

"Miss it?" repeated Floria as she turned her head to face Emilio.

"Home."

"Agrigento? Yes, sometimes I do. Well, if I am being completely truthful, all the time. But I'm happy here for the most part," sighed Floria.

"I miss it every day. I hate it here," said Emilio while stroking the bleach-blonde doll's hair.

"Oh, come on now, Emilio. It's not all bad."

"Yeah, for you, maybe. You speak flawless English. You have friends. If I had the things you have, I'd like it here too—well, a bit more, at least," said Emilio as he tapped the doll's porcelain forehead, producing a clinking sound.

"Well, I could teach you proper English if you would like, but your English is good considering you have only been here a short while. It will get better with time. I have just been here longer, that's all," said Floria, then she smiled. "And if you don't have any friends, then who am I?"

"Well—we're—we're—" began Emilio with a red face.

"Best friends?"

"Well, we are—yes. We're best friends," said Emilio as sweat formed on his forehead.

"Come on, let's do something fun. I was thinking we could go play a prank on the Carswell house," said Floria, then giggled. "Unless, of course, you want me to tell the boys at school you would prefer to play with dolls."

"Shut up!"

"Emilia, your doll's hair is almost as lovely as yours. Except her hair is blonde, while yours is more chocolate. A trip to the salon could fix that, Emilia." Floria giggled and then rolled on her stomach.

Emilio flipped her back and sat on top of her. "Call me Emilia one more time, and I will show you!"

"What are you going to do, Ms Emilia?"

Emilio gathered the saliva in his mouth and threatened Floria with it by moving his lips. As she laughed harder, he couldn't help but reciprocate it, and the saliva fell from his mouth, missing Floria's head as she swerved her neck to the right.

"You know that's not very ladylike of you to spit on my floor," Floria joked.

Emilio repeated her words back to her in a bass-heavy, sluggish tone, then stuck out his tongue.

"Come on! My mother has some apples that have spoiled so badly that they are practically liquid. We sealed them in jars last autumn, but the seal broke in the pantry. Let's teach those Carswell boys a lesson."

Reluctantly, Emilio dropped the doll and followed Floria.

*

The Carswell brothers, Donald and Joseph, were the epitome of privilege. They lived at the base of the escarpment in a Victorian mansion that, from the outside, exuded an old-world charm, with its ivy-clad red-brick walls and turrets casting long shadows over meticulously manicured English gardens. Inside, the house was exquisite, with crystal chandeliers dangling from textured ceilings and rooms filled with priceless antiques.

Despite their lifestyle, the brothers were starkly different in temperament. Donald, the elder, was a sharp and calculated thinker, always plotting his next move, whether it was in a game of chess or a family discussion. His demeanour went beyond his years. Despite this, he used his wit to manipulate and bully his younger brother.

Joseph Carswell, who was in Emilio and Floria's class at school, was a dreamer; his days were spent wandering the grounds or sketching scenes from his vivid imagination. His brother mocked his artistic talents, constantly telling him that men fight in wars or play bloody sports like rugby, not sketch drawings of trees or birds alone. Those things were for little girls in Donald's eyes. Their bond was superficial—a spectacle for their father to display to their guests and nothing more.

Although originally Joseph took a liking to Emilio, Donald asserted to his brother that 'dagos are not like us.' Eventually, the pressure eroded Joseph's ability to remain friendly to Emilio, and that's when the bullying started.

Floria tossed the jar of rotten apples at Emilio as they lay flat in the bushes below Donald's bedroom. They could hear the gardener raking last year's leaves in the front yard from the sound the rake made as it scraped the partially frozen soil. The half-melted ground was beginning to saturate Emilio's clothing, chilling his scrawny body to the core.

Floria poked her head out of the bushes, and her eyes met the back of Mr Michael Carswell's head, gasping as she jumped back into the bushes.

"You there!" called out Mr Carswell, hearing the commotion.

Floria looked at Emilio, whose face was frozen and pale.

"Hello?" said Mr Carswell again as he took a step off the porch.

Emilio gripped the jar and shuffled over to Floria. "What do we do?" he whispered.

"Run!" shouted Floria.

They both shot up, their faces concealed by the tall bushes. As they did, they heard the footsteps grow in velocity.

"Toss them!"

"I can't; the lid won't come off now!" replied Emilio.

"Toss the whole thing; nail the house, glass and all."

Emilio froze for a second, wound his hand back, and released the entire jar. Instead of shattering, he heard the jar make a thump sound, and then a delayed shatter followed.

"My god!" yelled Mr Carswell, covered in glass shards and rotten apples.

Emilio sprinted down the street, nearly knocking over the crate of empty milk bottles the milkman had been loading into the back of his wagon. Floria was three paces behind him, eventually matching his speed. They dashed past the corner grocery store, where the English people got their food—a brief but welcome distraction as they peered in to see the array of colours. Emilio's heart pounded in his chest—a mix of fear and adrenaline. Floria's breath came in short gasps as she kept pace.

They turned down a narrow alleyway, shadows barely visible under the sun that was poking through the clouds. The uneven stones beneath their feet echoed with each hurried step. Darkened doorways and shuttered windows lined the brick walls, with rubbish spread everywhere. The air was thick with the scent of dampness and decay. As they sprinted, they encountered a low, rusted fence. Emilio's shirt snagged on the jagged iron, causing him to stumble. Floria quickly pulled him free and guided him into another, even narrower passage, where the city sounds faded into a distant hum.

"Do you think he saw us?" asked Emilio, his face still laden with fear.

"Saw? Mr Carswell needs his glasses to see past his arms. I doubt it," Floria said and then smiled. "That was so brave of you. I can't believe you actually tossed the entire jar."

"You told me to!"

"I just didn't think Ms Emilia Bucci had the guts."

"Stop!" Emilio shouted, his face genuinely appearing annoyed.

"You know I'm only kidding, Emilio," said Floria as she shook her head. "Emilio, you're the craziest person I know. In a good way, though."

"Craziest?" repeated Emilio. "So I'm feminine, and I'm crazy. Thank you very much, Floria." Emilio rolled his eyes.

"I never said you were feminine. On the contrary, you're becoming a man. Did you see that throw back there? I don't think a boy could make that; only a man could."

"If you think I'm so manly, why do you call me Ms Emilia?" asked Emilio with a serious glare. "You know it bothers me, right?"

"I love bothering you. That's what best friends do." Floria smiled and crossed her arms.

"Yeah, well, keep it up, and my new best friend will be Raf. And that's saying a lot because that boy gets on my nerves."

"Oh, Emilio, I was only playing; you know I love you."

Emilio froze; the sound of the busy city was muted, and his vision went blurry. Then he repeated, "Love?"

"Not like that; come on, Emilio, you know what I meant," asserted Floria as she tilted her head to the left.

Emilio shook his head, turned around, and began running. Floria chased him down three city blocks, calling his name like that of a runaway dog. When she finally caught up to him, his face was red and puffy.

"What is going on, Emilio?" Floria asked as Emilio collapsed on the sidewalk, out of breath.

"I-I—" began Emilio, panting. "What if I told you I like you more than a friend, Floria? In fact, I fancy you. I love the way your hair shines even when the sun is dull in this grey city. I love the way you smile when you say my name out loud. I love the way you—"

"Stop! You're making this weird!" shouted Floria. "Do you realise what you are saying right now?"

"I have loved you ever since you kissed me on the day you were leaving for Canada. Did you know I still think about that every single day?" Emilio said, crying.

"Emilio!"

"But it's true, Floria."

Both Emilio and Floria sat on the sidewalk in silence for a few moments, allowing Emilio's comments to marinate.

"Well, what if I don't think of you like that?" asked Floria as she rubbed Emilio's hand. "Would you still be my friend?"

Emilio's eyes filled with more tears, and he took a deep breath. "Of course, I can't lose you, ever."

"Then be my friend first. The rest can come later."

Emilio wrapped his arms around Floria, yet his mind couldn't drop her final comment. The line replayed in his head on repeat, filling him with gentle shocks of electric waves each time he thought about it.

When Emilio arrived at the apartment, the streetlights had been on for an hour. As the door closed behind him, Salvatore sat under a single flickering light in the kitchen, the only thing visible from the door.

"Emilio," said Salvatore, his tone raspy.

Emilio placed his school bag down and untied his shoes. At a slow pace, he stumbled over to his father, making sure he took his time.

"Sit."

"What's the matter?"

"Sit," Salvatore asserted firmly.

Emilio pulled a dining chair out of the kitchen table, its wood legs scraping the checkerboard floor.

"Now, where have you been tonight?" said Salvatore with a stern glare. "You and I have some matters to discuss."

Emilio's complexion flushed, and his palms moistened, slipping from the sides of the chair he had been gripping.

"I'm not upset, Emilio," affirmed Salvatore. "I just want to know the truth."

"I was at the Savoia house."

"I'm aware, Emilio." Salvatore cocked his head. "You know, you can tell me things."

"Can I?" said Emilio quickly. He bit down on his lips, and his stomach dropped. "I-I'm sorry. What I meant—"

"You can, Emilio," said Salvatore as he extended his arm across the table. "You know, when I was a young man, your mother caught my eye instantly. I saw her brown locks in the breeze, and her half-cracked smile, and I was captivated by her beauty. I never saw a woman like her in Milan. Never."

Emilio didn't extend an arm back, keeping his tucked under the table until Salvatore slowly retreated.

"You're becoming a man now. And as a man, there are some things you must know. How to treat a woman, how to protect her, and how to be a gentleman."

"Protect? From what?"

"The world," Salvatore said hastily. "The world is full of men who only wish to harm women. It's your job to do something about it."

"Do something about it?"

"Yes, to be a man who's better than that." Salvatore rocked his head and grinned.

"May I ask what this is about?" said Emilio, crossing his legs. "I'm not a man yet. And I don't have a woman in my life."

"Do you take me as naive?" Salvatore's grin grew larger. "I know love when I see it."

"Love? What love?" Emilio said, then looked at the cupboards.

Salvatore shuffled his chair closer, his leg nearly brushing his son's.

"If you are talking about Floria, then you are mistaken. She is just a friend. We do not think of each other in that way," asserted Emilio.

Salvatore smiled, then shook his head as a slight laugh exited his mouth. "Oh, Emilio, don't hide it. Let it happen because if my experiences have taught me one thing about life, it's that everything can change instantly. The things you have tonight may not be here when your eyes open tomorrow. The things you love are all but permanent," Salvatore said as his grin faded into a slight frown. "One day, your friends are right beside you; the next, a stray bullet blows through their helmet, draining their lives from their skulls in a stream of maroon. No matter how many times you stuff the wound, their life will not return," he explained, a tear forming in his eyes.

"Must everything always come back to the Piave River?" Emilio asked as he shook his head.

Salvatore dabbed his eye with the top of his hand. "One day, you will understand, son."

"Will I?" said Emilio, shrugging his shoulders. "I would never sign up for war. I'm not a killer."

Salvatore's body filled with steam, and then he shuffled even closer. Emilio could feel his breath.

"I-I'm sorry, I didn't mean that," Emilio mumbled as he shuffled back.

"Do you truly believe I wanted to be there and that any of us young boys wanted to be there?" rambled Salvatore.

"I did things I am not proud of, sure, but it was because I had to. You see, the difference between my generation and yours is quite clear. My generation stands for justice, while yours is content to watch."

"Justice? Do you know what your generation did? You stole an entire part of Austria in the name of justice, yet—"

Salvatore swung at quarter speed, the backs of his fingers colliding with Emilio's lips. "That's enough!"

Emilio jolted, then covered his mouth with his hand.

"How dare you critique things you did not understand! The Austrians chased us, but unlike your generation, we responded. You may be becoming a man, but a light smack is what you need now and then," Salvatore said sternly. "As for myself, I was thrown down flights of stairs, beaten with a broomstick, and even had my back teeth smacked out of me," said Salvatore while exposing his missing molar.

"Who did this?" asked Emilio, his eyes wide while continuing to rub his lips.

"My uncle never loved me. I was his obligation and nothing more. Despite what you think, Emilio, I do love you. I just do not want you to become a man who refuses to act. You have Aldo's fac—" Salvatore began as he cut himself off, "spirit. You have my uncle's spirit."

"I am no such person!"

"His determination, his witty personality, but not the other parts," Salvatore said. "Don't let the good parts go to waste."

Emilio sat in silence and stared at his father. Both nodded at each other and then Salvatore retired to Leonarda. Emilio sat in the kitchen for an hour, lost in his thoughts.

He cracked open a window and watched the night creep by. The street below faintly hummed while Emilio stared off into the distance.

*

In school, both Emilio and Raffaele struggled immensely. Although both could speak English with some fluency, reading and writing were nearly impossible. Mrs Buchanan, Emilio's teacher, and Mr Blake, who was Raffaele's, both agreed that the boys could read and write at a second-grade level. Emilio received the bulk of the pressure as Mrs Buchanan went the extra step of making Emilio read out loud to the class, making him the butt of the joke among the students.

As they learned about Macbeth by Shakespeare, he was assigned the role of reading Lady Macbeth's lines to the class. Although Mrs Buchanan promised it was simply due to the fact that all the other roles had been filled, Emilio was not convinced. He had caught Mrs Buchanan giggling at a few of the comments, her inner bully shining through her façade of inclusive positivity. Her parted blonde hair was split like her personality—simultaneously kind and cruel.

As Joseph Carswell had been assigned the role of Macbeth, they bounced off each other with alternating reading speeds. Joseph had finished his soliloquy, which led to Emilio's turn to speak.

Glancing at his next lines, Emilio couldn't read them. The Scottish twang written on the pages was indistinguishable.

"Today, Emilio!" cried George, a fat boy with slicked-back hair.

The entire class erupted, repeating George's lines with laughter. The only person silent was Floria, who had turned around and shook her head at each student individually.

"George, that is enough!" shouted Mrs Buchannan with a stern glare. Her glare broke, and then she cracked a slight smile. "Now, ladies and gentlemen, when Emilio is reading, I would ask you to show him the respect he deserves and remain silent," she said as she fixed her hair with her fingers.

"Read? He's not reading anything. And if he manages to read a few words, they sound funny under that accent of his," said George as he stood up.

Once again, the room began to giggle.

Emilio's face went red, and he buried himself in his arm.

"George, that is enough. I will be speaking with you after class. And if you do not stop, I will be mentioning this interaction to your father and mother as I see them every Sunday at church," asserted Mrs Buchanan.

The entire class, except for Emilio, turned around to face George as they taunted him. George stood up and left, and then Mrs Buchanan followed him into the corridor.

Floria walked over to Emilio, placing a hand on his shoulder. "Don't worry, his house is next," she whispered, causing Emilio to let out a slight giggle.

"Why are you still here, Emilio? You're not going to college anyway. You should go paint houses or shine shoes, whatever it is that you people do," said Joseph then he made a sinister smile.

"Shut up!" Floria shouted then she shook her head at Joesph.

"Hey, look! Emilio has a girlfriend," cried Joseph, his gaze starkly focused on them.

"Maybe he does," said Floria with a sarcastic tone. "Are you jealous?"

"No," replied Joseph with his arms crossed.

Floria knew Joseph fancied her. His eyes told her every day.

"Are you sure?" Floria said, then, without thinking, pushed Emilio back and kissed his lips passionately in front of the entire class. As they finished, she looked over to Joseph, whose jaw was on the floor and his face pale.

Emilio smiled, then kissed Floria again, the entire class gasping.

"What I said earlier was stupid," Floria whispered into Emilio's ear.

"I knew you felt the same. I just knew it," he whispered back. "Is this the rest that comes later?"

"Perhaps."

10

1937

The butcher shop continued to sit empty. Most of its windows were boarded, but one had been damaged by a brick from a group of teenagers with nothing better to do. The sign had been removed; the only thing remaining was the bolts in the bricks, rusty and loose. Leonarda walked past the space each day, her dream of one day opening a pastry shop beginning to fester in her mind.

She remembered the busy life the butcher shop once had—the smell of fresh cuts of meat mingling with the scent of sawdust on the floor. Giuseppe, with his kind eyes and roaring laughter, was one of the only people capable of making her husband content. After the closure, the neighbourhood was never the same.

Each day, as she passed the old butcher shop, her steps would slow. She would pause, imagining what the space could become. Her mind buzzed with ideas: a warm, inviting interior filled with the scent of fresh-baked Sicilian bread and pastries, display cases brimming with colour. There would be a sign hung above the door, large enough to be seen from six blocks away. She knew the neighbours probably took her for a madwoman, standing in front of the door, eyes closed with a grin, but she paid their opinions no mind.

Inspired, Leonarda confronted Salvatore with her ideas when he returned from his job at the coal plant out in the countryside—a temporary job he had taken to keep food on the table, a job he despised as he came home caked in soot and miserable daily.

"And how would we do this?" asked Salvatore, wiping the soot from his eyes.

"Well, I would do the baking, the boys could run the front with their friends, and you could assist me when you return from work if you wanted to," Leonarda said, then smiled.

"It seems you have already given this some thought," Salvatore said as he paced. "And what exactly would you call this shop of yours?"

Leonarda paused, then said, "Mamma Leonarda's."

Salvatore shook his head in disagreement. "What if we called it Leonarda's Pasticceria?" he said, then grinned. "We could call it Leonarda's in short form."

"No. It doesn't fit."

Salvatore scratched his forehead. "Pasticceria di Bucci," he said excitedly.

Leonarda smiled. "I think that is it!"

"Imagine our name, famous, gracing the covers of the newspapers. The store is in the background while you hold up your pastries," Salvatore said as he motioned his arms wide.

"The people would come from all over, not just our neighbourhood. Every Italian from up the Ottawa River to New York would come just for my pastries."

Salvatore sat at the kitchen table with Leonarda, planning every minute detail of their proposed business. They drew a sign and planned a menu, smiling the entire time. For Leonarda, it was the first time she felt she had a purpose in her life. She planned on using all her grandmother's recipes from Sicily—ones nobody had ever seen before.

Salvatore looked at the ground, lost in his thoughts, as Leonarda tried to get his attention.

"It's just that there is one problem. Where would we get the money to finance such a shop? I make just enough to keep us fed and the rent paid, but not much more," explained Salvatore as reality shattered his spirits.

Leonarda sat quietly, thinking of all the money she wasted over the years from the sale of the necklace, her only inheritance of monetary value. "We could get a loan at the bank."

"A loan?" repeated Salvatore, and then he laughed. "Not here, not now. Nobody is getting a loan in these times," he said, his voice dull.

"Well, who owns the building?"

"When I worked there, it was a man by the name of Davide Scavo. He owned the entire block, but I'm not sure if that's still the case," said Salvatore as he scratched his scalp.

"I'm sure something could be worked out. The alternative, as it stands, is that he is making nothing if that store remains closed," added Leonarda.

"Well, you have a point," Salvatore said with his hands in the air, facing upwards. "Allow me to speak with Giuseppe and Davide, man to man, and settle something. Are you sure this is something you want?"

"I'm more than certain, Salva."

Salvatore nodded at his wife; her stare was intense, and her face was still.

*

Floria and Emilio had been spending the afternoon at the beach, the scent of Lake Ontario releasing its putrid odours. The sun shined through the clouds, casting a golden haze that kissed their skin. Floria lay on Emilio's stomach, looking up at the seagulls swarming the sky. They relished the tranquillity and the soft sound of waves hitting the shore. Emilio ran his fingers through Floria's hair, marvelling at its silkiness beneath his touch.

At this moment, time seemed to stretch, their worries silent. They shared their dreams and aspirations, with Emilio speaking about his desire to return to Sicily one day and start his own hotel overlooking the sea. Floria laughed at first, then warmed up to the idea. They laughed about the exorbitant price they could charge to stay there.

Floria's heart swelled, her fingers tracing patterns on his chest, etching her name on him.

"Do you think we could ever return?" Emilio asked, his face stern. "Aside from this stupid dream of mine, could we really return?"

"Why is it stupid?" Floria said. "I think it could work."

"You know why both of our parents left; there's no money back home," Emilio said with a defeated tone.

"Right, because we live such lavish lives here," Floria replied, then laughed. "We are not our parents; we have new, bright ideas to make a living. My mother is stuck in times gone by, and my father, wherever he is, is stuck chasing women half his age in some casino. I will not be like my parents, neither of them."

"Me either. My mother is alright, but she does nothing with her time except cook, bake, and clean. There's more to life than just housework. My father is a headcase. One minute, I'm his darling son, and the next, he hates me. I can't stand living like this much longer," Emilio said, then sighed.

"Your parents are not that bad," Floria said while she picked up handfuls of sand and then let it fall through the cracks of her fingers.

"From your perspective, I'd agree. From my perspective, I do not."

Emilio arrived home to find Raffale pacing around the apartment, his stare distant and his steps heavy. Raffaele was taking deep breaths, mumbling words that Emilio couldn't make out.

"What are you doing, Raf?"

"Stupid dago! Stupid dago!"

"Raf?" Emilio said, grabbing his brother's arm to snap him out of his trance.

"Stupid dago, go home!"

"Raf!" Emilio yelled, shaking his brother.

Raffaele's head shook, and he stared at Emilio. His face had been cut, and blood was slowly dripping below his eye.

"What happened?" shrieked Emilio. "Who did this?"

"Joseph—Joseph Cars—"

"Joseph Carswell?" repeated Emilio, his shoulders dropping and his arms tensing.

"Yes, him and a few other guys. They followed me home, and before I could turn down the street, one of them tackled me. My face hit the ground, scraping the sidewalk. I looked up, and Joseph was standing over me, his face red and his voice booming. He called me a dago and said we are better off back with the Duce," Raffaele cried. "Emilio, who is the Duce?"

Emilio, his body filled with rage as he jumped up and down on the spot, said, "The Duce is what they call Mussolini."

"What do I have to do with the Duce?"

"Nothing, Raf, nothing."

Emilio slammed the front door behind him and began marching down the street. People in his path cleared as he swatted them away like flies.

When he reached the Carswell house, the gardener had been pruning a boxwood. The gardener called out to Emilio, but he pretended the man did not exist.

As he slammed on the front door, Emilio heard the shuffling of feet, and then the door creaked open with an ominous screech.

"Hello there, how may I help you, sir?" said the butler, an older gentleman with a pressed white shirt and black trousers.

"Good afternoon. Is Joseph home at the moment?" Emilio said, then politely smiled through his teeth.

"I do believe so. Master Joseph usually is home at this hour. May I ask who it is that I have the pleasure of speaking to?"

"Oh, I am a friend of Master Joseph's from school," Emilio said confidently, then smiled again.

"Very well, I will send him down," the butler said, then nodded.

Emilio stepped back onto the porch, hiding behind the post next to the door. As the door opened, he heard Joseph call out, then closed the door behind himself.

"Master Joseph, is that what they call you around here?" Emilio said with a hint of mockery in his voice.

"What—what are you doing here?" replied Joseph, beads of sweat forming on his hairline.

"I was in the neighbourhood, and I thought to myself, I should pay my friend Joseph a visit."

Joseph quickly turned around and tried to open the front door. In a panic, the handle was too difficult to operate, his thumb not pushing down hard enough.

Emilio lunged, tossing Joseph into the door. As he stood over him, Joseph looked up, terrified. Emilio pulled his arm back, making a fist, then swung hard into Joesph's teeth. A slight crack violated the air, and then Joseph screamed as blood fell from his mouth. As he opened his mouth, his teeth remained intact, but they had punctured his bottom lip.

"Mess with my brother again, and next time, those pretty teeth of yours will be no more!" Emilio shouted as Joseph lay helpless on the porch.

The gardener, watching in horror, began to scream.

Later that evening, Leonarda had prepared sausages and mashed potatoes. Raffaele detested them, constantly reminding them that the sausages back home were not half-filler.

"I can see the grains in these. There's hardly any pork," explained Raffaele.

"Shut up and eat it. It's not often we get meat anymore," Emilio replied, then shoved another bite into his mouth.

"This is not meat!" Raffaele said, tossing his fork on the table, which made the plates bounce slightly.

"Boys!" Leonarda scolded. "Emilio, don't tell your brother to shut up, especially not at the dinner table. Raffaele, please stop complaining about every meal we eat. Your father works hard, very hard. The world is a different place now. We need to consider ourselves lucky for everything we have."

Salvatore nodded, agreeing with his wife.

A violent knock pounded the Bucci's front door as they continued to eat, startling Leonarda as she placed her hand on her chest.

Salvatore rushed to the door, opening it with a confused stare. Before him were Mr Carswell and his son, each standing side by side.

"Mr Bucci?" said Mr Carswell, his eyes squinting.

"Yes?" replied Salvatore.

"Is Emilio here, your boy?"

"I am," Emilio said confidently.

Salvatore took a step back, his face confused.

"Well, Emilio, I will say. When I first discovered my boy, I considered pressing charges," Mr Carswell began. "However, I am a man with the ability to reason. I pondered the many reasons a person would do this to my Joseph," he said as he shook Joseph's shoulder, who had been timidly staring at the floor. "I did somewhat of an investigation, if one would call it that, and Joseph's friend, Robert, finally disclosed to me after I crossed him like I do to opponents during mediation what they had done to provoke such a reaction. And for that, I am deeply sorry for I have failed to raise a gentleman; rather, I have raised a heathen in its place."

"I don't understand," Salvatore mumbled.

Mr Carswell shook Joseph's limp shoulder again and said, "Please, son, tell Mr Bucci here what exactly you have done."

"I-I-I was the one who beat up Raffaele," Joseph muttered.

Salvatore's eyes opened wide as Raffaele appeared behind him, the blood now dried and crusty. Raffaele had told both of his parents that he had fallen down the stairs leading up to the apartment.

"Perfect, now Joseph, what was it that you wished to say to Mr Bucci here and Raffaele?" said Mr Carswell, and then he grinned.

"I'm terribly sorry for what I said and did," Joseph said, his eyes rolling as he did.

"Come again, son. I'm not sure Mr Bucci heard you, as I barely did."

"I'm sorry Raffaele!"

Raffaele nodded his head as Emilio smirked.

"Now, back home, son. Leave the gentlemen to discuss other matters," Mr Carswell said, lightly nudging Joseph.

"Please, come in," Salvatore said, stepping out of the doorway.

Salvatore led Mr Carswell through the front entryway and past the kitchen. Leonarda, confused, stood up and asked her husband in Italian, the reason for his unexpected guest. Salvatore responded in English, making her more confused.

"Please sit down on the settee there. Would you like anything to drink?" asked Salvatore.

"No, I'm quite alright, thank you," Mr Carswell replied, taking in the petite nature of the room. "I will only be here for a short while; I have a client to meet tonight as his negotiations are set for two days' time."

"A lawyer, I presume?" said Salvatore.

"Yes, I deal in matters of property law and things of that nature, more civil matters. It's quite dull to those not in the business if I am being honest." Mr Carswell chuckled. "Tell me, Mr Bucci, what is it that you exactly do for work?"

"I work at a coal plant," Salvatore said while shuffling in his armchair. "I oversee a few men, making sure they don't injure themselves."

"I see. Have you always been involved in that industry?"

"No, before that, I managed a butcher shop, which has since been closed. And in Italy, I did the same. Going back a few years, I managed an estate in our hometown in the agricultural industry," said Salvatore proudly.

"It appears you are quite good at managing people, doesn't it?" Mr Carswell said, then he grinned. "You see, the reason I ask is that I heard through the grapevine that you are quite a hard worker. My people and I have many—tell me you have a work ethic most do not."

"Well, yes, this is true, but—"

"Now is not the time to be humble," Mr Carswell interjected.

"Yes, I do."

"Well, I have an opportunity for you, Mr. Bucci. Please, between us gentlemen and God only, how much do they compensate you at the coal plant for your work?"

Salvatore hesitated, then walked over to Mr Carswell and whispered the number in his ear.

Mr Carswell nodded, then said, "My offer is double."

"Yes, when can I start?"

"Well, Mr Bucci, I have not described what I need from you. You see, your people have been coming here in large numbers. This is not something I particularly see an issue with." Mr Carswell smiled. "As an opportunistic man, you see, the opportunity has been laid in front of my eyes ever so clearly. As time progresses, those of Italian backgrounds will need some form of legal representation as they seek to purchase properties. Seeing that you can speak English well, you could essentially be a bridge between those potential clients and my firm. In the meantime, I can have you file paperwork and do small tasks to keep occupied. Now, given this, do you still accept, Mr Bucci?"

"I do." Salvatore smiled and shook Mr Carswell's hand.

"Very well, I look forward to our ventures," Mr Carswell said as he sprung up from the settee.

*

That evening, Emilio lay in bed, staring at the ceiling. The entire house had gone to sleep, or so he had thought. In the dimly lit kitchen, Salvatore sat drinking a cup of stale coffee he had made hours ago. It tasted like a cigarette with a slight hint of sweetness.

As Emilio got up to get a glass of water, he spotted his father.

"What are you doing up at this hour?" asked Salvatore.

"Can't sleep."

"Why is that?" Salvatore said, sipping on his coffee.

"I'm not sure," said Emilio, shrugging his shoulders.

"You know, when things like that happen, you can tell me." Salvatore pulled a chair out for Emilio. "Please, sit."

Emilio reluctantly sat down, his anxious energy intensifying.

"Now, tell me exactly what happened. I promise I will not be mad. In fact, I'm quite impressed. Standing up for your brother—that's impressive. Emilio, you acted at a time when you could have done nothing. You truly are becoming a man."

"Really? So you're not mad?" Emilio said, his eyes wide and his mouth opening after he spoke.

"No. I'm proud." Salvatore smiled.

"Proud?"

"Yes, proud."

Emilio choked, and then a tear built up in his eye. He quickly wiped it so that his father didn't notice. "I have just never seen Raf so upset. His face looked terrible. Those Carswell boys are vermin, the scum of this town."

"Emilio, be careful," cautioned Salvatore. "I understand what Joseph did was bad, but never tarnish another man's name when he's not around to defend himself. Even if you believe, and rightfully so, that he is a terrible person." Salvatore took another sip of his coffee.

"Defend? There's nothing to defend. Joseph is a terrible person," explained Emilio, his breathing becoming more rapid as the images of Joseph flooded his mind.

"I agree, son. All I ask is that once your quarrel is finished with any man, no matter who, you remain silent so as not to continue to destroy a man's dignity, even if that man deserves it."

Emilio sat and reflected on his father's words, pensively staring at the wall behind his father. He noticed its cream colour was flaking, and the old red paint was showing through the broken pieces.

"I want you to have something," Salvatore said, reaching into his trouser pockets. "But promise me this. I hope to God that you never have to use it, but if you do, it can only be used to protect the ones you love and nothing else. This is not a weapon to use should you lose a fight or an object to flash around to appear as if you are tougher than your short Sicilian genes allow."

"Short? Who did I get that from?" Emilio said, then smiled.

Salvatore chuckled. "Now, this knife belonged to my best friend. Before we came here, he entrusted me with it. Now, I want you to have it," he said as he placed the knife in Emilio's hand.

Emilio pulled the blade from the sheath, its mirrored surface reflecting the lightbulb above them. "Why would you give this to me?"

"This world is a terrible place. In this lifetime, you will see things you wish you hadn't. Things that rob you of your sleep. Things that have you up in the middle of the night, drinking coffee and staring into the abyss. It's not about how we can prevent these things; rather, it's about being prepared for when these things happen," Salvatore said, his eyes watery.

"Thank you."

PETAWAWA

Emilio slid the knife into his pocket and went to his bedroom. After an hour, he faded away.

11

Four months later, Salvatore had enough money to cover a portion of the rent for the space Leonarda envisioned. The landlord, Davide, agreed to a deal in which Salvatore paid for half of the rent in cash and the other half was deducted from their gross revenue. Although not ideal, Leonarda agreed, so the paperwork was signed by the gentlemen in her absence.

First, the sign was installed—a large black-painted wood sign with golden lettering. The shimmer it made as the sun hit it was unlike anything the neighbourhood had seen. After cleaning the front and repairing the broken window, the façade came to life once again. The inside was the most difficult; the floors were caked in dust and years of neglect. Rats, mice, and spiders ran rampant, but they were no match for Leonarda. After a few weeks, the furry tenants had all been evicted.

The opening weekend was buzzing with excitement. Leonarda and Salvatore had worked tirelessly to transform the dilapidated space into a charming bakery that emitted the charm of Sicilian cuisine in the downtown core of Hamilton. As the doors swung open on that crisp Saturday morning, the scent of freshly baked bread and pastries wafted out onto the street, drawing in curious neighbours who had followed their every move since the renovations began.

The bell above the door chimed as their first customers stepped inside, greeted by the sight of shelves filled with biscotti Leonarda had baked in preparation. From crusty loaves of Sicilian bread to delicate, bright pastries, there was something for every customer. Leonarda stood behind the counter, her apron dusted with flour, as she expertly served customers with a smile. She wanted to be the first person they saw on opening day, to prove to the neighbourhood that she had what it took. If customers who spoke English entered the shop, she made her husband fill in for her.

Salvatore, meanwhile, manned the ovens with precision, ensuring that each batch of bread emerged from the heat perfectly golden brown. He had never baked bread in his life, but for his wife, he vowed to learn. Emilio supervised, remembering all of the baking he had watched his mother do while in Agrigento.

"Another five minutes," said Emilio.

"How can you tell? They look ready to me," Salvatore replied, shrugging his shoulders.

"Trust me, another five minutes."

"Lio is right," Leonarda said as she stumbled into the back. "Listen to your boss, Salva." Leonarda smiled as she rubbed Emilio's hair, his combed appearance now ruffled.

"My boss?" Salvatore grinned as he slid the loaves back into the oven. "The boy can't even toast a slice of bread; what does he know about baking it?"

Emilio shook his head, then grinned. "Where is Raf? Why isn't he helping?" he said. "Today is an important day for Pasticceria Bucci."

Leonarda put a tray down on the counter. "He's coming in about an hour. He said he would be here by the afternoon."

The towel Salvatore had been using to provide a barrier between the hot pan and his hand slipped. "Shit!"

Leonarda and Emilio turned their heads, witnessing the tray of bread crash to the floor. Both loaves slid, skidding across the tiles.

"I'm sorry," Salvatore began, "the pan slipped."

"That is coming out of your cheque," Leonarda said, then she grinned.

The front door opened slightly, and then the bell chimed. Floria stepped inside, her hair tied back and her clothing unusually casual. Emilio couldn't tell if she had stolen coveralls from a mechanic shop. There was even an oil stain on her knees, its colour black and pronounced upon the navy fabric. As Floria approached Leonarda, she explained that her mother had sent her over to work for the wage of a free loaf of bread. Leonarda agreed, countering her offer of employment by doubling it and adding a biscotti bonus.

"For now, there's dishes in the back if you wouldn't mind, darling," Leonarda gushed. "If you would like, you can work here, not just for bread."

Salvatore looked at his wife with wide eyes, lost in his thoughts about the tight finances.

"I'm not a baker, but thank you," Floria said. "But if you ever need a hand ever so often, I can be available."

"Careful, love. Mamma may take you up on that," Emilio added.

Salvatore looked at his son, mouthing the word that had just flowed effortlessly from his son's lips, a simple display of affection so unrestrained.

Emilio put his finger to his lips, then shook his head.

When Raffaele arrived, the sun had moved across the horizon at a great distance. He apologised for his tardiness, yet he remained evasive about his previous whereabouts. Salvatore had retired home, and Leonarda had locked the door about half an hour ago. She had been in the front, counting the sales for the day.

As she counted, Leonarda thought to herself that if they continued at this pace, the shop would be around for generations. She envisioned Emilio's future children working the cash register, yet she couldn't make out their faces despite the fact that they felt real to her. She imagined Raffaele, ten years older, whose face hadn't aged a day. His skin was still youthful and untainted by time.

For some reason, in her vision, Emilio had smile lines, and his hair slightly receded like his father's, following the same pattern. She knew both her sons would eventually have Salvatore's hairline, yet the thought brought her comfort and immense sadness at the same time.

Raffaele stepped into the storefront, apologising again for not showing up as he promised. Leonarda, already teary, grabbed his face and then pinched his cheeks. Taken back, he asked the reason she had been upset, but Leonarda wouldn't disclose the truth. Instead, changing the subject, she asked Raffaele to try the different cookies she had made.

First, he was fed taralli, a lemon-glazed cookie her grandmother baked every Sunday when lemons were ripe. Raffale nodded as he bit down for a second time, letting her know the recipe was just as he remembered it from back home. His eyes said otherwise.

Leonarda informed him that the lemons came from an importer in Toronto, that they weren't as fresh as the ones they knew, but that they were what she had. Raffaele couldn't grasp why they would pay an exorbitant price for flavourless lemons.

As he wiped his mouth, Leonarda cut a *tetu* in half, a spiced chocolate cookie with a white glaze.

Raffaele chewed the cookie, then shook his head. "The spices are wrong."

"I have to use what I can here," Leonarda explained with a defeated stare. "They don't have all of the ingredients I need, especially not now."

"They still taste delicious, Mamma," Raffaele said, then kissed his mother's cheek. "You will perfect these updated recipes, I know you will."

Leonarda contemplated tossing the trays, but her arms wouldn't allow her. She thought of the many people she had seen in her life, starving and half-naked, nothing but bones. Her grandmother's voice echoed in her head—an intense lecture on food waste.

*

Later that evening, as Emilio made his way past his brother's room, the tired floorboards groaned beneath his footsteps, bearing the weight of years gone by in their worn-out apartment. The hallway, dimly lit by a flickering bulb overhead, cast long shadows that danced along the walls.

Pushing open the door, he was met with a scene of organised chaos. English learning books lay scattered across the floor, their spines cracked and pages dog-eared from countless readings. Emilio lightly chuckled. Thinking about his brother studying the complexities of English was both adorable and dreadful. He considered the fact that, despite Raffaele's distaste for life in Canada, deep down, he had big, long-term plans for this country. Drawings covered the walls, overlapping in a kaleidoscope of scenes of home, each one a window into Raffaele's mind. Emilio knew his brother had liked drawing as a child, but he was ignorant of his talents now.

The scenes, detailed despite their lack of colour, reminded him of home. Each drawing evoked memories—ones that Emilio had long archived. The desk, cluttered with half-finished sketches and crumpled sheets of paper, also had stacks of journals, each labelled with different years. Clothes hung aimlessly from an overstuffed wardrobe, their colours intertwining. Despite the chaos, there was a sense of comfort in Emilio's eyes. He lingered for a moment, taking in the sights of his brother's domain, before reluctantly closing the door behind him.

"What were you doing in my room?" Raffaele said as Emilio stepped into the corridor.

Emilio, his face frozen and his stomach knotted, looked up to his brother. "I was—I was just closing a window, that's all," he stammered. "There was a draft, and I couldn't stand it anymore."

"A draft?" Raffaele said. "My window is always closed."

"Not today, it wasn't," Emilio replied as he moved his hair from his warm forehead.

Raffaele stared into his brother's soul, his eyes wide. "Did you read my journals, you bastard?"

"Journals?" Emilio repeated. "I did not see any journals. I did, however, notice your drawings. Incredible work! Why haven't you shown these to anyone?"

Raffaele's shoulders dropped, and he took a deep breath. "Because they are for my eyes, and my eyes only. Please stay out of my room because next time, I'm not asking questions."

"Relax, you dago goon." Emilio laughed as his brother's face turned red.

"Don't call me that, Emilio!"

"Dago!"

Raffaele's breathing became rapid. "Shut up!"

"Dago goon!" Emilio said, then gave a snarky grin. "Look at this hot-headed wop!"

Raffaele lunged at his brother, causing Emilio's smile to drop instantly. As Emilio fell to the floor, Raffaele sat on his chest with his arm up in the air.

"I was just playing, Raf!" Emilio cried, his eyes focused on his brother's fist.

"Call me a dago one more time; I dare you."

Emilio smiled again, unintimidated. "I won't; I like my teeth." He giggled again, which made Raffaele return a smile despite his own efforts not to.

"You're a real piece of work, you know that?" Raffaele said as he relaxed his arm. "I just hate that word; I really do."

Emilio stood up after his brother let him go. "Would you really punch me?"

Raffaele froze, his eyes shifting to the floor. "You just don't get it, do you?" he began. "Ever since we came to this country, the people here act like we don't belong. I feel like an intruder, out of place everywhere. That word, that disgusting word, makes me sick to my stomach. Every time I hear it, I see a Carswell brother sitting on top of me, spitting in my face. I see a stranger look at me funny on the train, and I see the shopkeeper roll his eyes as I ask Mamma a question. These people, these Canadian people, don't want us here, Emilio. Yet you seem so blind to it all."

"Blind? You don't think I don't understand what you have been through? Did you forget that I am also from the same town, speak the same language, and look exactly the same as you? Yes, we don't have blond hair and blue eyes; yes, we don't speak flawless English; and yes, we were not born in this country. Does that change the fact we could be Canadians if we tried?"

Raffaele laughed. "Canadians?" He shook his head. "No matter how hard you try, no matter how much you lie to yourself, Emilio, you will never be a true Canadian."

"I don't lie to myself. I know that I'm Italian; that will never change." Emilio took a deep breath. "I can't help the fact that I have an accent. But you know what? That accent makes me who I am. I will never be a true Canadian; that is true. But to survive here, we have to adapt to life here. Sitting in your bedroom, locked away and angry at the world while drawing stupid little pictures of home is not going to help you make friends here. Maybe try socialising every once in a while. Maybe, just maybe then—"

"Fuck you, Emilio. Fuck you!" Raffaele stormed towards the front door of the apartment.

"Raf, sorry, I didn't mean—"

The door slammed, cutting Emilio short. He sat down on the settee and cried—an intense cry, something he hadn't done in years.

12

The breakfast table was silent. Emilio cleared his plate, handing it to his mother to wash, while Raffaele sat facing the wall, avoiding all contact with his brother. Salvatore sat down beside his son and greeted him. He sensed Raffaele was lost in his thoughts, but he would rather not investigate.

Salvatore considered Raffaele the emotional son, the one better to leave to his own devices when silent. Salvatore poured himself a cup of coffee from the moka pot on the table, the aroma of nuts and tar filling the room. He glanced at Raffaele, noticing the tightness of his shoulders, which were held back and high.

Salvatore sipped his coffee, the bitter taste mingling with the sweetness of the sugar Leonarda had mixed in—the way he liked it. Emilio, the outgoing one, always ready with a joke or a smile, was easier to understand for Salvatore. But Raffaele, with his quiet introspection, often left Salvatore feeling like an outsider in his own home. He often wondered what troubled Raffaele and what demons lurked in the shadows of his mind. But he knew better than to pry. He reached across the table, placing a hand on Raffaele's arm, and Raffaele flinched slightly but didn't pull away.

Salvatore squeezed his son's arm gently. They sat like that for a moment, then, with a sigh, Salvatore released his grip and returned to his coffee, leaving Raffaele to his thoughts. The morning sunlight streamed through the window, casting long shadows across the room. Outside, the world was waking up—birds chirping in the distance, people stumbling down the street. But inside, at the breakfast table, time seemed to stand still.

"What do you want to eat?" Leonarda said as she stared at her husband.

"Nothing for me, just this coffee will do."

"Salva, you must." Leonarda began slicing the bread she had brought home from yesterday's close. "Please, at least a slice or two of my bread."

"Only if you made it," Salvatore said, then smiled. "Raffaele, are you not eating?"

Raffaele hung his head, then covered his face with his arm.

"Raffaele, when I ask you a question, you better answer it," Salvatore demanded.

Raffaele lifted his head and mumbled, "I'm not hungry."

"Well, that's going to catch up with you at church. It's Sunday; there won't be another meal until your mother makes us a delicious meal late this afternoon."

"I'm not going to church," Raffaele groaned.

"The hell you are!"

"Salva, please, not now," Leonarda cried. "He must be unwell. Maybe he can rest instead."

"He can rest after church," Salvatore affirmed.

"Why do we go to church anyway?" Do you really think if there is a God, that he cares if we sit in a room and say some ancient Roman prayer?" Raffaele said as he opened his arms like a preacher.

"It's not 'if' there's a God. There is a God. You will be going to church!"

"Salva, please!"

"Leonarda, I will handle this!"

"I will go. Just please, don't make me go up for the Eucharist. I want to sit in the back and ignore everyone there," Raffaele said, then rolled his eyes.

"Son, you don't make the terms. When Father calls us up for the Eucharist, as the good Catholic boy we raised you to be, you will go. I will not speak anymore on this issue," Salvatore asserted. "Now, eat a slice of bread, wash your face, and change into something more presentable."

Emilio had been standing in the doorway of his room, watching from afar while trying to hold in his laughter. As his brother stood up from the table, Emilio quickly stepped into his room to conceal his position, shutting the door behind him.

*

After mass, Father pulled Salvatore and Leonarda aside to discuss the new Sunday schedule. As they conversed, Emilio looked at his brother, but Raffaele quickly averted his eyes. They stood near the flowerbed; Raffaele's polished leather Oxford shoes were halfway in the soil.

Emilio sighed softly, his gaze lingering on his brother's bowed form. He wished he could ease the tension, but he knew he needed to apologise for that to happen. Instead, he focused on the conversation between his parents and Father, pretending not to notice the tension that hung in the air like a heavy fog. The discussion about the new Sunday schedule drifted over him, the words blending together into a meaningless hum. All he could think about was Raffaele, standing there with his shoes half-buried in the soil.

Emilio wanted to speak, to apologise, but he knew that Raffaele needed time. He wished things could be different that they could all be happy and carefree, like they used to be when they were children. But life here had a way of complicating things—it was just different now. Emilio glanced at Raffaele again, his heart yearning for a simple acknowledgement. He wanted nothing more than to see his brother's smile.

"I'm sorry."

Raffaele looked at his brother and shook his head. "Sorry?"

"I'm sorry for yesterday. I know those drawings mean a lot to you, Raf," Emilio said as their eyes met.

"Drawings? Do you seriously think this is about the drawings?"

"No, what I meant was the part after where I was mean to you. I was a fool, and for that, I'm sorry."

Raffaele let out a slight smirk. "You were acting like a fool."

"I know what I said was not right. I don't mean any of those things I said to you," Emilio explained. "You know that, right, Raf?"

"Maybe."

"Come on, stop!"

Raffaele smiled, then patted his brother's back. "Now, was it that hard?"

Emilio wrapped his arm around him and squeezed his brother's bicep. "These things wouldn't have even hurt me yesterday."

Raffaele shook his head with a smile. "You really are something, Emilio."

*

The next evening, Emilio planned to pick Floria up from her house for a date. As Emilio arrived at Floria's house, he couldn't help but feel a sense of excitement tinged with nervousness. Maria's enthusiasm about their relationship only added to the fluttering feeling in his stomach. He was determined to make this dinner memorable for Floria and to show her just how much she meant to him.

Floria emerged from her bedroom, glowing in a cream-coloured dress that complemented her olive skin and dark, wavy hair. Emilio couldn't tear his gaze away as she approached, his heart skipping a beat at the sight of her. He offered her his arm with a smile, feeling a surge of pride as they walked out the door.

As they strolled to the French restaurant, Emilio stole glances at Floria, admiring her elegance. He constantly reminded her of her beauty every day, but the dress changed things in his eyes. He couldn't help but feel a swell of affection for her, kissing her hand as he pulled it up to his.

Upon arriving at the restaurant, they were greeted by an arrogant server who eyed them with thinly veiled distaste. Emilio's smile faltered slightly, but he quickly recovered, determined not to let anything spoil their evening. Floria glanced around the restaurant, her eyes widening at the fancy decor and the well-dressed diners. She couldn't help but feel apprehensive at the prices listed on the menu, her mind calculating the cost of each dish.

The restaurant radiated elegance, with soft lighting casting a warm glow over the intimate dining space. Rich velvet curtains framed tall windows, allowing a glimpse of the city beyond. Tables were covered with crisp white linens and flickering candles. Detailed chandeliers hung from the ceiling, casting patterns across the polished wooden floors.

"Emilio, this place is somewhere I never thought we would go," she murmured, her gaze lingering on the menu. "But the prices are high, don't you think?"

Emilio chuckled, squeezing her hand reassuringly. "You're worth it, Floria. Besides, business has been good lately, and my mother gave me some cash that my father can't know about," he replied.

Floria nodded, though a small furrow appeared between her brows. She trusted Emilio's judgement, but the prices still made her uneasy.

"They were not supposed to give you the gentlemen's menu," Emilio said, shaking his head.

"The gentlemen's menu?"

"That's the one with the prices. Ladies usually receive the menu without the prices listed," Emilio explained.

Their server returned to take their order, and his attitude was noticeably frosty as he addressed them. Emilio couldn't help but notice the subtle sneer that accompanied his words, though he brushed it off as mere professionalism.

Floria, however, sensed the underlying hostility and frowned slightly, exchanging a puzzled glance with Emilio. She couldn't shake the feeling of being unwelcome despite their server's outward politeness.

Throughout the meal, their server remained distant and abrupt, his demeanour leaving much to be desired. Emilio did his best to engage him in conversation, attempting to lighten the atmosphere with jokes, but his efforts were met with only monosyllabic responses. His subtle disdain grated on his nerves, and he found himself longing for the warmth and familiarity of their favourite neighbourhood diner.

"Next time, let's go to Pete's," Emilio said abruptly.

"Let's go there now. This restaurant, although beautiful, left me hungry. Let's spend some of that cash and live a little."

"That's my girl!" Emilio laughed. "Shall we get some of those French fried potatoes they make?"

"Emilio, nobody says French fried potatoes anymore. It's just french fries."

"My Canadian girl," Emilio said, then giggled.

*

Pete's Diner was the only business open late for ten blocks, its sign illuminated by a few flickering light bulbs. If they hadn't known about it, like many who pass by, they would have assumed that the diner was closed.

As they entered, the door squeaked, which made the only two men sitting along the bar glance back. Pete had been working the night shift; his apron sopped in fryer grease, and his black hair, dishevelled, was swept to the right side. Emilio and Floria sat down in an empty booth while Pete poured their usual pop into a glass. He added a quarter pump extra of syrup with the soda water, as he knew Emilio liked his on the sweeter side. Behind Pete was the menu board; the options were limited.

"Good evening, lovebirds," Pete said as he placed the drinks on the table. "What can I do you for?"

Emilio grinned. "Good evening, Pete. We would love some of those fried potatoes."

"French fries?" Pete corrected. "Sure thing."

Floria shook her head and then said, "Oh, Emilio, you really are something."

They both laughed and mocked Emilio's request repeatedly.

Floria dug into her purse, fumbling with its contents. She pulled out a package of Camels, sliding one from the box. Emilio looked at her in shock, unaware of her habit.

"I need a smoke after that cad at the restaurant," Floria sighed.

"Cad?" Emilio said, his eyes wide. "And since when do you smoke?"

"You know, cad. He was rude," Floria expressed as she pulled a box of matches. "Why, are you going to tell my mother?"

"What if I do?"

"My mother has done far worse in her life, I assure you," Floria said as she shuffled from her seat. "I would smoke in here, but I know you would judge me, won't you?" Floria smiled.

"I would, yes." Emilio shook his head with a grin.

Standing in view of Emilio, Floria took in the sights and sounds of the city at night. The darkness crept into every corner, swallowing the edges of buildings and streets, leaving only the faint glow of distant streetlights and the occasional flicker of neon signs. The air was thick with the distant murmur of voices drifting from nearby alleyways.

As she exhaled a plume of smoke, it danced in the faint illumination, swirling and dissipating into the night air. Her cigarette glowed amber, like a beacon between her fingers. The city was alive with restless energy, yet amidst the chaos, there was a sense of stillness—a quiet moment of solitude—that engulfed Floria. But as she stood there, lost in the sounds of the night, her solitude was interrupted by the sudden appearance of a figure beside her.

A man dressed in a white button-down shirt and navy trousers approached with a confident stride, his features illuminated by the soft glow of the streetlight. He was young, his eyes gleaming with an intensity that mirrored lights in the distance. With a casual 'hello,' he asked for a cigarette, his voice smooth. As Floria reached into her pocket to retrieve one, she vanished from Emilio's view for a moment; however, he was unaware as Pete was lost in conversation with Emilio, filling each other in on updates with their own families.

Floria handed the man a cigarette, yet he complained about the brand. He told her he smoked a brand she had never heard of before, assuming it was some affluent underground cigarettes that cost double that of her Camels. He leaned forward to Floria's lit match, then puffed out the first hit of smoke that engulfed his face.

"So, what's a fine young woman like you doing out here all alone?" he said, moving the middle-parted curtains from his forehead.

"Same as you, I suppose."

"I mean, what is a woman like you doing out here alone in the dark? Especially near an alleyway? Don't you know there's bad folks out here at night?"

"I do. But I'm not afraid of folks around here," Floria said, then rolled her eyes.

"And why is that?"

"Just not."

The man introduced himself, yet Floria felt the name was too generic and simple. Jacob Smith is not a real name, she thought.

"So, Mr Smith. What brings you to this part of Hamilton?" Floria said as she sucked the second last drag from her cigarette.

Jacob looked at her, and his eyes went narrow. His face went flat, showing zero emotion.

"Mr Smith?"

He took a step towards Floria, which instantly caused her palms to become moist. Jacob then tossed his cigarette into a puddle; most of it remained unburned.

"Are you sure you're not afraid?" he said as he stepped closer again.

"Mr Smith! What are you doing?"

Jacob stood directly in front of Floria, making her take three steps back. He made the same three steps forward.

"Your hair—it's not like the English girls I know. It's quite pretty."

"Excuse me?"

Jacob pushed Floria into the brick wall behind her, then pushed her again to the ground. As she lay on the concrete, her vision went blurry, and the sounds of the city bounced off the brick wall, filling her head with a cluster of noises. The weight of Jacob's body brought her awareness back, and she screamed.

"Shut up, whore! You know you wanted this; I could see it in your eyes!"

Floria cried out Emilio's name until her vocal cords nearly gave out. Her screams echoed down the alleyway like a sonic boom of fear.

Emilio heard the final scream, jumping up from the booth as Pete trailed him. As the front door swung open, Emilio and Pete took a moment to take in the horror scene in front of them. Jacob had been lying on top of Floria in the dark, his trousers at his ankles.

"Get off of her!" Emilio wailed. "I'm going to kill you, you bastard!"

Jacob looked over his shoulder and smiled—a kind of sinister smile that the most intense of exorcisms could not undo.

Emilio reached into his trouser pockets, unsheathing the knife his father had given him. His thumb rubbed against the engraved handle, and then the blade reflected the faint glow of the streetlamp across the road. Grabbing Jacob's head with his left hand, Emilio slid the blade between Floria and Jacob, turning the edge towards Jacob's neck. He pulled the blade closer and rested it on his skin.

"Now, give me one reason I don't pull my arm back and cover this alleyway in blood," Emilio said as Jacob untangled his legs from Floria. "Better yet, I could cut it off and then slit your throat."

Emilio held the blade still as he pulled his torso towards his own, and then Pete held Jacob's naked legs still, allowing Floria to slide out from under him. Her dress had not been lifted, which allowed Emilio to exhale.

Placing the tip of the blade on his back, Emilio again asked why his life should be spared. "If you were going to kill me, you would have already, dago."

"Are you testing me? You don't know what I'm capable of!" Emilio replied, poking the blade through his shirt. A small stream of blood came from the hole as Jacob cried out in pain.

"Now, what is going on here?" a voice shouted from in front of the diner. "You there, drop that knife!"

Emilio looked over his shoulder, pulling the knife away. He caught a glimpse of the police officer, who had his hand placed on his half-unholstered revolver.

"Drop the knife, son!" shouted the officer. "I'm not going to ask you again!"

Emilio threw the knife, which made an awful scraping noise as it slid under a stack of crates lining the wall.

As Emilio began to stand up, Jacob attempted to blitz his way down the alley, falling three paces later as his ankle-level trousers brought him back to the concrete.

"You there, stop running!"

Jacob bent down and pulled his trousers over his naked body, then disregarded the officer's commands, making it down the alley and vanishing into the night.

"Put your hands where I can see them, son!"

Emilio raised his hands as Floria cried out his name.

The officer placed his revolver back into the holster and approached Emilio.

"Son, when you lose a fight, you can't pull a man's pants down and pull a knife on him. That's how you know you have gone too far," the officer said sternly.

"That's not what—"

"Enough!"

"Sir, that man was trying to rape me!" Floria cried.

"It's true! I saw it with my own eyes, officer," Pete added.

"You expect me to believe that he was trying to rape you while your friend over here had him pinned to the ground with a blade, and you were standing over here, completely clothed?" The officer chuckled as he crossed his arms.

"Sir! You must believe us!" Emilio said, his face warm and his shoulders tight. "I was in the diner, having a conversation with Pete over there, and I heard a scream, so I ran outside to find that man on top of my girlfriend," explained Emilio.

"Yes, see, look at my legs; they have red marks from being pressed to the concrete," added Floria, exposing her legs to the officer.

"Enough, enough!" the officer said. "Now, why don't you all just run along? I will forget this little incident ever happened, and we will all go on our ways."

"No, but sir," began Emilio.

"That is unless you wish for me to take you in?" the officer said abruptly.

Emilio shook his head, looking at Floria and Pete. Floria met his gaze, telling him with her eyes to back down.

"Are we finished here?" said the officer. "Shall we all go on our own ways?"

Emilio groaned, then took a deep breath while Floria's face filled with tears. She wiped each one as they formed, concealing them with her fingertip.

"You people better not cause trouble in my neighbourhood again, understand?" asserted the officer. "Life was peaceful before you all came here, and I intend to keep it that way!"

Emilio looked at the officer and nodded, biting down on his tongue in the process.

The next day, Floria lay in bed for the entire day. Emilio had his brother cover his shift at the shop, offering him a few dollars to do so. When Emilio was let into the Savoia house, the air lacked the usual smell of Maria's cooking. Instead, it smelled of nothing; the lack of aromas confused him.

"My love," Emilio whispered. "How are you?"

Floria lifted her head from her pillow, then sank back into it.

Emilio lifted the covers and slid beside her.

"Emilio," she said with widened eyes. "You know we can't be laying in the same bed. My mother would kill me if she walked in on this."

"Walked in on what?" Emilio covered his body with the sheets, pressing his body against hers. "I just want to hold you." Emilio kissed her shoulder, then collapsed his head onto it.

Floria, with tears running down her face, began to sniffle. "I was so scared, Emilio."

"Me too," he said as he placed his arm around her stomach. "I will never let anybody hurt you. I would have killed him; you know that, right?"

"I do," she said, then sniffled. "I wish you had time to."

"That's my girl," Emilio said, then smiled.

"What about that knife?" said Floria. "That knife was so important to you."

"Wrong." Emilio turned Floria over onto her back, then looked into her eyes. "You are important to me. You and only you."

Floria's face softened, and she extended a hand to Emilio's hair, ruffling it, gel sticking to her fingers.

"And besides, Pete did retrieve it for me. He dropped it off early this morning, before his shift. The man is a saint."

"That he is," Floria whimpered.

"I love you."

Floria paused, then a slight smile cracked from her red face. "I love you too, Emilio."

13

1939

The law office, as predicted, saw an increase in Italian clients over the past few years. Salvatore's bilingualism paid off immensely, Mr Carswell constantly referring to him fondly as 'my Italian investment.' At the office, Salvatore processed paperwork; his desk was filled with stacks of sheets, and his pen was constantly moving. His fingertips were always black, covered in ink.

Despite the mundanity of his tasks, Salvatore took pride in his work, finding satisfaction in the meticulous process of paperwork and legal documentation. Each signature, each stamp, carried with it a sense of accomplishment.

The clients that frequented the office varied in their needs and backgrounds, but a significant portion of them were Italian immigrants like himself. Salvatore's fluency in both English and Italian proved invaluable, allowing him to bridge the gap between his clients and the complexities of Canadian law.

Today, the office buzzed with activity as Salvatore assisted a client with the purchase of his property—a common occurrence in a city experiencing rapid growth. The client, a young Italian immigrant named Antonio, had worked tirelessly to build a life for himself and his family in Hamilton. He came from Reggio-Calabria, yet his dialect was easily understood by Salvatore. Now, with the opportunity to purchase a property, Antonio sought Salvatore's expertise to navigate the intricacies of it all.

PETAWAWA

As Salvatore guided Antonio through the paperwork, explaining each clause and provision in meticulous detail, he couldn't help but feel a sense of pride in his role as a trusted advisor and advocate for his fellow immigrants. For Salvatore, the law wasn't just a profession; it was a means of empowerment, a tool to help his community navigate the challenges of life in a new country, a country that increasingly did not want people like them.

*

Raffaele had been strolling the streets with Dominic Mancuso, a boy two years older who lived in their building with his mother. Dominic was a brute, often throwing fists before asking questions. He towered over Raffaele and had about thirty pounds on him—thirty pounds of muscle. Dominic kept his black hair gelled back and meticulously combed straight back. He spoke English better than Italian, as he had only left when his father died at age two. His mother did what she could to keep them fed, which meant he saw her once a day for a period of thirty minutes before bed.

"Let's grab a bite," Dominic said, pointing to Pete's.

"I could kill for a hot dog," Raffaele said. "Something about a fresh hot dog."

"Your mother hates that you eat those; you know what she calls them."

"My mother hates a lot of things I do, Dom. Eating hot dogs is low on the list," Raffaele said, then laughed. "I hope ol' Pete is working today."

Dominic and Raffaele stepped inside the diner, the bell announcing their arrival. Inside, the booths were packed, filled shoulder to shoulder. The bar had a few seats open, so the boys sat on the fixed stools and hollered for Pete.

"The usual?" said Pete. "Two colas, a hotdog, and a plate of meatloaf?"

"Oh, you know us too well, Petey!" Dom grinned, then nodded.

"Did you make that pie?" said Raffaele, pointing to the cherry pie resting in a glass dome. "Maybe a slice of that after as well."

"Baked it yesterday. The cherries are from my mother's trees."

"Chef Pete," Raffaele said, then smiled.

As they ate, the normal bustle of the diner carried on. Families came and went, workers sipped their black coffees, and Pete refilled drinks constantly. The sound of sizzling burgers and frying onions filled the air, mingling with the aroma of savoury soups simmering on the stove. Pete, the master of multitasking, deftly juggled orders while engaging customers with his quick wit and friendly banter. Amidst the energetic scene, the sense of comfort that permeated the room remained constant, offering a break from the outside world.

"That Adolf Hitler fellow has done it," a man said, reading a copy of the Toronto Daily Star.

"A war is brewing," said another man, and then he sipped from his coffee.

"That's right, and this time, not only are we going to be fighting those dirty Germans, but also the Italians too. They are foes this time around!" replied the first man as he stroked his chin and then cut his meatloaf with his fork.

"Alright. That's enough, gentlemen. There will be no talk of politics in my diner. If you wish to speak of these matters, I will have to ask you to settle your tabs and make way," Pete asserted.

Both the men looked down and remained silent.

"What do you mean, foes?" Raffaele said abruptly. "Do you think of me as your foe?"

The first man's eyes shot through Raffaele's chest, then met his eyes. "Well, not you, but your people, rather."

"My people? Last time I checked, the people here are 'my people.' I've lived here for years; is that not enough? Am I not a Canadian?" Raffaele added.

"Not a real one," the second man mumbled.

"Come again!" said Raffaele.

The first man, embarrassed by the scene he caused, averted his eyes and stared into his plate.

"Alright, that's enough!" Pete said, his arms crossed and his head tilted.

"I'm not going to stay quiet. If these fools have something to say, then by God, say it!" Raffaele yelled.

The second man tossed his fork onto the table, grabbing the attention of all the diners. "Have you no class? In this diner, screaming like your Duce?" the man said, then shook his head.

"The Duce?" Raffaele said, then began breathing rapidly. "And so what? Maybe I love the Duce. Maybe his policies aren't half bad. That's what you wanted to hear from me, isn't it? My family and I have his poster in our kitchen, and we worship it every morning before leaving. Long live the Duce!"

The onlookers' mouths were wide open as they all stared at Raffale. Embarrassed, Dominic threw a couple bills onto the counter and dragged his friend into the streets with force.

"What's the matter with you? Do you understand what is going to happen?"

"I'm not afraid of these fools!" Raffaele said, then spit onto the sidewalk.

"We can never come back here, not for a while at least," said Dominic as he began marching down the sidewalk.

"Who cares? Pete's got nothing special. There's a diner on every block."

"Raf, what's not clicking in that thick skull of yours? Do you not understand that people love to talk? That little solo you pulled back there is going to come back to haunt you."

"I'd love to see the day. Besides, nobody could actually be stupid enough to believe me. I mean, come on, worshipping a poster? How ridiculous."

"I really hope so, Raf. I really do."

*

The phone rang six times before Emilio, who had been spread across the settee, walked over to answer it.

Emilio, leaning against the wall, absorbed Pete's words. "Thanks for letting me know, Pete," he said, his voice steady despite the urge to scream. "I'll handle it from here. Just keep an eye out for any further trouble, okay?"

"Sure thing, Emilio," Pete replied, his tone easing slightly with relief. "You know I've always got your back. Just hope that brother of yours realises the mess he's gotten himself into."

Emilio sighed, rubbing his temples as he pondered his next move. "He'll understand, one way or another," he said, more to reassure himself than Pete. "I'll talk to him, that idiot. Better yet, I'll talk to my father first."

With a final nod of gratitude, Emilio hung up the phone and returned to the settee. He only lasted a moment before a surge of electricity jolted him from his position. As he paced the room, his mind raced. He began questioning if Raffaele had tarnished their name indefinitely. He kept repeating out loud that they would have to move and that showing their faces around this neighbourhood would be too much to handle.

Emilio sat on the floor and began hyperventilating. "What a bloody fool!" He kicked the settee, yet it didn't budge, sending the shockwaves back to his knees.

As Emilio lay on the floor, Leonarda returned from the shop, caked in flour and icing. She untied her filthy apron, and it fell to the floor.

"Hello?" Leonarda called out, tossing the apron into a hamper with the others by the front door.

"Mamma!" Emilio cried. "Please come here. I need to talk to you."

"Lio?" said Leonarda as she entered the room. "What are you doing on the floor?"

"Sit with me, please."

As Leonarda sat, the front door opened again; this time, it was Salvatore. Emilio cussed under his breath, then buried his face into his palms while grunting.

"What is going on?" Salvatore inquired as he placed his briefcase down on the kitchen table, then approached his son. "Is everything okay?"

"No. Everything is not okay. We're fucked!"

"Lio!" Leonarda shrieked, "Don't talk like that."

"Emilio, if you would prefer to tell me in English first, then we can tell your mother—if and when she is ready—if this is a conversation better suited for us gentlemen," Salvatore said.

Emilio shook his head. "Well, it involves all of us, so it's better we all know," Emilio whimpered.

"How could anything possibly be that bad?" Leonarda said as she crossed her arms.

Emilio took a deep breath, then exhaled slowly. He began recalling Pete's message, his father frozen with his jaw wide open. Leonarda gasped at each detail, and then tears began to flow. She couldn't stop thinking about what this meant for the pastry shop. With a son who made remarks such as that, she feared having to face the neighbourhood customers.

Salvatore nodded but remained silent. The kind of silence that either meant he was so furious that no sound could exit his mouth or the kind of silence where he didn't believe his son would say such a thing. Emilio studied his face intensely, yet he couldn't decipher his father's true emotions.

"If Raffaele said that, then our family name is ruined. What if my boss hears of this?" Salvatore said, then took a deep breath.

As they absorbed the information, Raffaele opened the front door with Dominic behind him. Salvatore rushed to the door and excused Dominic instantly.

"Raffaele Bucci, my idiot son, have you the slightest clue what you have done?"

Raffaele hung his head, and his face became pale. "I'm sorry—"

"Sorry?" Salvatore shouted. "Do you realise we're going to have to move? Do you realise the people here are already weary of us because of the tensions back in Europe, yet here you are, throwing a sack of coal onto the hungry fire? I could lose my job or, worse, the right to hang my head high when I introduce myself to another. No apology can give us back our name!" Salvatore took a deep breath once again. "If you wish to tarnish your name, don't use ours."

"Ours?" Raffaele repeated. "My name is Raffaele Bucci, and I am proud of that."

"Then start acting like it!" Salvatore screamed.

Walking to his bedroom, Raffaele avoided eye contact with his mother. He could hear her sobs, yet he couldn't stomach looking into her soul. He shut his bedroom door and collapsed on his bed, drifting away after replaying the day's events twenty times.

*

The morning glow of the streets hinted at the industrious spirit that defined the city, with a calmness that belied the active industrial zones just beyond the horizon. In the distance, the faint sound of the factories hummed steadily; their rhythmic churn carried across all the rows of modest homes lining downtown. Emilio had gotten used to the sound of the industry, hearing it only once someone pointed it out. To his surprise, not a single person gave him a strange look, as if the neighbourhood had forgotten about Raffaele's scene. He even passed by Pete's, yet not a single person stopped to stare at him.

As he arrived at the pastry shop, everything was the same. He expected the place to be burned to the ground by some mob or for the windows to be smashed with bricks, yet everything remained intact and orderly. After the first hour of serving customers with his mother in the back, the day felt as ordinary as any.

The aroma of freshly baked bread and pastries consumed him as he folded pastry boxes, a comforting scent that instantly transported him back home. He greeted each customer, expecting each to throw something at him, envisioning a rotten tomato or an egg slipping from their fingers, yet it didn't happen. Despite the looming shadows of the unknown, he continued to assist his mother. Each interaction with the customers, each exchange of pleasantries, made him doubt whether or not Raffaele's outburst happened the way Pete described it.

Emilio glanced out the window, his gaze lingering on the familiar sights of the street outside. Despite the apparent calmness of the morning, he couldn't shake the feeling that Hamilton, like the rest of the world, stood on the brink of change—a change he didn't know what to call yet.

PETAWAWA

With a heavy sigh, Emilio began folding boxes again, then made himself a coffee to take the edge off.

14

1940

Mr Carswell dropped a stack of papers on Salvatore's desk, as he did every morning. He smiled, then handed Salvatore a cup of coffee and began discussing the day's work. There was an urgency to his tone, an urgency that confused Salvatore as his posture was relaxed and his pace remained slow.

"Salvatore, we have a new case that's come in, and it's rather time-sensitive. A Mrs Evelyn Whitaker has reported a legal issue with her late father's property. There's a dispute regarding the title of their cottage in Muskoka. She believes there's been some kind of fraud, and her sister, who was managing the matter, has been unreachable. She believes her sister's husband has forged documents to falsify the transfer of the property to himself rather than Evelyn."

Salvatore took a sip of his coffee, letting the warmth seep into his hands. He squinted his eyebrows, considering the details. "And there's no clear indication of fraud yet? We have nothing tangible?"

"Nothing that we've found yet," Mr Carswell replied. He paused, his eyes drifting to the window. "Even beautiful Muskoka isn't immune to problems."

Salvatore nodded. But there was something else in Mr Carswell's demeanour today, something personal.

"Salvatore," Mr Carswell said, breaking the momentary silence, "I know things have been rather challenging for you lately with the war. There have been rumours and whispers about your family and their affiliations."

Salvatore stiffened, his grip tightening around the coffee cup. He had heard the whispers and felt the judgmental eyes on him whenever he walked through the office. It was an unspoken weight he carried, one that consumed him daily. "They are just rumours. My family are proud Canadians. This is our home, sir."

"I know that. However, let me make one thing clear," Mr Carswell continued, his voice firm and sincere. "I don't think anything less of you because of these rumours. I know you, Salvatore. You're a good man and a dedicated worker. Your son's choices are his own, not yours."

Salvatore felt a lump form in his throat, a mix of gratitude and relief washing over him. He had always respected Mr Carswell, not just as a superior but as a person of integrity. Hearing these words meant more than he could express, yet they stabbed him at the same time. Nothing he could say could revive Raffaele's name. "He's a good boy, just troubled, I suppose."

Mr Carswell nodded, a faint smile on his lips. "Good. Now, let's get back to work. We need to gather all the information we can on the Whitaker property dispute. Start by interviewing Mrs Whitaker, checking property records, and any communications or documents that might provide insight."

Mrs Whitaker was waiting in the reception area, her face pale and drawn. Salvatore approached her with a gentle smile, introducing himself before leading her to a small, private room for their conversation. Evelyn recounted the last days before her father's death. She noted the small details—the mundane tasks she and her siblings carried out after he died. Her sister's husband became obsessed with property, arriving there one week after the funeral to clean it out.

At first, this struck Evelyn as odd, noting his unusually shortened grieving time, yet she didn't want to believe her suspicions. It wasn't until her sister mentioned the fact that her father had left the cottage out of his will—something Evelyn knew to be untrue. She vividly recalled seeing the document ten years prior—her own name in bold.

"Thank you, Mrs Whittiaker. We'll do everything we can to resolve this," Salvatore assured her, standing up to shake her hand.

The phone rang at the office multiple times before Salvatore could answer it. On the other end, his wife had been sobbing; the sound of her voice was piercing and incoherent. When he finally got a severed message from her cries, Salvatore hung the phone back in its place, then excused himself from the office. Mr Carswell could tell by the panic in Salvatore's face that he had a good reason to leave. In the years he had worked for the firm, Salvatore had never left a minute early.

*

The crimson paint that covered the front of the pastry shop was still fresh. Emilio had begun scrubbing it with Floria, yet their sponges shredded on the bricks. As the sun baked the paint, the word became increasingly impossible to wash away. Although they made slight progress, the word 'FASCISTS' read across the façade, still entirely legible. The sight of their dream's demise twisted the knife in Salvatore's abdomen, forcing him to the sidewalk in tears on his knees. He glanced up at the window, which now had sharp shards of glass clinging to the frame. Inside, glass covered the entire storefront.

"These bastards," Emilio said as he shredded yet another sponge.

Salvatore began wiping the tears from his face. "I hate that word. I hate it!" he said. "If your idiot brother hadn't opened his mouth—"

"Salva!" Leonarda yelled, her face red and her eyes puffy. "We have to fix this together."

"Together?" said Emilio. "That bastard brought this upon our family, yet he's roaming the streets somewhere with his pal, Dom."

"Lio, you watch your mouth! You may think you're a man, but I'm still your mamma. You will not speak that way in front of me."

Emilio rolled his eyes as he continued to scrub. "Sorry, Mamma."

Floria's fingernails chipped as she scrubbed. She managed to remove a quarter of the second 'S,' yet the rest of the letter had cured.

Salvatore stood up, his knees aching from the hard pavement. He joined his family in the futile effort to erase the hate scrawled across their livelihood. The rhythmic scrubbing of sponges on brick filled the air, a futile battle against the sun-baked paint. He knew his family's rumours had made them targets, and the whispers around town had only grown louder. This attack to him felt like the culmination of everything.

Half an hour passed, and the sun was climbing higher in the sky. Neighbours walked by, some casting sympathetic glances, others quickly averting their eyes. No one stopped to help. Salvatore's hands were raw, his back aching, but the word still appeared large in front of them.

"We need stronger cleaner," Floria said, her voice laced with frustration. "This isn't working."

Salvatore glanced at Floria, then at his wife, her hands sweaty and her face streaked with tears. "I'll go to the hardware store," he said to them. "Maybe they will have something stronger."

He wiped his hands on a rag and set off down the street, his mind racing. The neighbourhood felt different; every face was a potential enemy. He hadn't felt this way since the front lines, unsure of where his enemy's position was. Eventually, he reached the hardware store, where Mr Thompson stood behind the counter.

"Salvatore," Mr Thompson greeted, his tone wary. "I heard about the shop from Angelo, who was just buying nails. Terrible thing, I'm sorry."

Salvatore forced a nod. "Do you have any strong paint remover? Something that can get rid of it?"

Mr Thompson hesitated, then nodded. "I do in the back. I'll get it for you." He disappeared into the back room, leaving Salvatore alone.

A few minutes later, Mr Thompson returned with a can of industrial-strength paint remover. "This should work. Be careful with it, though. It's potent stuff."

Salvatore paid him and hurried back to the pastry shop. His family looked up as he approached, hope flickering in their eyes. They applied the remover, watching as the paint began to bubble and peel. It was slow, painstaking work, but bit by bit, the word started to disappear, and order was restored with each bubble.

Even once the word had disappeared, Leonarda's tears did not. She repeated the word like a broken record, saying it even in her sleep for a week straight.

*

One evening, after Emilio's shift, he made his way to the Savoia house. He leaned his rusted bicycle against the side of the house and gently tapped the door. There was a stillness to the house; the lights were out, and the door was locked as Emilio tried to turn the handle after nobody reacted to his knocks.

Moments later, Floria shuffled down the stairs, her feet barely making a sound as they clicked down the wooden steps. Emilio could see her silhouette moving through the tiny glass window beside the door and studied its shape intensely until he realised it had been her. As the door opened, her white linen dress emerged first, flowing in the breeze.

Emilio greeted her with a sense of curiosity in his tone, unsure as to why she had been home alone. Floria could sense his confusion, explaining that her mother had left to stay with their cousins, who had moved from Palermo a few years prior. They had a house an hour north of the city, yet Floria couldn't stand the family.

Her cousin's friend, who hung around the house, had made a pass at her only four months ago, yet she struggled to tell her mother the truth. He had cornered her into a bedroom upstairs and shoved her into a wall, only stopping once her young cousin, Vincenza, had caught him, causing a stir. To her youthful ignorance, Vincenza hadn't the slightest clue what had happened, only investigating the noise.

"Come, I can make us some coffee," Floria said, tilting her head towards the kitchen.

"I think I have had enough for today." Emilio smiled and then said, "But a cold pop will do."

Floria handed Emilio a chilled glass bottle, then poured herself a cup of coffee. The coffee was nothing like what she knew back home, yet she tolerated it, among other things.

"How was the shop today?" Floria asked. "The front came out good. I walked by this morning; you can't see the paint anymore."

"It was quiet," Emilio said, then looked down. "And, yes, it looks better. My mother wanted to thank you again for your help. She told me she doesn't think she could do half the things she does around the shop without you." Emilio grinned.

"She's family. You're all my family."

"Family?" Emilio said, then smiled. "Is it wrong to be so dumbstruck by your family?" Emilio laughed as he placed his bottle on the table, approaching Floria.

"You know what I meant, you fool." Floria's face went scarlet. "You really are something, Emilio."

"Is that so?"

"You are."

"When is your mother coming back?" Emilio said, his eyes pointed at Floria's figure, scanning it with a grin.

"Emilio!" Floria shrieked. "What are you doing?" she said, then cracked a slight smile.

"Come with me to the sitting room."

Floria placed her coffee cup down, the sound of porcelain clinking violently as she did.

Emilio threw himself onto the settee, its emerald-coloured velvet brushing the back of his shirt. Floria jumped on top of him, laughing as her head crashed onto his chest.

Stroking her hair, Emilio said, "Do we have the entire house to ourselves?"

Floria grinned, then nodded. "Why do you ask?"

"No reason. No reason at all."

Floria reached her hand back and began caressing his brown hair, playing with the strands between her fingertips. "We could get in a lot of trouble, do you understand?"

Emilio tilted his head and said, "Trouble? We haven't done anything that could get us in trouble." He bit his lip. "Not yet," he mumbled.

Floria turned around so that she was facing him, then sat up so that her face was above his, then sat on his stomach. She reached down and began unbuttoning his shirt. Emilio's face became red and sweaty. His eyes widened as she undid the last button. He felt the cool breeze caress his torso, and then he swallowed the buildup of saliva in his mouth, which let out a sound.

"Maybe this isn't such a good idea. What would your mother think? I mean, we are unmarried—"

Floria silenced Emilio with a kiss, her lips soft but insistent against his. He responded with a hungry urgency, their breaths mingling as his hands found the hem of her dress, tearing it away in a frenzy. She mirrored his actions, their clothes falling away in a desperate cascade until they were naked and flushed.

The air around them seemed to crackle with electric tension; every light touch and every caress charged with anticipation. The stern faces of Maria's relatives glared at them from their framed prison on the walls, but Floria barely noticed at first, too consumed by the heat of Emilio's body against hers.

When she did notice, Floria broke away, her chest heaving, and flipped the frames over, their disapproving Sicilian eyes no longer an intrusion. Returning to Emilio, Floria's movements became more fluid, her initial awkwardness melting away. Their bodies intertwined with a growing rhythm, moving together in a dance that neither had experienced before. The intensity of their connection grew with every kiss and every touch—the pleasure intensified. The sitting room seemed to disappear around them, their world narrowing to just the green velvet beneath them.

Emilio paused occasionally, his eyes searching hers, ensuring she was with him and that she was enjoying every moment. Each time she responded with a sincere nod or a whispered affirmation, energy surged through both of them. They moved together in perfect harmony.

As the moments stretched, Emilio and Floria found themselves lost in their unity, their bodies communicating in a language only they could understand. The awkwardness was gone, replaced by a primal connection that left them both breathless and yearning.

*

Emilio lay on the settee unclothed and content. Floria returned from the kitchen, a smile gleaming on her face as she handed him a glass of chilled Scotch.

"This tastes awful," Emilio said, the Scotch dripping from his mouth back into the glass as he lifted his head.

"One of my mother's friends gave it to her. An Englishman, Mr Collins, I believe."

"Does he dislike your mother?" Emilio said, then smirked.

"She thought the same thing when she tried it."

Emilio shot the glass back, then shook his shoulders. He rested his hand on his stomach and began to hysterically laugh. "What did we do?"

"Unmarried too; what a scandal that could be if our families found out."

"Well, I could change that," Emilio said, then paused. "Mrs Floria Bucci."

"Emilio!"

"It sounds splendid, actually. Mrs Bucci. Mrs B—"

"Don't mess around with me." Floria's smile faded as her face appeared stern. "Don't say things you don't mean, Emilio."

"Well, what if I do mean it?" Emilio said as he sat up to stare into her eyes. "What if you were my wife? We walked down the aisle, we bought a big house somewhere in the countryside, and we opened that hotel in Sicily, our dream."

"Your dream." Floria smirked yet again. "I can't take you seriously with your penis pointed at my family portrait."

Emilio let out a huff of air, then smiled. "Well, if I put on a suit, then come back, get down on one knee, and ask you to be my wife, would the answer be yes?"

"Perhaps it would." Floria looked down. "You see, the problem is that two women can't get married; it's against the law, Ms Emilia."

"Oh, so I'm not masculine enough? I haven't heard that nickname in years." Emilio smiled. "You're going to pay for that one."

"Am I, Ms Emilia?" Floria said. "Funny, you sinner."

"Well then! If we are counting, then you sinned twice. Homosexual premarital intercourse. Wait until the nuns back home get a hold of this story. They will shun you for the rest of your life."

Floria shook her head and said, "If they will shun me, they will shun you also."

"In that case, we might as well sin again," Emilio said, then sat beside Floria. "Unless that is within the past ten minutes, you have found God."

"God and I are strangers," Floria said, then smirked.

*

The next morning, Emilio woke up in Floria's bed, still unclothed. He had no recollection of how he ended up there, yet he was in bliss. Floria was downstairs, preparing breakfast, as the scent of burnt bread travelled up the stairs and penetrated his nostrils. Emilio put on his trousers and made his way to the kitchen.

Upon pulling up a chair, Floria greeted him with loving eyes, showing not a sliver of regret for the choices they made. As they sat and enjoyed their meal, Emilio looked at the clock ticking above the doorway, then panicked at the time.

He kissed Floria and then wished her farewell, buttoning his shirt, which had still been on the floor of the sitting room in a ball prior.

Emilio opened the front door to the Bucci apartment, yet the entire place was silent. All the lights were off, and the curtains were closed. He quickly sprinted to his bedroom and put on some clean clothing, then shut the apartment door behind him, cycling to the pastry shop as if he were in last place for the race.

The pastry shop had a few customers, but Leonarda scolded Emilio as if she had been serving the masses. Salvatore had stopped by to pick up pastries for a client of Mr Carswell and decided to spectate Emilio's public shaming.

"Mamma, I'm sorry!" he pleaded. "I lost track of the time."

"Yet, you won't tell me where you were last night!"

"Oh, Leonarda, leave him be. He's a man now, you know," Salvatore said, then winked at Emilio.

"A man? He can't remember to eat enough during the day. I still pick up after him and all of his messes around the house. Where is this man you speak of?" Leonarda said frantically.

"Mamma, I'm nearly twenty in a few weeks."

"When you are thirty, then you can be a man," Leonarda returned with fire in her voice.

"And then, when I'm thirty, will the bar be set at forty?" Emilio cracked a slight smile, yet his mother did not return one.

"Go, help the next customers. I need to pull the bread from the oven. Go!"

"Yes, ma'am!"

Salvatore raised his hands to show he remained neutral to both his son's and wife's banter. Salvatore's neutrality angered his wife even more than if he were on the other side of the battle.

15

The sound of boots echoed in the storefront, clicking against the floor in a uniform march. Three Royal Canadian Mounted Police officers stepped into the store, forming a barrier from the outside world. Emilio looked past the officers and noticed a small crowd gathering across the street, all spectating the shop's affairs. The first officer nodded at Emilio and tipped his brimmed hat.

"Good day, gentlemen. We are looking for Mr Salvatore Bucci, Mr Emilio Bucci, and Mr Raffaele Bucci," the officer on the left said briskly.

Emilio looked at his father and mouthed a few curse words.

"That is me. I'm Salvatore Bucci, and that is my son, Emilio Bucci. May I ask what this is regarding?"

All three officers took four steps closer, then moved in behind Salvatore, and one walked behind the counter to Emilio.

"Gentlemen, you are both under arrest under the War Measures Act. As you know, your homeland, Italy, is at war with us. We have reason to believe you have affiliations with the fascist regime there, which has declared war on Britain and her allies. That includes Canada," the first officer said while the others began handcuffing Emilio and Salvatore.

"I don't understand," Salvatore said. "We have no ties with any of that fascist business. My son and I are not involved."

"Well, we will discuss this at the station. As for now, both of you are to come with us."

Leonarda ran to the front of the store, screaming. She tried to speak to the officers, yet her severely broken English did not string together coherent sentences. Salvatore silenced her out of fear that she would be arrested for obstruction. Leonarda put her hand on Emilio's cheek, and a tear fell onto her fingers. The officer who had Emilio in cuffs gently pushed her back, asking her for space.

"We have a right to an attorney. I work in the legal field. You will be hearing from my boss, my lawyer," Salvatore asserted.

"Mr Bucci, we know all about your job as an assistant. Unfortunately for you, property lawyers have little pull in a time of war," the first officer said, then made a sinister grin. "Now, we can either walk you out the front door with dignity, or we can drag you out with force. Please let me know which path is your preference."

"Dignity?" Salvatore yelled, then bit his tongue and paused for a moment. "We can sort this out at the station." He turned to Emilio. "Don't worry. I will fix this."

*

The cell was painted sterile white and had a dampness to it. The iron bars were so tight that Emilio couldn't get his arm between them past his elbow. Emilio turned to his father and begged for him to assist them, yet Salvatore's face appeared ghostly and defeated, a sight that gutted Emilio.

Raffaele was led into the holding cell by the same three officers. When he entered, he hung his head and could not look at either his brother or father.

Emilio waited for the officers to step out of the room, then cocked his arm back and sent his fist into his brother's jaw, knocking him into the floor.

Salvatore picked his son up and stood between the boys as they cursed at each other. Emilio kept repeating that the reason they were in this mess was because of Raffaele. Raffaele didn't deny the allegations but instead broke down and cried, returning to the concrete floor in a ball.

"Emilio, if you ever hit your brother like that again, I will hold you down and let him hit you twice as hard. Do you understand?" Salvatore grunted.

"Hold me down?" Emilio scoffed. "Maybe ten years ago. You haven't lifted a finger since you started settling property disputes. What strength do you have left, old man?"

"Enough!" Salvatore commanded. "You are not too old to—"

"To what?" Emilio blurted.

Salvatore looked down and cried. He hung his head and mumbled, "I'm sorry."

After an hour of silence with all three men in separate corners of the cell, the main door squeaked open, and two officers walked into the room. One was holding a stack of papers, and the other stood crossed-armed, examining the Buccis with a hint of disgust in his stare.

"As you are all aware, you are classified as enemy aliens of the state," said the officer with the papers. "Mr Salvatore

Bucci, Emilio Bucci, and Raffaele Bucci. You will be detained here for the week until your departure."

"Our departure?" Salvatore shrieked. "You can't deport us, my wife; their mother is here. Our life is here. I work here, I pay taxes here, and I contribute greatly to the city. My boss, Mr Carswell, is one of the best lawyers in the city. We operate—"

"Enough! This is not a trial; your fate has been decided, Mr Bucci. You and your two fascist sons will be shipped to a camp for the duration of the war that your Duce and his little accomplice started. If you are looking for somebody to blame, blame them. This is out of our hands, I'm afraid," the officer said, his arms crossed.

"Camp?"

"Yes. I am not at liberty to discuss any further details."

"You cannot do this to us; we are Canadians," Salvatore asserted.

"Well, your file says otherwise. It wouldn't matter to me if you had naturalised. You and your sons are a threat to Canada."

"There's some kind of misunderstanding," Emilio said as he grabbed onto the bars. "My brother may be stupid, but he's no fascist. Neither am I, nor is my father. We are hard-working, average people."

"Enough! I am not looking for a background story. You three will be out of here within the week. That is final."

Both officers exited the room, and Emilio began screaming at his brother once again, then Raffaele returned with louder screaming. Salvatore, who could not take the noise, silenced both of them, and for some reason, they both complied. Emilio and Raffaele took different corners of the cell and spent the rest of their time sobbing. Emilio cried himself to sleep eventually, but Salvatore sat in his own corner, awake for the entire night.

*

The dim light of dawn crept through the small, barred window of the cell. Salvatore remained in his corner, his eyes red and puffy from lack of sleep. The cold concrete floor had left an ache in his back, but he barely noticed it. His mind was a whirlwind of worry and regret. He couldn't help but feel responsible for his part in moving his family to Canada in the first place. Salvatore pondered the life they would have had back home, looking back with rose-coloured glasses to fabricate some alternate future. He kept replaying the officers' words, their disrespectful tone when they called them fascists, and the way Emilio had lashed out in frustration.

The morning felt as tense as the night before. His sons' sleep did little to ease their sorrows. A guard pushed a cart down the corridor, the wheels squeaking and echoing off the hard walls. He stopped at their cell and slid three trays of food through the slot. The smell of the food was unappetizing—a slop of oatmeal, a slice of stale bread, and a small cup of brown hot water.

Salvatore stood up slowly, his joints protesting. He picked up one of the trays and handed it to Emilio, who was only partially awake. Emilio took the tray without a word, his eyes avoiding Salvatore's. Raffaele had already been fully awake for an hour, staring blankly at the floor.

Salvatore handed him a tray as well. They ate in silence, the food doing little to fill the void in their stomachs.

Hours passed in a haze. The clanking of keys and the occasional shout from down the corridor were the only interruptions. The Bucci men spoke little, each lost in their own thoughts. Emilio sat on his bunk, picking at the bread, his mind far away. Raffaele lay down, staring at the ceiling, his face rosy and his mind blank.

The cell door opened again with a metallic squeal. The same two officers walked in, their expressions hard and uncompromising. The officer from yesterday who ran through the paperwork glanced around the cell, his gaze cold and calculating. He scratched his dirty blond moustache with his fingers, then tapped on the bars with the tip of his baton.

"You three, stand up," he ordered.

Salvatore, Emilio, and Raffaele complied, standing in a row facing the officers. The other officer stepped forward, his blue eyes narrowing as he looked at each of them with disgust.

"There has been a change of plans, gentlemen. You will be moved tomorrow," he announced. "Until then, you will remain here under close watch."

Salvatore took a deep breath, struggling to maintain his composure. "Please, there must be some way to prove our loyalty to Canada. We are not fascists," he implored.

The officer sneered. "Loyalty? You are loyal to one man only."

Emilio clenched his fists, his anger bubbling to the surface. "We are innocent! This is bullshit!"

"You should have thought about that before aligning with a fascist regime. Your Duce has made his bed, and now you must lie in it."

The officers turned and left, leaving the Bucci men in stunned silence. The sound of the cell door locking behind them was like a final, resounding verdict. Emilio's anger flared again, and he turned to Raffaele, his face twisted in frustration.

"This is all because of you and your stupid outbursts at the diner. You brought this on us!" Emilio shouted, his voice cracking. "Do you realise that because of that moment of stupidity, every person in our neighbourhood assumed that when you were sneaking around at night with Dom, that you were going to some underground fascist meeting?"

Raffaele stood up, his eyes flashing. "Me going out? You were the one who told me to get out more, and when I did, it's now my fault that people assumed I was professing my love to Mussolini at some underground meeting. I know nothing about him."

Salvatore stepped between them, raising his hands. "Stop it, both of you! This is going to stop now!"

Emilio shoved Raffaele, and in the confined space of the cell, it turned into a brief scuffle. Salvatore intervened, grabbing Emilio and pushing him back. Raffaele stumbled and hit the wall but didn't retaliate. The three men stood, breathing heavily.

Suddenly, Emilio collapsed onto his bunk, his shoulders shaking with sobs. "This isn't right," he whispered. "We don't deserve this."

Raffaele, leaning against the wall, wiped a tear from his cheek. "I know," he said quietly. "But fighting each other won't help."

Salvatore looked at his sons, his heart aching. He stepped forward and wrapped his arms around them, pulling them into a tight embrace. Emilio resisted for a moment, then melted into the hug, his body trembling. Raffaele joined in, his grip firm and reassuring.

"I wish we never left home," Raffale cried.

"We will get through this," Salvatore murmured. "Together."

The day passed slowly, marked by the routine sounds of the jail and the distant echoes of other prisoners. The Bucci men sat in silence for the entire day. As night fell, the cell grew colder. They huddled together for warmth, sharing whispered words of comfort. The future was uncertain, and fear consumed their minds.

*

The next morning, the guards returned with more trays of unappetizing food. This time, it was less than before, with a small piece of bread and lukewarm tea.

Hours later, the cell door opened once more. The officers entered, flanked by guards who moved with a sense of purpose. "It's time," the officer with the papers said.

Salvatore, Emilio, and Raffaele stood up, their hearts pounding. They were escorted out of the cell and through the maze of corridors of the detention centre. The cold, sterile walls seemed to close in on them as they walked, their footsteps echoing in the silence. They were led outside to a waiting truck, its engine idling. The guards helped them into the back, where they sat on hard benches, the door shut behind them. The truck rumbled to life, and they were on their way to the unknown.

*

As the truck wound its way through the countryside, the sun set, and Emilio rested his head on his brother's shoulder. Instead of flinching, Raffaele's head collapsed on top of his. Around them, five other men of Italian backgrounds sat in silence; their faces displayed worry and fatigue. None of them spoke English well enough, and the heavy silence in the back of the truck was broken only by the occasional jolt as the vehicle navigated the rough terrain. The men communicated with glances and small gestures.

One of the men, an older gentleman with a thick moustache and deep-set eyes, clutched a worn rosary, his lips moving in silent prayer. Next to him sat a younger man, barely out of his teens, whose eyes darted nervously around the confined space. Across from them, two middle-aged men huddled together, their expressions a mix of fear and resignation. The last man, who appeared to be in his early forties, stared blankly at the floor, lost in his own thoughts. None of the men shared their names with one another.

The older man with the rosary caught Salvatore's eye and gave a small nod, a silent acknowledgement. Salvatore returned the gesture, feeling a faint sense of solidarity with these strangers. The truck continued to jostle along the uneven road, the hours stretching. The cold night air seeped into the truck, making the cramped space even more uncomfortable. Emilio and Raffaele remained close, drawing what little warmth and comfort they could from each other. Salvatore, seated across from them, watched his sons with a mixture of pride and sadness.

As the truck pressed on, the men occasionally exchanged quiet words in Italian, their conversations hushed and tentative. They spoke of their families, their work, and their fears for the future. The young man, encouraged by the presence of others who shared his language, finally mustered the courage to speak, his voice trembling as he asked about what might await them at the camp.

One of the middle-aged men, who had a kind face and a reassuring demeanour, tried to offer some comfort. He speculated that they would be put to work and that their skills and labour might be valuable. His words, though speculative, provided a sliver of hope.

Eventually, the truck slowed and came to a stop. The door was flung open, and the guards ushered them out. They found themselves standing before a high barbed wire fence, beyond which lay the camp. Guard towers loomed overhead, and the camp stretched out before them, a bleak and unwelcoming sight.

"Petawawa," Salvatore whispered. "I haven't the slightest clue where we are, boys. Neither does your mother."

PART THREE

16

The men were ushered into a single-file line and led into a building. Two guards marched behind them with their rifles drawn from their backs, unlike the others. Emilio followed his father, trembling with growing intensity as it was their turn to enter.

"Wait for your names to be called!" a guard shouted.

The men complied, reforming the queue as a roll call commenced. The guards checked their names against a list to ensure everyone was accounted for. The process was impersonal and efficient; Emilio felt as if this had been planned for years.

One by one, they were led to a registration area, where they faced a desk with clerks and officers. Salvatore, Emilio, and Raffaele were called forward together. A stern-looking clerk began the process, asking for their personal information.

"Name?" the clerk demanded.

"Salvatore Bucci," he replied, his voice steady.

The clerk recorded the information and spoke to them as if they were inhuman, savage animals of some sort. Emilio and Raffaele provided their details next, their voices trembling slightly. Raffaele began to spell his name out but forgot the order of the letters temporarily. The guards then accused him of trying to stall, making him forget even more of his personal details.

Next, they were photographed. The flash of the camera was blinding, capturing their expressions well—each photograph radiating fear. After their photographs, each man was then assigned an identification number. Salvatore was handed a tag with his number, followed by Emilio and Raffaele. The numbers were to be worn at all times. Next came the medical examination.

They were led to a makeshift clinic, where the camp's doctor conducted a basic health check. Salvatore stood in the queue, watching as the older gentleman with the rosary was examined first. The doctor checked for any signs of contagious diseases and noted their overall physical condition. Fortunately, none of the men required immediate medical attention, though the doctor's indifferent manner added to their sense of savagery.

Following the medical check, the guards conducted a thorough search of their belongings. Salvatore clutched a small photograph of his wife, the edges worn from years of handling. The guards confiscated any items they deemed dangerous or suspicious, though most personal items were returned. Emilio felt violated, yet he had little choice but to comply. He thought about Floria and the fact that she may never see him again. This thought brought a tear to his eye, which he quickly rubbed away as a guard began examining his face with an intense stare.

"Follow me to your barracks," a guard ordered, leading them through the camp.

The camp was a sprawling complex of barbed wire fences, guard towers, and rows of utilitarian barracks. The wind whipped through the camp and made an eerie screech as it did. The Buccis and the other men were escorted to a long, narrow building. Inside, rows of metal cots lined the walls, each with a small space for personal belongings.

Raffaele and Emilio chose a bed beside each other, and Salvatore chose the one on the other side of Emilio. As they lay down to test the mattresses, each man felt the springs dig into their spines, the beds all screaming as they did.

In the centre of the barracks, a rack of uniforms was hung in a row, and each man was instructed to strip and wear one. The backs had a large red circle—a place for the guards to aim their rifles in case one of the men escaped. Emilio struggled to find trousers that were long enough, each exposing his midcalf as he tried them on. The uniforms appeared to be tattered, like scraps of fabric sewn together for a school project.

As they settled in, the older gentleman with the rosary introduced himself. "Giuseppe," he said, his voice soft but steady. The young man, who had been silent until now, introduced himself as Marco. The two middle-aged men were Pietro and Alessandro, brothers originally from Calabria, and the last man was named Vincenzo. They exchanged brief stories of their arrests and the circumstances that led them to this point. Emilio noticed they had all been at an Italian club, and they picked up their allegations from this club.

The fact that none of his family had been to this club made Emilio angry. He kept reciting in his head that he had nothing to do with these men, even blaming them for attending such a place. He began wondering if, in fact, his brother had attended, but he felt it was no use to accuse him of such things.

As the night wore on, the men attempted to sleep. The cold seeped through the thin blankets, making rest difficult. Salvatore lay awake; his thoughts were centred around

Leonarda and Pasticceria Bucci. His mind then drifted to the law firm, pondering what Mr Carswell had thought of him now.

*

The guards woke the barracks up early, the harsh sound of metal on metal jolting them from their restless slumber. They lined up for breakfast in a communal dining hall like pigs waiting for slop. The meal consisted of watered-down porridge and a piece of dry bread. Emilio complained to his father, yet Salvatore immediately silenced him.

"This food is tasteless," Raffaele whispered. "This bread was made last week; it's practically ready to be made into breadcrumbs."

Salvatore placed his finger on his lips and shook his head. "Eat, boys, eat. This is the only place we can get something to fill our stomachs. It's about survival now."

Emilio touched the cold porridge with his index finger, and it stuck, then dripped off in a clump. "I'm not eating this," he said.

"This is war. You do not have a choice," a guard said as he towered behind him. "A word of advice: given your new schedule, I would take any chance you get."

Emilio looked back, but the guard had continued on his stroll before he could get a good look at his face. Emilio noticed his youthful stride as if he ran from him like a boy playing a prank.

"You heard him; now eat," said Salvatore, then he shoved a spoonful of the porridge into his mouth.

"How can you eat that?" Emilio asked, his face slightly disgusted.

"I have eaten much worse. Do you know what I had to eat during the Great War?"

"What?" said Emilio as he dropped his spoon.

"Everybody rise!" a guard commanded. "Now!"

The men all stood from their seats, then turned their heads to face the guard. He was an older man; his moustache was grey, and his uniform was slightly different than the rest.

"I am Colonel William Mountsberg, the commanding senior officer of Petawawa for the time being. I am sure you are all aware of why you are here; no further explanations need to be made. I expect you all to arrive in ten minutes time in front of your barracks for orientation. You will be assigned roles based on yesterday's intake. There will be no accommodations should you dislike the role you have been assigned because, gentlemen, if you were unaware, we are at war. And as such, you men have pledged your allegiance to a man who is an enemy of the king and an enemy of our country. Therefore, as his majesty's loyal servant, you are my enemies and will be treated as such. Is this understood?"

The room was silent until Marco mumbled, "Yes, sir."

"Please, I will not ask again!" commanded Mountsberg.

The entire room replied in sync, and Mountsberg was satisfied, nodding his head.

The men stood in a single file as they called their names and identification numbers. When they called Emilio, he stumbled over to the guard in a defeated stride.

"Emilio Bucci. You have been assigned to the kitchen. Please report there at once."

Seeing that some men were given roles such as being assigned to dig ditches or chop wood, Emilio felt a sense of relief as he heard his role.

"These roles are not permanent, but rather what is needed in this current moment. We will move you around as needed," said the guard.

"Raffele Bucci. You will be processing wood."

Raffaele groaned, and then the guard silenced him.

"Salvatore Bucci. You will be processing wood as well. Report there at once."

Emilio followed the rest of the men in his group to the kitchen. A guard led them to their workspace; the building was cramped, hot, and dark. The men quickly learned that they were not doing much cooking; rather, they rehydrated oats, peeled potatoes, and, on the odd night, sliced odd ends of meat into portions for children. When the guards were not looking, Emilio and the other cooks would sneak a bite to stop the pain in their stomachs.

Outside, Salvatore and Raffaele chopped wood under the supervision of three guards, constantly being reminded by them that they could not trust them alone with an axe. Raffaele contemplated swinging at a guard each time he placed his hands on the wooden handle, yet his mind was not fully convinced. Salvatore found chopping wood too hard on his back. His youthful structure had departed years ago, long before his work at the law firm. Lifting the axe above his head took every muscle he had; oftentimes, he nearly dropped it on his feet below. The wood was piled higher than their heads, and the supply was abundant.

Each night, the pile seemed to grow without any of the men in their group knowing how. That was until they spoke with a man in their barracks who informed them it was his job to cut down the trees and that his group had to brave the wilderness with rifles pointed at their backs in case they decided to run.

Salvatore could not imagine that group, as he hadn't had a rifle pointed at him since the Piave. He didn't know how he would react to such a sight or if it would trip a wire in his brain and cause him to fight back involuntarily. He prayed each night that God would spare him from the logging group. Each morning, his prayers were answered as he remained a firewood chopper.

*

One night, after Emilio arrived back at the barracks smelling of grease, he noticed a rat had eaten the bread he had stashed under his cot. The crumbs were the only evidence left. Salvatore awoke as he frantically searched the floor for any leftover pieces.

"Emilio, what are you doing?" he whispered.

"Nothing. It's nothing." Emilio then curled up in a ball on the floor and cried. "I want to get out of here."

Salvatore grinned. "We all do. If you know a way, by all means, tell me."

"If we all charged the front gate, they couldn't shoot all of us, could they?"

"Well, no, but most of us. What if you made it out, but your brother didn't? How would that make you feel?" Salvatore said as he joined his son on the floor. "Please don't incite any ideas like that. If enough people believe it, there could be a riot in here."

"Wouldn't that be a good thing, though?" Emilio sniffled. "Some of us could be free."

"Yes, but at what cost? If we were to get out of here, we would be in the middle of the forest. Nobody knows how deep we are in the wilderness. The wolves would get you, or worse, the police."

Emilio tilted his head. "Now, why would the police be worse than a pack of hungry wolves?"

"Do you know what happens to escapees? You don't want to."

"I do. I do want to."

"Bad things, son. Very bad things."

"Tell me. I'm a man. I can handle it." Emilio wiped the tears from his face and ruffled his hair.

"I'll leave that to that big imagination of yours. I'll tell you one thing: no matter what part of you they kill in here, don't let them kill that." Salvatore put his arm around Emilio's shoulder.

Emilio sat and stared at the cot in front of him, confused.

"When I was a soldier, I let them kill parts of me I wish I hadn't. But I will tell you this: once they die, they do not come back," Salvatore said with a sombre face. "But you and only you have the power to let them die. They may lead you to believe that they have that power, but that is wrong. Only you do."

Emilio lay in bed, pondering his father's words. He hated that he spoke in riddles and that a direct answer was nearly impossible. As he began focusing on the roof above him, his vision faded to darkness.

*

On a Sunday afternoon, amidst the grim routine of the camp, a rare moment of fun emerged as Emilio and Raffaele organised a football match. The makeshift pitch, a patch of uneven ground between the barracks, was a far cry from any real field, but to the men, it was World Cup-worthy.

Emilio, ever resourceful, had found an old leather ball, its surface worn and patched yet serviceable. He wasn't sure where it had come from, but he thanked the heavens for its existence. The other men, their faces brightening at the prospect of the game, quickly formed two teams. Emilio captained one side, while Raffaele, more reserved, led the other.

As the game began, the tension of the confines seemed to fade away, replaced by a temporary warmth. Emilio's agility and quick footwork, although he had never played before, turned the match into a thrilling dance. The ball, though battered, flew across the pitch with surprising speed, passing from player to player. For the first time, shouts of encouragement echoed through the camp, a stark contrast to the usual sombre silence.

Emilio's team scored the first goal, sending a surge of energy through the players. Raffaele, undeterred, rallied his team, and soon after, they equalised with a powerful shot that sent the ball straight into the net. The guards, often stern and watchful, allowed this rare indulgence, standing back and letting the men savour their fleeting freedom. One of the guards watched on with a smile but quickly corrected himself as Colonel Mountsberg came to investigate the ruckus.

"Men, what have we here?" said Mountsberg. "You have an ounce of free time, and you decide to interrupt my paperwork with your God-awful noise. Everyone to the dining hall at once. We will be having an impromptu meeting."

"Oh, come on! We were supposed to have free time," Emilio said, then instantly panicked, shoving his teeth into his lips. "Sir, please, I'm sorry."

"You, boy, come here." Mounstberg straightened his back and puckered his lips.

Emilio approached slowly, his head tilted downward.

"What is your name?"

"I-I-I."

"Funny one, are you? Well then, what is your name?"

"Emilio, sir. Emilio Bucci." Emilio looked up at the colonel as his cheeks became rosy.

"Well, Mr Bucci. When I tell you to do something, I am not seeking a rebuttal. This is your first and final warning. I will not be embarrassed by a boy again. Understood?"

"Yes, sir!"

"Very well." Mounsberg turned to one of the younger guards, the same one who watched the match with delight. "Now, Private Ramsey. Escort this boy away to his cot. I do not wish to have him in my sight for the rest of the day. His privileges of free time are hereby revoked for today. He will be changing the linens on each cot, sweeping the floors, and making sure each corner of the barracks is dust-free. I will be doing a personal inspection tomorrow morning, and if this is not done, both you and the boy will be responsible. Am I clear?"

"Yes, Colonel Mountsberg!" said Ramsey. "He will have this in order by then; you have my word, sir."

Private Ramsey led Emilio back to his barracks, pushing him with force as they walked, which pleased the colonel. Emilio pushed back a few times, yet Ramsey did not use additional force to correct him.

As they shut the barracks door behind them, the empty chamber echoed their footsteps as they entered.

"Well, you heard the man. You are to start by changing the linens, Emilio," Ramsey said, crossing his arms.

"Emilio? Did you just call me by my first name?"

"Sorry, Mr Bucci." Ramsey's eyes widened as he corrected himself.

"Emilio is what I prefer," he said with a slight snarkiness in his tone. "That is, if you care what I prefer, Private."

Ramsey chuckled, then tried to contain himself. "Private, right? I'm a private. That's what they call me in this place."

Emilio looked over at the man, then quickly realised he was no man at all, but rather a boy a year younger than himself, if he had to guess. His skin was soft and rounded, its pale complexion still spotted with the red pricks of youthful hormones emerging to the surface. His eyes, blue and sparkly, had a sense of naivety about them. His uniform barely fit his scrawny body, drooping at the shoulders like a boy in a costume.

"Well, what do you call you?" Emilio asked, then stopped himself, quickly realising he had gone too far.

After a ten-second pause, Ramsey inhaled, then looked down. "Before the war, I was Thomas. Now, I'm not quite sure."

"Thomas. Can I call you Thomas?" Emilio's said as his gaze softened.

"Thomas doesn't live in this body anymore. Private Ramsey does. Now, get the pillows stripped from each cot, or we are both in trouble with the colonel."

Emilio began stripping the pillowcases while Thomas stood watching him with a slight grin.

"Am I supposed to do this all by myself? I'm going to be here for hours," Emilio sighed. "All I did was stand up for myself."

"The colonel doesn't like being stood up to. That's how it works around here, Emilio," Thomas said, then smirked. "The longer this takes, the better. I was supposed to be on watch at the front tower this evening. I'd rather be in here where the mosquitoes can't get me."

"It's not just the mosquitoes that suck the life from your veins out here in Petawawa," said Emilio as he piled the pillowcases into a basket.

"What do you mean?" Thomas blurted, his face filled with boyish curiosity.

"What do I mean?" Emilio shook his head. "The guards here treat us like dogs. Us Italians, anyway. You know, I'm not the person you probably think I am."

"Well, tell me, Emilio. Who do I think you are?" Thomas said, his eyes focused on Emilio's.

"A fascist. Well, I'm not. And I'm not a dog either, so tell the other men that too," said Emilio, then his stomach dropped, feeling he had gone too far yet again. "I'm sorry, I didn't mean it like that, I just—"

"You look like a boy to me. A harmless boy, in fact. Emilio, you have no idea what I think of you."

"I just assumed because—"

"I'm not the person you think I am either. This uniform, this rank—it's all made up. Before this, I was me, Thomas. I loved to go to the cinema with my friends on the weekends. I was going to study at Oxford in England before all of this. My father had my entire life planned out until, you know, the war. If I'm being honest, I don't want to be here anymore than you do," Thomas exclaimed. "My God! What has gotten into me? Please forget I said that, Mr Bucci."

Emilio swore he could see a tear in Thomas's eyes, but he wasn't certain. His soldier veil dropped, and his boyish personality emerged only for a brief second.

"I think it's best we do not speak as you finish your duties," Thomas said as he shook his head in self-disgust.

"I don't think you're like the rest of them, Thomas." Emilio shook the last pillow violently from its case. "Not in the slightest."

*

The following morning, Emilio arrived at the kitchen and began adding water to the oats to make the pig slop. The oats absorbed the water reluctantly, as if they, too, knew that concoction was a crime. As he stirred, a guard entered with a cart of luxurious-looking ingredients: fresh breads, fruits, and real coffee grounds. Shocked, the men stopped what they were doing and looked at each other in confusion.

"Men. You are to prepare this food and have it ready in twenty minutes time. This morning, there is an inspection of the camp, and we must be in tip-top shape," a guard commanded as he began handing items off the cart to various cooks.

Stunned, Emilio took the tray of bright red and fragrant raspberries. His eyes could not believe the sight, and his brain was fighting the urge to pop a few in his mouth.

"So what? We are supposed to put on a show for your inspection? How about we serve the same slop to show these fancy inspectors the truth?" blurted one of the men.

"Silence!" screamed the guard.

"And why the hell should I be silent? Who gave you that authority anyway?" returned the man, his face red.

The guard tossed the coffee grounds at another cook and stormed over to the man, drawing his rifle from his back. Without saying a word, he jammed the butt end of his rifle into the man's stomach, sending him to the floor of the kitchen with a groan.

Emilio turned his head as if he did not see the guard and began picking through the raspberries.

"Now, does anybody wish to protest any further?" said the guard as he fixed his cap.

Nobody said a word, each returning to their tasks with hyper-focused eyes.

As the food came out, the men sat confused as their regular porridge was dressed up with fresh raspberries. There was even a basket of fresh bread in the centre of the tables, and next to it were more berries in a ceramic dish. As the inspector walked around making notes, the satisfied look on his face disgusted all the men, yet they knew speaking the truth was pointless.

Salvatore forced as many berries into his mouth as his cheeks could allow, with many of the men doing the same until the supply depleted. After his tongue turned bright red, Salvatore met the other men near the firewood, the axe moving slightly faster than normal.

17

Three months later, Salvatore stood in the cold morning air, a dull ache settling into his middle-aged bones as he swung the heavy axe. The woodpile before him seemed endless, as it did every day. Each swing of the axe grew more laboured, his breath coming in gasps. He could feel his strength waning, but the task had to be completed; he knew he had no choice. The guards watched from a distance, their eyes always on the men, ensuring they worked without rest.

Salvatore's hands, calloused and raw, gripped the axe handle tightly. His muscles screamed in protest with each stroke, the weight of the tool pulling him forward. He paused, trying to catch his breath, but his breathing did not slow down. He knew the consequences of slowing down; the screaming from the guards was echoing in his mind. His vision blurred for a moment, and he shook his head, trying to clear the fog.

The crisp autumn air burned his lungs as he inhaled deeply, forcing himself to focus. He lifted the axe again, but his movements were sluggish. He felt a sudden, sharp pain in his chest—a searing bolt that radiated down his left arm. Salvatore staggered, dropping the axe as he clutched his chest. The pain intensified, and his heartbeat became a wild, erratic drum in his ears. He fell to his knees, gasping for air, his vision darkening at the edges.

Raffaele, working nearby, noticed his father's collapse and rushed to his side. Panic gripped him as he kneeled beside Salvatore, his hands trembling. He shouted for help, his voice breaking through the stillness of the morning. The guards glanced over, their expressions hardening as they approached. One of them, a burly man with a scar across his cheek, barked orders at Raffaele to step back.

Raffaele refused to move, his fear and desperation evident in his eyes. He pleaded silently, his hands hovering over his father, unsure of what to do. The guard grabbed Raffaele by the arm, yanking him away from Salvatore with force.

Raffaele sprang to his feet, shoving the guard in a futile attempt to get back to his father. "Don't touch him!"

"Get back! How dare you lay a hand on me?" the guard shouted, drawing his rifle from his back.

The other guards converged quickly, restraining Raffaele as he struggled against their grip. The burly guard struck Raffaele across the face with the butt of his rifle, the impact sending him to the ground. Salvatore lay motionless, the pain in his chest subsiding, only to be replaced by a numbness spreading through his body. His breathing was shallow; each breath was a battle.

The guards forced Raffaele to his feet, dragging him away as he continued to fight, his shouts turning to sobs.

Salvatore's vision dimmed further, the sounds around him growing faint. He could hear Raffaele's voice—a desperate, distant plea. The cold seeped into his bones, and the weight of his exhaustion was pressing down on him. He closed his eyes, surrendering to the darkness. His chest tightened, and all of a sudden, he felt nothing.

Raffaele's struggles grew weaker as the guards restrained him, their rough hands gripping his arms tightly.

His mind raced, the image of his father lying helpless on the ground searing into his memory. The guards' voices were harsh, their commands sharp, but Raffaele barely heard them. His focus was entirely on Salvatore and the fear of losing his father.

The guards dragged Raffaele away, his feet scraping against the ground. The numbness in his limbs spread—a cold heaviness that made it difficult to move. He could hear the distant sounds of the camp, the routine noises that had become a backdrop to his daily existence. But now they felt distant as if he were drifting away from the world around him.

Inside the infirmary, the camp's doctor, Dr Rawley, worked quickly, his hands efficient, and practised. Salvatore was placed on a makeshift bed, with the thin mattress offering little comfort. The doctor examined him, his expression grim. He could see the signs of a heart attack, the pallor of Salvatore's skin, and the heavy breathing that was unmistakable.

Raffaele was allowed to be nearby, but he was restrained by two guards, as per the doctor's orders to the guards. His face was as pale as his father's. The doctor barked orders at the nurse, who hurried to fetch the necessary equipment. The tension in the room was palpable, the urgency of the situation pressing on everyone present.

Salvatore's consciousness wavered, the pain in his chest subsiding into a dull ache. He could feel the presence of his son, yet he could not see him as his head was pressed to the bed. He tried to speak, to offer some reassurance, but the words caught in his throat.

"I'm here!" Raffaele cried. "Please, please, I'm here!"

Minutes felt like hours as the doctor worked, his focus entirely on Salvatore. Raffaele sat in silence, his eyes filled with tears, as the doctor appeared helpless.

Salvatore's breathing once again increased momentarily, and then he looked up at his son with fearless eyes. Raffaele began to scream as Salvatore placed his head back down. He took one deep breath, then on the next, his lungs collapsed, then deflated, but they did not rise again.

"I'm sorry, son. I did all that I could. He's gone," said Dr Rawley, shaking his head.

"No!"

"I'm sorry. If you need a moment, please take it."

Raffaele fell from his chair and collapsed to the floor. His screams intensified as the doctor left the room.

Two guards rushed into the infirmary, investigating the blood-curdling screaming, their hands on their rifle straps.

One of the guards, an older yet muscular man who was bald under his cap, barked, "What's going on here?" He glanced at Salvatore's lifeless body, then back at Raffaele, who was now on his knees, tears streaming down his face.

"It's your fault!" Raffaele shouted. "If it wasn't for you bastards making him work like a dog, my father would still be alive!"

The guard with the scar stepped forward, his expression hardening. "Watch your mouth, son. We had nothing to do with this."

Raffaele's anguish morphed into a fierce rage. He scrambled to his feet, and his fists clenched. "You're responsible for this, you bastards!" He launched himself at the guard, swinging wildly.

The guard easily deflected Raffaele's blows, his face twisting with irritation. "Son, I will tell you once and only once. Stand down," he growled, shoving Raffaele away.

But Raffaele's thoughts went momentarily blank; all he could feel was the rage pent up in his shoulders. He charged again, this time managing to strike the muscular guard's jaw. The guard staggered back, more surprised than hurt.

"How dare you?" the guard hissed. He grabbed his rifle and, in one swift motion, slammed the butt of it into Raffaele's stomach. Raffaele doubled over, gasping for breath, but he didn't back down. He tried to stand, but the guard struck again, this time hitting Raffaele across the face. The force of the blow sent Raffaele crashing to the concrete floor.

There was a sickening crack as Raffaele's head hit the ground. Blood began to pool around him, a dark crimson stain spreading rapidly. He lay there, unconscious, his breathing shallow.

The second guard, a younger man with wide, fearful eyes, took a step forward. "Sir, what have you done?"

The older guard sneered, wiping the trickle of blood from his own lip. "He had it coming. Besides, what's one less dago to feed for a few weeks while he rests?" He began to laugh. "He will bounce back. In fact, sort him out it will."

Raffaele lay on the cold, hard floor. The doctor, hearing the commotion, rushed back into the room. His face paled at the sight of Raffaele's motionless body and the blood seeping from his head wound.

"What in the bloody hell happened?" Dr Rawley demanded, kneeling beside Raffaele and checking his pulse.

"He attacked us," the older guard said defensively. "Even threatened to kill me and Private Richards here."

The younger guard, Richards, gulped nervously, then bit his lip.

Dr Rawley ignored both of them, focusing entirely on Raffaele. "We need to get him stabilised and to a bed immediately," he barked at the younger guard. "Help me move him carefully."

As they lifted Raffaele, his head lolled to the side, blood dripping from the gash on his forehead. The doctor worked quickly, applying pressure to the wound, but he knew it was severe. They had to move fast if Raffaele was going to survive.

They laid him on a bed beside his father, then rolled Salvatore's corpse out of the room. The older guard watched with a grin, his face completely unbothered. The doctor began working, Raffaele coming in and out of consciousness as he did. Tears kept falling from his face, but not tears of sadness, rather, tears of pain. The doctor's uniform became sopped in blood, but after using an entire medical kit's worth of gauze and stitches, he stopped the bleeding.

Emilio returned to the barracks after dinner service, finding Thomas and another guard waiting by the door before he could enter.

"Mr Bucci, is it?" said Thomas with a commanding voice yet softened eyes.

Emilio, confused, said, "Yes?"

"We have orders that you must come with us. There has been an incident," said Thomas.

"What do you mean, an incident?" Emilio said, his knees loosening.

Thomas did not break his silence despite Emilio's many pleas as he led Emilio to the infirmary. As they arrived, the second guard saluted Thomas, then departed on his way.

Thomas pulled Emilio down the corridor of the infirmary, then into a dark corner where the light had burned out.

"Thomas! What is the meaning of this?" shrieked Emilio. "Please, what is it?"

"Emilio, please keep your voice down. I'm breaking so many protocols right now," explained Thomas, then he put his index finger to his lips. "It's your father."

"What about my father?"

"Emilio, your father, he had a heart attack today. They expected me to tell you at your barracks, but I thought you needed somewhere more private."

"No, that's not possible; my father is not—my father—"

"Emilio, he's gone. I'm so sorry," Thomas whimpered. "He's gone."

Emilio's complexion faded, his skin white and clammy. "No. He's not gone. Why would you say such a thing? You're a bloody liar!"

"I'm sorry, Emilio." Thomas began to cry. "And your brother, he—"

"Where's my brother?" Emilio demanded. "I need to see him!"

Thomas's sobs became more defined, and then he took a deep breath to control himself. "He's fine, but he did get hurt." Thomas wiped his tears. "He hit his head after an altercation with a guard. Apparently, he blamed one of the older officers for your father's death."

"Why are you crying? This is my family," said Emilio, his face cold. "What an idiot! He fought a guard?"

"I didn't sign up for this," replied Thomas. "And yes, he did. I was instructed to take you to see him after I told you about your father. I figured it wasn't right to make you walk across the camp as a wreck."

Emilio fell to the floor, but the tears did not flow, no matter how hard he tried to make them. Thomas stood above him, uncertain of what to do.

"Sit with me, please," Emilio cried. "I need a moment before I see him."

Thomas froze, looked over his shoulders, and then peered down the empty corridor. He grabbed onto the wall with his palms and slid down beside Emilio. The two boys said nothing, both staring at the wall across the dark corner of the corridor. After five minutes of silence, Emilio began to weep, putting his face into his palms. Thomas awkwardly placed his hand on Emilio's shoulder, which at first made him flinch, but then he relaxed, submitting to the gesture.

"I'm ready; I want to see my brother."

Thomas led Emilio down the corridor, playing the role of guard once again. As the door swung open, the doctor nodded at Thomas and then pouted at Emilio.

"Dr Rawley, sir." Thomas nodded again.

"Right this way," said Dr Rawley to Emilio. "Your brother is asleep now; best we don't wake him, but you can at least see him."

"Please, sir." Emilio sniffled. "Thank you."

The door to Raffaele's room opened, and his still body lay in bed with his head completely bandaged above the eyebrows. Emilio shook his head, thinking he looked like an Egyptian mummy he had learned about in his school days. There was a glass bottle connected to a tube that ran directly into his brother's arm and a nurse with a white cap standing beside it, adjusting the bottle.

"He's a lucky boy," the nurse said, then walked away.

Emilio crouched beside his brother and placed his hand on his arm. He was relieved to feel warmth radiating from Raffaele's body, expecting it to be cold.

"You stupid bastard," Emilio whispered, a tear falling from his cheek. "Wait until I tell Mamma; she will smack you harder than that guard did."

A slight smile cracked on Raffaele's face, but he was too weak to respond. He opened his eyes slightly, then shook his head at Emilio with a grin.

"Come now, son. It's best he sleeps." Dr Rawley placed a gentle hand on Emilio's back. "You as well, son; at least try to."

*

Emilio awoke the next morning, looking over at the two empty cots. The sight stabbed him, making him realise yesterday hadn't been a dream. A guard walked through the barracks, tapping on the iron bed frames to wake up the men.

As Emilio walked to the kitchen, he held his tears in, masking his cries with deep breaths under the watchful eyes of the guards. When he arrived at the kitchen, an older, plump man had been standing in his station.

"Mr Bucci. You have been reassigned," said the guard watching the kitchen. "You have been assigned to the logging group. There's a shortage of men capable of cutting down trees, and we feel you are better suited there."

"Cut down trees?" Emilio groaned. "I've never cut a tree down in my life."

"Well, you're going to learn." The guard smirked as he adjusted his cap.

Emilio met the logging group in the courtyard beside the barracks. A group of younger men, all in their twenties, stood in a circle. They all introduced themselves, but Emilio didn't listen to a single name. The only man he recognised was Marco, a man he entered the camp with. After a few minutes, Private Richards and Thomas emerged from one of the guard cabins, each holding a crate of tools. Behind them, three more guards carried additional crates.

As the guards handed out the axes, Emilio's mind departed, thinking of his father.

"Your axe. Take it," said Richards. "Hello?"

Emilio re-entered the compound, shaking his head. "Thank you."

The men marched into the woods, Thomas and Richards leading the pack, with the three additional guards on their tails, all with their rifles drawn in case any of the men made an attempt to run. Emilio wondered if any of the boys playing men in their costumes had the guts to fire if he actually did run. He knew it was best not to test his hypothesis. Behind them, an empty wagon led by two chestnut-coloured Clydesdales was being driven by a guard. Emilio thought it was ridiculous that they had to walk, as the wagon sat empty on the way out.

After ten minutes, Richards stopped and nodded at Thomas. "This is the spot, men. Now, stay where we can see you; you know the drill. We have a new member with us today."

Emilio looked around, but the men all appeared dead inside, not one acknowledging him.

"I expect you to show him how we do things out here," Richards said. "Now, get to cutting."

The men began selecting trees, a few of them taking swings. They made a pile of the trees they had cut, only selecting ones they could drag back to the camp on the wagon. Thomas made it clear that they could only cut what they could haul, as the horses were exhausted this morning, believing they would only get one trip out of them.

Marco swung his axe, yet it bounced back at him. The maple tree was barely dented. Another pushed Marco aside with an arrogant tap. He took five swings, cutting only a third of the way into the trunk.

"I think it needs more of the saw before we go at it with our axes," said Marco, wiping the sweat from his brow.

"Nonsense. Let the new boy try." The man motioned for Emilio. "Come!"

Emilio approached the maple tree with his axe in hand. The tree was decrepit yet strong-looking. With one swing back, he launched the wedge of the axe into the trunk, the tree making a crack so loud that the men all watched in disbelief. Emilio, with tears budding, grunted and then screamed. He cocked his arm back again and swung harder; this time, the tree made a crunching sound and began to lean. It remained like that for five seconds, then fell. All of the men, including the guards, watched on with horror and amusement as the maple tree lay flat on the ground, once alive, now to be burned into nothingness.

"You were the right pick," said Marco, his eyes wide.

Emilio said nothing, ignoring each of the men. He paced around the men with a pale face in tears until one of them noticed, asking him if he was alright.

Thomas approached Emilio and took the axe from him. "I think he is unwell. He needs to rest."

"We can't leave yet," said Richards. "We have only chopped down four trees!"

"I can take him back. He looks like he is going to be ill." Thomas placed a hand on Emilio's back.

"Should I send an additional guard back with you?" asked Richards. "We don't need all of them here."

"No." Thomas began gently pushing Emilio. "I can manage, thank you."

The boys strolled back to the camp along the trail, both not saying a word to each other.

The silence between Thomas and Emilio grew heavier with each step. Emilio's mind swirled with memories of his father haunting his thoughts. He kept his eyes on the ground, trying to steady his breathing, but the pain was too raw, too overwhelming. Thomas glanced at him occasionally. He was concerned, but he respected Emilio's need for silence. The path was rugged, the ground uneven, and the forest around them seemed to close in, the tall pines and dense underbrush creating a sound barrier. The silence of it all was haunting. Emilio's legs felt like lead, each step a struggle. When they finally reached the end of the trail, seeing the camp in the distance, Thomas stopped Emilio and took a seat on a boulder off the path.

"Sit with me," Thomas said softly, his voice barely above a whisper.

Emilio nodded but remained silent, his hands trembling slightly. The camp's sounds echoed in the distance. Emilio sat beside Thomas.

"Look, Emilio, I know it's hard," he continued, choosing his words carefully. "Losing your father is—"

"How the hell would you know?" Emilio barked, and then a tear fell from his face. "You don't."

"I lost my mother last year—cancer."

Emilio's eyes finally met Thomas's, a flicker of understanding breaking through the veil of sorrow. "I'm sorry," he mumbled. "I didn't know." He swallowed hard, trying to regain some semblance of composure.

Thomas sighed, understanding all too well the importance of finding the right words. "I hate it here as much as you do."

"I doubt that."

"No, truly, I do."

Emilio took a deep breath. "Let me go then." He smirked for the first time.

"If you can find a way out of here, let me know," said Thomas. "If I abandoned my post, I'd be in a worse place than this," he sighed.

"At least they wouldn't shoot you if you tried."

"The men here all have a terrible shot. If they were any good, they would have sent us overseas." Thomas began to laugh. "But you didn't hear that from me."

"Hear what?" Emilio grinned.

"Good."

Emilio sat and marvelled at the realness of Thomas. His hair poked out from under his cap, swaying in sync with the trees. He wanted to reach out and touch it, but fear prevented him from doing so. The locks reminded him of Floria's, healthy and full of lustre.

They entered the camp, playing their assigned roles once again. As Thomas walked away, Emilio leaned back against the rough wall of the barracks, closing his eyes. The noise of the camp faded into the background, replaced by the rustling leaves and the distant call of a bird. He took a deep breath, trying to centre himself.

18

The following Sunday, Emilio had to bury his father. The colonel informed him that moving the body back to Hamilton would not be in the cards for now, and Emilio could not stand the thought of him decomposing on a table at Petawawa. The burial was lacklustre, a far cry from the traditional Sicilian procession line he was used to. A few guards and about ten men, none of whom Salvatore knew, joined for the lowering of the pine box. There was no headstone, no flowers, no pool of relatives—just the faces of the men around Emilio who looked like they could care less.

He knew they felt nothing, yet the surrealness of it all made Emilio feel the same—nothing. The fact that his own brother could not be there gutted him, yet he knew his hands were tied. Emilio didn't believe his father was in the pine box that dropped into the hole in the earth; rather, it was empty.

He almost convinced himself that it was empty, expecting his father to return to the barracks after a long day of processing firewood in the compound. Emilio made the sign of the cross as the box hit the bottom of the pit, wiping away a single tear that crept its way from inside. Thomas watched on, swallowing the lump in his throat that reappeared about twenty times.

That night, Emilio sat up in his cot, drafting a letter to his mother to inform her of his father's passing. He knew they had probably sent her an official letter; however, it was important to him that she heard it from his own words, his own fingers touching the paper. The handwriting was messy, yet he knew she would be able to make out most of it with help from Maria.

When he finally posted it, the letter was returned to him the same day. Emilio, confused, flipped the envelope over. The seam had been opened, and the letter was written in words he could not make out. He then took the letter to the guards who controlled the postal office. They informed him that he was to write in English if he wanted to send a letter home.

Despite explaining his mother's inability to understand English, they persisted, so he rewrote the entire letter in English, addressing it to Maria Savoia of Dundurn Street. He assumed that they wanted to probe through it, as they did with every letter, so he kept his sentences brief and factual, sparing any distaste for the camp. The letter read like a news report rather than a personal note, which was painful to draft, yet he knew he had no choice but to oblige.

After breakfast, Emilio was permitted a twenty-minute visitation with his brother before the daily logging expeditions, who appeared to be improving with each passing day. The bleeding had stopped, and he was awake most of the time that Emilio visited. Raffaele was quiet, though, not his typical self. Emilio thought of him as a castrated steer, once a force to be reckoned with, now docile and submissive. He hated the version of his brother that lay before him. It made him ill to see Raffaele teary-eyed.

*

One afternoon, Emilio had been logging in the forest with his group. They had all been trying to cut down an oak tree, but for some reason, this tree gave great resistance to all the men. One of them pointed out that it must be filled with knots, while the others agreed. Emilio took five swings at it but only made a slight dent compared to the last man.

"Stop!" shouted Thomas. "You're going to hurt your back."

Emilio relaxed his arms as Thomas approached him.

"Now, stand up," Thomas instructed. "Feet, shoulder-length apart."

Emilio did as he was told, with the other men watching in confusion.

"No, Emilio. Stand up straight." Thomas placed a hand on Emilio's stomach gently, then used his other hand to pull his shoulders back straight. "Now bend this arm slightly, but not all the way. Then point the bottom of your elbow towards the base of the trunk."

The other men watched on, their faces a mixture of smiles and shock.

"Now, when I step back, strike it with a hard blow," Thomas said, then stepped back. "Now, strike!"

Emilio struck the same spot he had been hitting before, yet nothing happened.

"Again, Emilio, again!"

The axe only moved an inch further into the trunk. Some of the men began to laugh and shake their heads.

"Watch and learn, gentlemen." Thomas placed a hand on Emilio's back and patted him twice. "The axe, please."

"Is everything alright?" asked Richards, shocked by the sight.

"Everything is more than alright, private," said Thomas, then he turned back to the men. "Now, I may have grown up in Toronto my entire life, a city boy if you will, but my father used to take us up to a lodge with my grandfather. Do you think we had firewood up there, boys?"

Thomas took a step back, and with one blow, he made the tree crack. A second blow sent the entire tree to the forest floor, the men watching in disbelief.

"Thomas!" Emilio shouted, the other men looking at him as if he were about to be sent to the gallows.

"That's Private Ramsey to you," Thomas said with a stern tone.

"Sorry, Private Ramsey," Emilio cried.

Thomas waited until the men looked away and then winked at Emilio. For some reason, the wink ignited something he hadn't felt in a long time—a sensation that warmed his chest. In Emilio's head, a few of the men grew increasingly suspicious of him, yet none of them said a thing. In reality, they were afraid, believing that Emilio was going to be reprimanded. Their glares towards him made Emilio nervous, yet he figured it was best to ignore them, as they would forget about it.

On the way back to the camp, the men followed in a march behind the log wagon. Thomas was at the end of the line, and Emilio paced in front of him.

"Mr Bucci. A word, please."

Emilio turned around, and the men towards the back all turned their heads.

"You will not disrespect me or my men like that again. Now, I will not bring this up again, and neither will the men in this group. When you address one of us, it's either sir or our rank, if you know it. Understood?" Thomas barked.

"Yes, sir."

"Good." Thomas smiled. "All of you, face forward; enough of the spectating. This will stay out here, in the woods."

The men all turned around and faced the back of the wagon as commanded. As Emilio followed, Thomas tapped on his shoulder and handed him a note. He placed it in his palm and quickly glanced down.

Meet me tonight, behind the barracks, at midnight.

Emilio turned his head back, and Thomas just nodded with a grin.

*

After dinner, Dr Rawley met Emilio in the dining hall. The doctor stood in the corridor, his face set with a stern yet sympathetic expression, as he waited for Emilio to finish his meal. The evening light cast long shadows through the small windows. Emilio pushed his tray away as he spotted Dr Rawley, making him uneasy. He quickly made his way over, his heart pounding in his chest.

"Emilio," Dr Rawley began, his tone serious, "I need to speak with you privately." He led Emilio to a quieter corner of the corridor, away from the curious eyes of the other men.

"Is Raffaele okay?" Emilio asked immediately, his voice trembling.

Dr Rawley sighed, running a hand through his greying hair. "Raffaele has come down with the flu. His condition is serious, but I can manage. I'm doing everything I can to help him."

Emilio's face fell. "I need to see him, Doctor. He needs me."

Dr Rawley shook his head firmly. "I'm sorry, Emilio, but I can't allow that. The flu is highly contagious, and we must prevent an outbreak in the camp. I'm under strict orders to keep everyone away from him until his symptoms subside."

Emilio's fists clenched at his sides, a mix of frustration and helplessness surging through him. "But he's my brother. I can't just do nothing while he suffers."

"I understand how you feel," Dr Rawley said, his voice softening. "But we have to think about the health and safety of everyone here. If the flu spreads, it could be disastrous."

Emilio's shoulders slumped in defeat. He knew Dr Rawley was right, but it didn't make the situation any easier to bear. "What can I do, then?"

"Focus on taking care of yourself," Dr Rawley advised. "Raffaele is in good hands, and we're monitoring him closely. I promise to keep you updated on his condition."

Emilio nodded. "Why can't he go to a real hospital, one that's not that room?"

"He's too unwell to travel, Emilio."

"How can that be? He was fine earlier today."

"The body can work in mysterious ways. Even I, a doctor with twenty-five years of experience, don't understand things sometimes," Dr Rawley said, his tone slightly annoyed.

Emilio nodded, then stormed back to his barracks. On the way back, he ran into Thomas on the way to Thomas's evening watch of the compound.

"Raffaele has the flu," Emilio said. "I'm not allowed to see him until he gets better."

Thomas placed a comforting hand on Emilio's shoulder. "I'm sorry, Emilio. But if he's tough, just like you, he will pull through this."

"I hope so," Emilio replied.

"He will," Thomas said gently.

Thomas patted Emilio's shoulder, then said, "Remember my note. I will be on patrol here well into the night." He winked, making Emilio feel warm yet again.

"Everything alright, gentlemen?" The colonel said, approaching the boys.

"Yes, sir. I'm on patrol, sir." Thomas asserted. "Mr Bucci is on his way to his barracks, sir."

"Very well."

Emilio nodded at both men, then excused himself. As he walked towards his barracks, the rocks crunched under his feet, and he began to hum a song from his childhood that his mother used to sing. It was the Sicilian song *Ciuri, Ciuri*, a song about flowers and sunny skies. The folk song brought Emilio comfort, and he dreamed of a world beyond the barbed wire and trees. One of the men recognised it as he passed and began singing the chorus and bobbing his head. Emilio smiled, then looked around, and his smile faded.

As Emilio lay in bed, he remembered Thomas's instructions. He waited for the clock in the sleeping quarters to strike midnight, making sure all the men in his barracks were sound asleep. He looked around, and everyone was asleep. The sound of heavy breathing and a few snores filled the room, echoing off the walls. Emilio placed his shoes on his feet, then crept towards the back door of the barracks. As it opened, the hinges made a screech that he thought had blown his cover, but to his surprise, the men remained asleep.

Emilio crouched behind a crate that was resting on the back exterior wall and sat in complete darkness. Behind him were rows of barbed wire and then, beyond that, darkness. The moonlight was about the only source of light he had; aside from the light pollution seeping from across the compound, its effect was faint. His eyes became heavy, but he fought the urge to sleep. The feeling of the cool night air caressing his face kept him awake—the only thing doing so.

"Emilio," Thomas whispered as he followed the building to the back of the barracks.

"Here," he replied, his voice a faint hum.

Thomas slid in the shadows, avoiding the faint, distant light of the gates that barely cast its way to his position. He pressed his back against the wall, then sat down in the dirt beside his friend.

"What are we doing out here?" asked Emilio. "We could be in so much trouble."

"Isn't it great?" Thomas smiled. "A little bit of fun is needed every once in a while. Besides, I think you need a break from all the rules and formalities."

"Tell me about it. Do I ever."

"I brought you and me a treat."

"A treat?" Emilio said, his face focusing on Thomas's veiny hands.

Thomas reached his hands deep into the pockets of his jacket, pulling out two chocolate bars.

"I haven't seen one of those since I was, you know, free," Emilio said, his eyes widening.

"Sorry, I wish I could have gotten more."

"Don't apologise. This is the best thing ever. You don't understand, private." Emilio paused, then smirked. "Permission to call you Thomas again, private?"

Thomas mimed Emilio's voice with a slow and mocking tone, then laughed.

"No, seriously, Thomas, this is the best gift a man in my position could ask for," Emilio said as he unwrapped his chocolate bar.

The sensation of the chocolate melting on Emilio's tongue brought him back to the pastry shop, where he would snack on the supplies as his mother baked. The flavour instantly brought back a thousand memories, each flashing before his eyes, evoking a range of emotions from him.

"You like chocolate, don't you, Lio?"

Emilio froze; his complexion faded, and his shoulders tightened. "Thomas, please don't call me that."

"What, why? It's the end of your name, like a nickname. It has a nice ring to it."

"Just don't." Emilio began to cry. "My mother is the only person on this planet allowed to call me Lio."

"I'm so sorry; I didn't know, Emilio." Thomas took a deep breath and then exhaled. "Can I call you E?"

"I don't really like nicknames, sorry."

"Me either. My father calls me Tom, and I hate it. He says it in his posh London accent in a way that lets me know I'm stupid. If I ever mess up, he will use Tom as a way to belittle me, like a little boy."

"Your father is from London?" asked Emilio.

"Well, so am I. We left when I was a baby, so I don't remember it at all. I have an aunt who still lives there, but that's about it. Our relationship consists of her sending me money or chocolates from England, yet unlike my father, I never question if she loves me."

"I'm sure he loves you, Thomas." Emilio took another bite of his chocolate bar, then tossed a pebble at the barbed wire fence.

"How can you be so sure? I have hugged him maybe twice in my life. Once when my mother died and once when my grandmother died. They were not real hugs either; rather, he patted my back when the relatives were watching so that they didn't think he was a monster. But he is a monster, Emilio. He truly is."

Emilio nodded, then rested his head on Thomas's shoulder. At first, Thomas panicked, but then he warmed up to the sensation of Emilio's warm head on his cold shoulder.

"I wish we knew each other outside of this God-awful place, Emilio. When this is over, we could spend time at my family's cabin up north, or you could come to see me in the city."

"I'd like that." Emilio smiled. "I'd like that very much."

"Besides your mother, do you have anybody else at home?" asked Thomas, then he bit his chocolate bar.

Emilio stayed silent for a moment, then said, "I had a girlfriend. Although it's been so long, and I have no idea how much longer I'm going to be here, she has probably moved on. I loved her, though. I just know that she can't sit around and wait forever. So, no, other than my mother and my brother, I don't have any other people in this world."

"I had a girlfriend once, well, kind of. Our relationship was mostly over the telephone. Beautiful broad from New York, if you believe it. She was blonde with blue eyes; Mary was her name. She was a half-Italian, half-English girl. She left me for another man in New York," Thomas sighed. "That's just the way life works, my friend."

"New York? How did you meet?"

"I was visiting with some friends; I walked into a bar, and there she was." Thomas grabbed a cigarette from his pack and lit it. "Do you want one?"

"No, not for me; I don't smoke."

"Good. Good boy."

"Good boy? What am I, some kind of mutt?" Emilio began to laugh, and then Thomas placed his hand over Emilio's mouth, sending a shockwave down both of their spines.

"We can't be too loud; someone might hear us," explained Thomas, then smiled. "Those other guards treat you like one, but you are not, Emilio."

"If they bark one more command at me, I'm going to start barking like one," said Emilio.

Thomas took a long drag from his cigarette, then puffed the smoke sideways, away from Emilio. "I will make sure they aren't too rough on you. I have my eye on you."

"You better."

Thomas once again mimed Emilio's voice, and then both began to laugh. The faint sound of the wind drifting through the branches echoed across the compound, and then Thomas excused himself, wishing Emilio a good night. They discussed meeting there again, claiming the spot as their own. Emilio returned to his cot and tried to sleep, yet the howling wind kept him awake. He took the pillow from his father's cot, buried his head in it, and sobbed. The pillow still smelled of him.

*

Late in the night, Raffaele awoke as Dr Rawley began examining his head. He noticed that although the bleeding had stopped, his neck had red-brown webbing across his skin, travelling down his chest.

"My God. You haven't got the flu at all, do you?" said Dr Rawley out loud to himself.

"What's the matter, Doctor?" Raffaele mumbled.

"Son, please spare your energy; rest, please."

Dr Rawley began making notes on his chart; his face panicked. He noted Raffaele's sweating, his clammy skin, his pale face, the skin marks travelling past the site of injury, and his short breathing. Raffaele had closed his eyes, unable to see the doctor's facial expressions as he made notes.

PETAWAWA

"I must wake your brother; he must know," Dr Rawley said to himself as he exited the room in a hasty march.

19

The door to the barracks crept open, and the moonlight cast a shadow on the doctor's silhouette. Emilio rolled over, and his heart raced at the sight of him.

"Mr Bucci," whispered Dr Rawley.

Emilio sat up, then slid on his shoes. He approached the doctor reluctantly, then shut the barracks door behind him.

"What is it?"

"Mr Bucci, your brother, he's a lot worse than I thought." Dr Rawley looked down and avoided eye contact. "I believe he has a blood infection. He may not have much time."

"Liar!"

"I wish I was," said Dr Rawley as he looked up at Emilio's shocked face. "These kinds of things can happen after a deep flesh wound. The site becomes infected, and the infection has spread throughout the bloodstream."

"Don't be an alarmist; it's only the flu!"

"Listen, it's not the flu."

"Raf has beat the flu many times before, and he will beat it again. My mother used to make our broth with little balls of pasta; it helps with the flu," explained Emilio frantically.

"It's an infection, I am certain."

"Sometimes, she would make herbal tea with dried lemon peels and a few spices. A day or two later, the flu would be gone." Emilio wiped the sweat from his palms on his shirt. "I can sneak into the kitchen and see what I can make him."

"Please, listen to me, Mr Bucci," pleaded Dr Rawley. "Your brother may not make it through the night, and if he does, in the morning, the chances of survival will be even more grim. You need to come with me."

"Nonsense!" Emilio shouted. "I will get some hot water going in the kitchen; the door should be unlocked then—"

"Come with me!"

"No!"

Dr Rawley pulled Emilio by the arm across the compound. At first, Emilio dug his heels into the gravel, but finally, he cooperated. As they reached the doors to the infirmary, Emilio took a deep breath and swallowed the lump in his throat.

Raffaele was sitting up; his eyes appeared to be entranced, staring at the blank wall across the room.

"Raf!"

Raffaele tilted his head towards his brother, and then his head fell.

"Raf, you bastard. If you die on me, I'm going to hate you forever!"

Raffaele smiled with his eyes slightly shut. "Hello," he whispered, his voice dry and cracked. "I don't feel so good, Emilio."

"You just have a fever," pleaded Emilio as he sat on the corner of the bed.

"I'm tired."

Emilio's eyes filled with tears. "Remember when we were young, you would beg me to stay for lunch at school, telling me that I had to eat lunch with you? I knew it was because you were scared of eating alone because of the other boys who used to pick on you. I never used to listen, but if they did anything to you when I wasn't around, I'd beat them up the next day." Emilio sniffled. "Well, I'm scared now, Raf. You can't leave me here alone with the bullies."

"My brother will get you for that." Raffaele grinned, and then his face fell. "I'm so tired."

"You need to rest; that's it."

"No, Emilio, this is different."

"Don't say that!"

"My stomach aches like it's been stabbed, and it hurts to breathe. Every time I breathe out, it burns." Raffaele groaned as he exhaled.

"Dr Rawley, please, do something!" Emilio begged. "Surely, there must be something that can be done."

Dr Rawley swallowed the salvia built up in his throat, fighting the urge to cry. "We need to make him as comfortable as possible. I can administer medication for the pain."

"Please, something!" replied Emilio as he held his brother's hand.

Normally, Raffaele would have swatted his brother away, yet this time, he grabbed onto Emilio's hand, closed his eyes, and smiled.

Dr Rawley, in the next room over, began searching the cabinets for supplies. He grabbed the medication, then stormed over to Raffaele. "He needs to take this for the pain; that's the best I can do."

"Raf, are you listening?" said Emilio.

"I just need to sleep, that's all," Raffaele said, then began to groan. "I can't breathe; it burns."

As he counted the correct dose, Raffaele gripped Emilio's hand tighter and began to breathe in short, mechanical breaths. He cried out in pain, and then his head collapsed, and his grip on Emilio's hand loosened.

Dr Rawley placed a hand on his jugular and waited, then shook his head. "I'm sorry, he is gone."

"No, he can't be. He needs some of that medication, that's all." Emilo slid up the bed and tapped his brother's face gently, then smacked it, but Raffaele did not respond. "Wake up, you idiot!"

"Mr Bucci, he is gone. I'm so sorry, son."

"Shut up!" Emilio said, then slapped his brother again. "Don't you dare leave me, you bastard!"

"Mr Bucci!" Dr Rawley placed the medication down on the counter and picked up his notes.

Emilio lay beside his brother, his tears flowing and landing on the bedsheets below him. He kissed his brother's forehead, then stepped off the bed. As he walked across the floor, Emilio collapsed in the middle of the room, his mind off to the abyss of darkness.

*

Emilio woke up disoriented and groggy. He was lying on a bed in the infirmary, the events of just an hour ago flooding back. He glanced around, his heart sinking, when he realised Raffaele's bed was empty. Panic set in, and he tried to sit up, but his body felt weak and uncooperative.

Colonel Mounstberg was there, watching over him with an emotionless expression. He nodded at Dr Rawley, then excused himself.

Dr Rawley approached, carrying a glass of water. "Drink this," he said softly, handing the glass to Emilio.

Emilio took it with trembling hands, his throat dry and tight. The cool water provided a momentary relief, soothing the walls of his throat.

"I informed him you are medically exempt from work for four days. You need the rest, Mr Bucci."

Emilio nodded, then whimpered, "Thank you."

Dr Rawley gave a sympathetic nod and left the room, leaving Emilio alone. Emilio's gaze drifted to the empty bed again, his brother's absence cutting through him like a knife. His breath hitched as he tried to process the loss and the hollow space that Raffaele once occupied. The silence of the infirmary echoed his inner desolation. The air felt thicker and heavier, pressing against his chest as if the room itself mourned with him. Each breath was a struggle, a reminder that he still lived while his brother did not.

The emptiness was an abyss, vast and unyielding. Emilio's heart ached with a profound loneliness, the kind that words could never fully capture—a void that stretched endlessly. He threw the empty glass at the wall, its shards sprinkling across the room, some landing on Raffaele's bed. He then lay on his back and stared at the ceiling, once again drifting away.

Emilio awoke a few hours later, with Thomas gently tapping his arm.

"Private Johnson and Private Ramsey, please take Mr Bucci back to the barracks," instructed the doctor. "He is permitted a four-day absence from any labour. He is under my orders to rest, understood."

"Yes, Dr Rawley, sir," said Thomas firmly. "We will take him from here."

"Hold his left arm; I will take his right," said Private Johnson.

The two men lifted Emilio from his bed, then supported him as Dr Rawley slid Emilio into his shoes. As they left the infirmary, Emilio lightly shook his way free from their grips.

"I can walk, thank you."

"Mr Bucci, please," said Thomas with a sombre face. "Private Johson, I can take him from here."

Private Johnson appeared confused but did not press. "Right then, I will leave you to it."

Thomas shut the door to the empty barracks behind him, and Emilio then locked it. He wrapped his arms around Emilio as Emilio began to saturate his shoulder with tears.

"I'm so sorry, Emilio." Thomas patted his back. "I'm so sorry."

"He was fine just a day ago; I don't understand. Now he's just gone; he's gone!"

Thomas squeezed tighter. "I'm here."

"Thomas, he was just here. And now he's not." Emilio let go of Thomas, then sat down on an empty cot. They sat in silence for half an hour as Emilio continued to sob.

Thomas reached out and touched Emilio's arm, then said, "I don't know what to say, Emilio. There's nothing I can say."

Emilio looked at him and then wiped his own face. "How did you get out of supervising logging?"

"I've been reassigned to the watch tower during the day, and we take shifts for a few hours on patrol of the compound. But I won't get into that mess right now. If you would rather I just sit here in silence, I can do that."

"I'd rather you leave."

"Emilio?"

"Sorry, I didn't mean that." Emilio pulled Thomas's arm and let his body collapse on top of his. Thomas's face hovered over his, feeling each other's breath on their faces. Thomas smelled of aftershave and mint.

"I can go if you prefer," Thomas whispered.

"I need you, Thomas." Emilio began to cry. "You're all that I have left here."

Thomas took his thumb and smeared the tears on Emilio's cheeks. He rubbed Emilio's lips, and then Emilio, without thinking, licked Thomas's thumb, which made Thomas jolt, his eyes wide and confused. Thomas then threw his pack onto the floor, placed his rifle beside it, and returned to Emilio, tears running down both of their faces. He placed a hand on the back of Emilio's neck, then placed his lips on his, connecting his tongue with Emilio's.

Emilio sniffled, and then his face became stiff. He shoved Thomas hard, sending him to the empty cot beside him. "What are you doing?"

Thomas looked at him with softened eyes, stood up, and then sat beside Emilio again. This time, Thomas sat still, and Emilio crawled up towards him, placing his hand on the back of Thomas's neck. He kissed Thomas on a whim, then pulled his head back. "We could get in so much trouble for this."

"I know."

"This is so wrong, immoral even." Emilio sighed. "What are we doing?"

"Is it?" Thomas slightly smirked. "I love you, Emilio. I truly do."

"Thomas!"

"I love you, Emilio. When I first saw you, I knew you were something special."

"Thomas, that's wrong. You can't speak like that. You could be arrested; what are you saying to me right now?" Emilio took a deep breath, choosing his next words carefully. "Your secret is safe with me; you're my friend, but this cannot be. I have a woman back home, maybe."

"I'm sorry, Emilio." Thomas got up and placed his rifle over his shoulder. "I should go."

"No, please, stay."

"I need to go."

Thomas left the barracks and placed his cap back on his head. He began marching towards the guard tower, and with tears rolling down his cheeks, he fought the urge to scream. His teeth dug so far into his bottom lip that he tasted blood.

Emilio's chest tightened with each laboured breath, his fists clenching at his sides as he stood alone in the barren barracks. The weight of his turmoil bore down on him like a suffocating blanket, threatening to smother him under its oppressive embrace. With a primal scream, he tore the sheets from his cot, the fabric ripping apart in his trembling hands as he flung them across the room in a frenzy of despair.

The echo of his pain reverberated through the empty space, and the sound of his breathing bounced off the walls. Emilio's heart pounded in his chest like a relentless drumbeat. He paced the length of the barracks, his footsteps a hollow echo in the silence that enveloped him like a shroud.

Tears streamed down his cheeks, and his vision blurred. He sank to his knees, the cold floor pressing against his skin like a cruel reminder of his isolation. With a trembling hand, he reached for his pillow, his fingers curling around the soft fabric in a desperate grip.

In one swift motion, he hurled it against the wall with all his strength, the impact sounding through the empty barracks like thunder. While on his knees, Emilio collapsed onto the floor, his body pressed against the coldness.

"I can't do this," he whispered hoarsely. "I can't."

But even as he spoke the words, he knew deep down that there was no turning back. The forbidden desires that had awakened within him could not be denied or suppressed. They were a part of him, a primal force that pulsed through his veins like a wildfire, consuming everything in its path.

Minutes stretched into hours as Emilio lay on the floor, his body trembling with the aftershocks. The barracks remained silent for an hour until he heard the footsteps of the men returning from a day's work.

The men entered as Emilio had already picked himself up. They all greeted him like a funeral procession, shaking his hand rather than hugging, expressing their forced sorrow for his losses.

At dinner, Emilio sat in silence and poked his fork at the half-boiled potatoes in front of him. They stuck to his fork a few times, but he flicked his wrist to release them. The rest of the evening, he continued to sit in silence, spending his free time in his cot, crying under the covers.

20

The next four days, Emilio remained in his cot, only leaving to eat. On the fifth day, he was expected in the compound to assemble for yet another logging expedition. His group, led by Private Richards and Jonhson, departed the compound. The walk was about thirty minutes, with some of the men complaining about the distance.

As the horses came to a stop, Private Johnson told the men to begin logging. Emilio's mind wandered as he swung his axe, the rhythmic motion almost hypnotic. His thoughts kept drifting back to Thomas.

As he worked alongside the other men, Emilio couldn't help but wonder how Thomas was faring in his new posting. He imagined him standing watch at the edge of the forest, his gaze scanning the horizon for any signs of trouble. He wondered if Thomas hated him, imagining Thomas drafting a list of lies about him, ready to make his life hell with the colonel.

Lost in his thoughts, Emilio barely noticed the passage of time as they chopped down the maple trees and loaded them onto the wagon. His muscles ached with exertion, but he pushed through the pain, his mind consumed by memories of his family.

He began to see Raffaele's face in his mind, swearing he could hear his voice rustle among the trees. Emilio couldn't shake the feeling of emptiness. And as he loaded another log onto the wagon, he made a silent vow to stay alive until the end of the war for Raffaele.

As the day wore on and the sun began to sink towards the horizon, Emilio and the other men finally finished loading the last of the logs onto the wagon. Wiping the sweat from his brow, Emilio surveyed their work with a sense of satisfaction. Despite the ache in his muscles and the weight of his heart, he felt proud.

As they began the journey back to the compound, Private Jonhson collected their axes. When he collected Emilio's, he nodded his head and placed it back into the crate. Emilio attempted to speak to the private, yet Johnson ignored him as if he didn't hear him. Emilio knew he did.

"What's for dinner?" said Marco to the other men.

"What do you think?" said one of the men. "More colourless slop."

The other men all laughed and shook their heads.

"Somebody call an inspector; maybe we can get something decent," shouted another man.

The men's laughter erupted.

Private Johnson huffed. "Silence!"

"And what if I don't?" shouted the same man.

"You better!" Johnson returned.

"What are you going to do? A little boy with a rifle, I'm trembling in my boots." The man laughed.

Private Johson's rage intensified. "Get in line! Shut up and march!"

"What if I were to just turn around and run? Would you really shoot me?"

"Order!"

"You wouldn't, would you?" said the man, taunting Johnson.

"Johnny, don't be so stupid," shouted another man.

Johnny shoved Private Johnson, then turned the other way and began to lightly jog, grinning as he did. "C'mon, shoot me, you gutless little boy."

"Return at once!" commanded Johnson, drawing his rifle from his back.

Johnny took another step forward, then began pumping his arms in a mocking way, mimicking a sprint while still walking.

An explosion went off, and Johnson's rifle launched him back. As it did, Johnny began to scream in agonising pain.

"Men, pick him up; I only hit his leg; he will be fine."

Emilio and Marco shrieked, then ran to Johnny on the ground, blood spilling from his calf. As they dragged Johnny with the other men, his cries arrived at the camp before they did.

They pulled Johnny into the infirmary, and Dr Rawley laid him down on a bed.

"What's the meaning of this?" shouted the colonel.

"He made a run for it, sir. I told him to stop, but he tried to run." Johnson adjusted his cap proudly. "I could not let one get away."

"Very well. Clean shot; he's still breathing; it looks to be a flesh wound. We can discuss this further in my office."

Emilio and Marco rolled their eyes and shook their heads as Mountsberg and Johnson marched down the corridor.

"Thank you, gentlemen. I will be fine from here," explained Dr Rawley. "He's in good hands."

Emilio returned to the barracks while the rest of the men sat for dinner in the dining hall. Emilio's clothing was sopped in blood. As he tossed his shirt in the dirty laundry,

Thomas sprinted to the barracks, witnessing Emilio's bloody appearance.

"Emilio!" Thomas cried, shutting the door behind him.

"I'm fine, thanks."

"What the hell happened?" Thomas said, his eyes wide.

"The truth, or?"

"The truth," Thomas demanded.

Emilio took a deep breath, then sat on an empty cot. "One of the guards, Johnson, the one who helped me out of the infirmary the other day, shot him."

"What? Why?" Thomas shrieked. "Why would he do such a thing?"

"To prove a point, I suppose. Johnny was acting out of line, and Johnson saw it as an opportunity to show off. The thing is, I don't believe he was aiming for his leg. I think you were right, Thomas; the men here have terrible aim. I could see it in his eyes as he fired; he was going for the kill shot."

"Jesus!"

Emilio began to cry. "I want to break free. I can't do this day in and day out."

"Me too."

"Thomas." Emilio took a deep breath, in and out. "Thomas I'm sorry for what I said to you in one of your most vulnerable moments. You didn't deserve any of that. I was terribly rude."

"No, it was honest. Look, if you don't feel that way about me, that's just life, my friend. I'm just glad you didn't run off and tell the colonel. My life would have been ruined. I would have been discharged from the army or, worse, arrested. But you said nothing to anybody, why?"

"Because I care about you, Thomas."

Thomas nodded, and then a tear formed in his eyes. "Yes, but—"

"Thomas, I love you too." Emilio paused, not believing his own words. "I love you, Thomas."

"Stop this now. You can't play with me like that, Emilio." Thomas buried his face in his arm and began to sob.

"Thomas, I love you. You make me feel things I haven't in a long time."

"Emilio, stop it now!"

Emilo shuffled beside him, wrapping his arm around him. He gently removed Thomas's head from his arm, then held his chin straight, kissing him.

As they kissed, Thomas threw his gear onto the ground, then wrapped his body around Emilio's. Emilio began unbuttoning Thomas's jacket, then tossed it on top of his rifle, concealing it underneath the pile.

Just as they reached the peak of their desire, a sound shattered the silence—the creaking of the door as it swung open once more. Emilio's heart leapt into his throat, panic flooding his senses as he realised they had been caught.

Thomas threw the sheets over himself, curling into a ball under them.

"Marco, Giacomo is looking for you; he said it was urgent," Emilio called out hastily, his voice strained with urgency as he stood in front of the lump of Thomas's body under the sheets. "I think it was Giacomo, but I don't recall completely."

"Oh, thank you," Marco said. "What are you up to?"

"Bastards made me switch the bed linens again." Emilio sighed. "Look at this pile I have going."

Marco stood in the doorway, his expression unsuspecting as he glanced at Emilio. "Bastards. They sure know how to work you."

Marco tossed his belongings onto the ground by his cot near the front and quickly exited, leaving them alone.

Emilio and Thomas stared at each other, their breaths ragged as they struggled to process what had just happened. Thomas took a deep breath, and Emilio grinned.

"Lock the door," said Thomas, and then he smirked. "That could have been bad."

Their bodies still hummed with desire, the heat of their passion lingering in the air as they held each other close. Emilio leaned in, pressing his forehead against Thomas's, their breaths mingling in the quiet space between them before they kissed once again.

"I love you," Thomas whispered. His eyes searched Emilio's face, his expression softening as he reached up to cup Emilio's cheek.

"I love you too," Emilio murmured.

Emilio pressed his lips to Thomas's once more, the kiss tender and sweet as they lost themselves in each other's embrace. And as they held each other close, their bodies intertwined.

As their clothing slipped off, Thomas kept repeating that they had to be fast, his voice filled with fear. Emilio laughed each time he did, telling him it would be.

Emilio handed Thomas his gear as he redressed. Both of their faces radiated contentment, fully satisfied with one another. Emilio placed a hand on Thomas's cheek, kissed him once more, and then Thomas departed.

*

The next morning, Raffaele was laid to rest beside his father. Emilio stood by the pine box, watching it lower into the soil as one of the men said a prayer in Italian. There was no priest, no family members, no flowers, and no music. Instead, the cold wind blew across Emilio's face, chilling him to the bone as he stood there, alone in his grief.

The barren landscape of the cemetery offered no comfort, only a gloomy reminder of Emilio's isolation. Some of the men tapped his back, slightly acknowledging his loss as his brother's coffin hit the bottom. The rope was not let down as gently as it was for his father. The sound the box made as it collided with the dirt was so distinct, so final, that Emilio knew he'd forever hear it on his darkest of days from here on out. It was a sound that echoed his harsh reality, a cruel punctuation to his despair.

With trembling hands and a scratchy voice, Emilio made a speech, barely coherent, as he wiped the tears from his eyes. His words were a jumbled mix of memories and sobs, a desperate attempt to honour his brother amidst a group that never knew him well. He wanted to throw himself into the hole and lay on top of his brother, yet he knew he couldn't.

The weight of responsibility and the need to survive held him back. Emilio felt an unbearable heaviness settle in his chest. Each shovelful of earth sitting in a pile beside the hole was a reminder that Raffaele truly was dead. The dirt haunted him, and he thought about the fact that his brother would become one mass with that very dirt.

As the men dispersed, Emilio lingered by the gravesite, his heart heavy. The sky was overcast, greyer than his mind. Emilio kneeled beside the freshly turned earth, his fingers digging into the cold, damp soil. He whispered a final goodbye, his voice cracking.

"Raf, I'm sorry," he choked out. "I should have been there."

He sat in front of the hole for an hour, lost in his thoughts, until he felt a hand on his shoulder. Startled, he looked up to see Thomas standing beside him, his eyes red.

"Emilio," Thomas said softly, "all the guards and other men have left. I told them I would stay with you."

Emilio nodded, grateful for Thomas's presence. Thomas helped him to his feet, and together, they stood silently by the grave, the silence between them filled with an unspoken understanding.

The cold wind continued to blow, carrying with it the scent of pine and earth. Emilio shivered, pulling his coat tighter around him. Thomas remained by his side, remaining silent as Emilio sniffled.

"I wish I could fix this," Emilio murmured. "I wish I could have been there to stop him from doing the stupid thing that he did."

"I know," Thomas replied softly. "But you must not blame yourself. You did everything possible. He became ill from an infection; you couldn't have stopped it."

Emilio shook his head, tears streaming down his face. "But I could have stopped the fight. My brother listened to me."

Thomas placed a hand on his shoulder, weary of physical touch where wandering eyes may see. "Raffaele wouldn't want you to do this to yourself," he said.

Emilio took a deep, shaky breath, trying to calm himself. "He was such an ass sometimes."

"That's okay."

"The bastard did this to himself. I'm so angry with him!" Emilio kicked a bit of soil onto the coffin below.

Thomas nodded, then said, "I love you, Emilio."

Emilio collapsed into Thomas's arms, and then Thomas looked over his shoulder to ensure they were, in fact, alone. After confirming, he embraced Emilio and kissed the top of his head.

As the wind howled around them, Emilio kneeled once more by Raffaele's grave, placing his hand on the cold earth. "I love you," he whispered.

*

On the way back to the camp, a few of the men were walking in the opposite direction towards the grave with spades in their hands under the supervision of a few guards. One of the guards nodded at Thomas, and he returned one instantly.

"Do you think they saw us?" whispered Emilio. "Is it possible?"

"If they had, they would not appear so calm."

"You're right." Emilio exhaled deeply and dropped his shoulders.

Once again, as they reached the confines of Petawawa, both playing their roles, Thomas lightly shoved Emilio as they walked to the barracks.

"They told me you have the day off for special circumstances." Thomas adjusted his cap. "You need to rest, Emilio, so please do. I hope to see you before tomorrow, but if not, meet me out back again tomorrow night, same time." Thomas winked.

"I would like that."

Thomas grinned. "Good boy."

21

In the morning, after the daily roll call, Emilio had been informed his time logging was finished. He was instructed by a guard that he was to join the other men in the compound to chop firewood. With a resigned sigh, he made his way to the designated area, the weight of the axe in his hand both familiar and dreadful.

The compound where they chopped wood was a cold, utilitarian place, surrounded by high barbed wire fences and patrolled by the guards. Emilio hated this part of the camp the most, feeling a tightness in his chest as he stood where his father once did. Emilio lined up with the other men and began working.

As he approached the pile of logs, he felt a sense of weariness settle over him. The act of chopping firewood was repetitive, something he hated. He selected his first log, a thick piece of maple wood. Setting it upright on the chopping block, he positioned his feet, grounding himself. He heard Thomas's voice in his head, instructing him how to hold an axe, then smiled.

A few of the men stared at him in confusion, like he had been intoxicated for smiling unprovoked. With each swing, he felt the muscles in his arms and back tighten and release, a physical exertion that momentarily distracted him from the fences. The axe's blade gleamed in the sunlight, arcing down with a satisfying clap as it split the log cleanly in two.

Emilio paused for a moment, wiping the sweat from his brow, and glanced around at the other men. Some worked with quiet efficiency, while others seemed to struggle with each swing, their movements jerky and uncoordinated. As he continued to chop, the pile of split wood grew steadily, and each piece that was added made him feel useful. The sound of axes striking wood filled the air, a chorus that echoed across the compound. Despite the tedious nature of the job, Emilio found comfort in the work, feeling like he was truly his father's son, proud to be working.

Finally, as the sun began to dip towards the horizon, the guards signalled an end to their work. Emilio set down his axe, his body heavy with exhaustion but his spirit unbroken. He looked at the neatly stacked firewood, feeling a small sense of accomplishment. He didn't care if the other men thought of him as mad. He knew the camp had, in fact, made them all a bit mad in one way or another.

Emilio walked down the path that led to the dining hall for dinner, but as he did, Private Johnson stopped him.

"Off to dinner, I suppose?" Johnson sneered.

"Yes, sir. A long, hard day has made me quite hungry," replied Emilio, wiping the sweat from his eyebrow.

"You know, I have been watching you, Mr Bucci. A few of us have. I can't help but notice you're one of the only men in this camp who doesn't seem to have any friends. I discussed this with some of the other guards, and we have a hunch."

"A hunch?" Emilio said, his palms beginning to sweat.

"Yes." Johnson pulled on his rifle strap to adjust its tension. "You see, to be quite frank, I don't believe you are truly from Hamilton."

"What do you mean?"

"I'm quite sure you know what I mean." Johnson smirked.

"Well, I was born in Sicily, if that's what you mean." Emilio shook his head.

"I believe you to be a spy. Your great strength, your shyness, and your quiet demeanour. Me and a few of the other guards have our suspicions, and I'm never wrong. You can tell me the truth if you are working for the Duce. You are already in here; what's the difference now?"

"You're mad!" Emilio exclaimed. "After everything I have been through, can you please just leave my name alone?"

"I beg your pardon."

"I am not and never have been a spy." Emilio sighed. "If I were a spy, why would I tell you anyway?" He smirked, then shook his head again.

"Forget I said anything then. But know this: I can see your eyes hold secrets, and I can smell something perspiring from you. Just know that I will always be watching you."

"May I go to dinner?" Emilio rolled his eyes.

"You are free to do whatever you desire, Mr Bucci."

*

That evening, Thomas was on night patrol with a group of the guards. Before their shift, they discussed the duties for the night. Private Johnson waited for the officers to depart the meeting, then began his normal banter with the other guards.

"You boys ever hear the one about the dago who walked into a bar?" Johnson said, his voice arrogant.

The others chuckled, leaning in to hear more. Thomas felt a knot tighten in his stomach, but he remained silent, his face betraying none of the pain inside.

"It's a trick question; we all know those dagos can't read signs. He walked into the pharmacy instead and asked for a pint."

The room erupted, yet Thomas just bobbed his head awkwardly.

Johnson's grin widened as he took the lack of protest as encouragement. "Yeah, those Italians are always trying to act tough. But they're nothing but cowards. One of them tried running from me in the woods. Thought he could escape. I showed him." Johnson's eyes gleamed with cruel satisfaction.

"What did you do?" one of the other privates asked, his tone eager, almost idolising.

Johnson puffed out his chest. "Shot the bastard point blank. Didn't even see it coming. Dropped like a sack of potatoes."

The guards erupted in laughter, slapping each other on the back, their cheers echoing in the darkness. All except Thomas. He stood still, his face a mask of stoicism. Inside, however, his mind was a storm of rage.

Thomas thought of his father, an immigrant who had come to Canada. Although they came from England, he couldn't understand why that made him any better. He thought of Emilio, then huffed, a sound finally escaping his lips. The thought of Johnson, a man he had to call an equal, speaking with such disregard for people made him ill.

"What's the matter, Ramsey? You look unwell, chap," Johnson sneered, noticing his silence. The others turned to look at Thomas, their laughter dying down, curiosity piqued by his irregular quietness.

Thomas forced a smile, though it felt like his face might crack from the effort. "Just tired, I guess," he muttered, hoping it would end the scrutiny.

Johnson shrugged, seemingly satisfied with the answer, and continued his tirade. The guards' laughter resumed, louder and more rambunctious than before. Thomas felt like he was on the outside, looking in. Each laugh felt like a dagger to his conscience.

The patrol continued, the group moving through their assigned areas, their banter continuing. Thomas walked at the back, his steps heavy and his mind distant. He felt the weight of his silence bearing down on him, each moment of inaction a condemnation of his own moral compass. He felt that his silence had made him complicit, and the realisation gnawed at him, eating him alive from the inside.

"Johnson," Thomas cried, "why would you shoot an unarmed man?"

Private Johnson's glare became demonically content, then his smile dropped, and his face was focused on Thomas's, anger radiating from his eyes. "Unarmed?" Johnson jeered. "He was trying to escape. Did you forget that these are prisoners we have in here?" Johnson spit onto the ground, the soil absorbing it instantly. "Not just any prisoners, fascists, or Nazi supporters."

"Yes, that may be true, and some may be. But do you think all of them are? Like the old man, I forget his name—the one who can't hold an axe to save his life. Do you think he's a threat?" Thomas crossed his arms. "Or what about the one who told me he has a son flying with our boys in the RCAF? Why would he support a man who wants his son dead?"

"Oh, Ramsey, of course they all are. If we were on the battlefield, any of those dagos would gladly place a bullet right through that pretty head of yours. Don't forget it." Johnson shook his head. "Now is not the time for a philosophical debate on what is right. Those men sleeping in those barracks a hundred yards in front of you would gladly take a shot if they had one."

"Yes, maybe they wouldn't miss either," Thomas mumbled, catching Johnson's attention.

"Come again?"

"Oh, nothing."

"No, speak up, Ramsey. I think I heard you."

"I said you're a bloody coward!" Thomas shouted, and the other two guards on patrol were looking on with stunned faces.

Johnson shook his head, then grinned. "Shut up," he said. "You know what I find peculiar? It's that we always hear about how splendid your father is—an old English chap from London, prestigious, royal-like. But the thing is, we never hear anything about your mum. For all we know, she was one of them dagos, making you a half-breed." Johnson smiled, extending his arms towards the other guards like he was preaching a sermon. "Who knows, boys, the half-breed private could be a dago in a costume."

Thomas threw his gear onto the ground, making a clunking sound as it hit the earth. "You bloody bastard. I could fucking kill you for that! How dare you bring that sweet woman into this!"

One of the other guards jumped between Jonhson and Thomas as the scuffle began to develop. "Both of you, enough!" He shoved Thomas hard. "If Mountsberg were to see this, we would all be fucked."

Thomas picked up his gear and then began to walk in the opposite direction on his way towards the other patrol unit on the west side of the camp.

"Where are you going?" Johnson yelled.

"To swap with some poor bastard that has to spend their shift with you." Thomas stormed away.

*

At midnight, Emilio snuck out the back door of the barracks, parking himself in the same spot as before. The darkness never failed to amuse him; its sight was terrifying yet the only sliver of beauty in his environment. He stacked one of the empty crates beside him, trying to provide an extra sliver of privacy in case someone walked to where he had been sitting. He waited ten minutes, yet Thomas had yet to appear from the abyss.

The minutes ticked by, and Emilio's anxiety grew. The night was unusually quiet; the typical sounds of the camp muted as if the world around him were holding its breath. He shifted the crate, the wood creaking softly. His mind raced with possibilities, each more unsettling than the last.

Finally, he heard the faint crunch of gravel underfoot, the sound growing louder as a figure emerged from the shadows. Emilio's heart lifted as Thomas came into view, though his usual brisk pace seemed slower, almost defeated. Thomas approached, his face partially obscured by the darkness, but the tension in his posture was unmistakable.

"Sorry I'm late," Thomas said, his voice low. He glanced around nervously before sitting down next to Emilio, his eyes darting to the stacked crate as if it provided a flimsy shield against prying eyes.

"What happened?" Emilio asked. "Are you alright?"

Thomas sighed heavily, running a hand through his hair. "It's been a rough night, Emilio," he admitted, his eyes down. "Johnson was going on about how much of a hero he was for shooting that poor man. Saying things that...well, it doesn't matter. It just got to me, I guess."

Emilio nodded slowly. He knew all too well the venomous remarks that circulated among the guards. "I'm sorry," he said. "It must be hard being around him."

Thomas's jaw tightened. "It is," he said, "but it's harder not saying anything. So I did. I might be in trouble with the superiors."

Emilio placed a hand on Thomas's arm. "You're no coward; that's what I love about you," he said firmly. "You have always seen me as a person first."

"Because you are," Thomas cried. "I don't know how much longer I can keep this up."

"Us?"

"No, the role I play. I would give the world to escape this place."

Emilio smirked. "Would you? I know the feeling." He pulled Thomas's hand up to his mouth and kissed it lightly. "That bastard told me he knows that I'm a spy working for the Duce."

Thomas grunted, then took a deep breath. "I'm going to kill him."

Emilio laughed. "Imagine me as a spy. All they would have to do is hit me once, and I'd give away all the secrets." He kissed Thomas's hand again, and Thomas smiled.

"A spy? What an idiot."

"I missed you today. I had to chop wood in the compound. Can you request I get moved into whatever group they assign you to next?"

"Yes, any further requests?" Thomas grinned. "I have this adjusted at once, sire."

"Very well, kind servant boy." Emilio kissed Thomas's cheek, making both of them smile.

Thomas began drawing a heart into the dirt but stopped at half of the shape.

"Where's the other half?" said Emilio, resting his head on Thomas's shoulder.

"While we are both trapped in this prison, I can't give you my full heart, only half. No matter how much I want to love you fully, we can't with all these watchful eyes and barbed wire closing in on us. But one day, Emilio, one day when we are out, I will draw the complete heart."

Emilio's face was filled with tears. "I love you," he said.

"I love you, Emilio. I promise, one day you will get my full heart."

"Half will do for now." Emilio laughed as Thomas began to carve their initials into the half.

"One day," Thomas smiled.

"We can't stay here then, lover boy. Our love is illegal here."

"You have a point," Thomas said as he ran his fingers through Emilio's hair. "Where can we go?"

"Is there really anywhere we can go?"

"Far, far away from people, as far as we can drive." Thomas began to cry. "Why does it have to be this hard?" His sobs intensified as he buried his head into Emilio's shirt.

"The world is a terrible place, Thomas," he said. "But I don't think it will always be that way. I like to hope it won't be; that's the only thing keeping me going."

Thomas held Emilio's hand tightly, then pressed his lips against Emilio's neck.

"Careful, we're outside."

"I don't want to have to be careful," Thomas whispered into Emilio's ear.

"We have to be."

"It's dark; nobody can see." Thomas reached a hand into Emilio's shirt, caressing his chest with his hand. "You must be freezing."

"Shut up," Emilio said. "Make it quick; I'm nervous," he said as he reached his hand for Thomas's trouser button.

"What in the bloody hell do we have here?" screamed Johnson, lighting their faces up with his torch. "Bucci? Private Ramsey?" he belted, his face ghostly white.

Thomas curled into a ball, his trousers undone.

Emilio shot up, charged, and attempted to tackle Johnson. "Wait!" he shouted. "It's not what—"

Johnson shoved Emilio as he read his body language well, silencing Emilio as he collided with the ground face-first.

"Stop!" Emilio shouted as Johnson sprinted away. "Stop!"

Emilio looked over at Thomas; he remained curled, his sobbing and heavy breathing a piercing sight.

22

Thomas sat in front of the colonel's desk, all the colour draining from his face. The colonel said nothing, his pen moving swiftly across the papers in front of him. They continued in that manner for half an hour, then Colonel Mountsberg lifted his head.

"Private Ramsey." Mountsberg cleared his throat. "Shall we begin?"

Thomas nodded silently, staring at the wall behind Mountsberg, avoiding eye contact.

"When I address you, private, you must address me back. Now, shall we begin?" Mountsberg said, his tone short.

"Yes, Colonel Mounstberg, sir."

"Splendid. When I met your father many years ago, you were only a small boy, about two years of age. You see, your father did a lot for me; he may be the reason I hold this very rank. I did a lot of stupid, foolish, and barbaric things in my youth. Your father was a guiding light to pull me from my stupidity and lead me down a path on which I continue to trek this very day." Mountsberg poured himself a glass of Scotch from the cabinet behind him and then took a massive swig quickly, avoiding its aromas. "I can't say I ever did something as deplorable as kissing another man, yet I have done things the Lord would disapprove of, Private."

"Sir, I just wanted to—"

"You will have your opportunity to speak!" He poured another glass. "Now, listen here."

"Yes, sir."

"I'm not sure you are aware of the repercussions your actions can have, Thomas. I will, from here on out, refer to you as Thomas, as you are no longer one of my men," said Mountsberg as Thomas began to cry. "As a soldier, you defy me by sneaking behind my back, disobeying orders, and fornicating or doing whatever it is you have done with that Italian boy, Mr Bucci, your friend. As a man, you have committed one of the worst sins possible." He took a deep breath. "Now, I don't know if you are a man of God or not; however, that is beside the point. Thomas Ramsey, you have broken the law of this country while under my watch, and for that, I have deeply failed you. I hope you understand that I could have you in handcuffs right now, awaiting trial in Ottawa. Quite frankly, I believe that people of your type, homosexuals, deserve that. However, I am a fair man. Your father gave me a new start in life, and I intend to repay my debts. You will not face trial, and you will not face your father; however, I never wish to see your face here again. I am beyond disgusted with you, but that is between you and God now, son."

"Am I no longer in the military?" Thomas sniffled as he rubbed his face.

"How would I explain this to your father if I discharged you here? The truth is, I couldn't. I have not informed your father and will not, as I leave that to your prerogative. I have requested your transfer to another facility where you will be far away from Mr Bucci. As for him, we have reasons to believe, as Private Johnson has presented—"

"He is not a spy!"

"Thomas, I will not have you interrupt me again, son!" asserted Mountsberg. "Now, you must be careful who it is you share a bed with. Though you may think you know him, you do not. In fact, I believe the stories that I have heard; they all seem to check out in my books. Now, son, I don't know how long this bloody war will continue; none of us do. But I would not count on seeing your friend for a very long time."

Thomas began to sob uncontrollably, making the colonel deeply uncomfortable.

"Now cheer up, dear Thomas. You have just been spared. You are going to leave this office, put on a fresh uniform, await your departure tomorrow, and you are going to accept this new chance I have given you. You are to remain in your chambers until tomorrow morning. I will have food brought to you until then. Son, you may hate me now, but mark me: one day, when you have your own wife and family, you will be forever grateful for my actions here today. Now that our conversation is through, I want nothing more from you. Goodbye, Thomas."

"Sir, is there—"

"Goodbye, Thomas!"

*

That night, Emilio lay in his cot, fighting the urge to cry in case one of the other men woke up to find him. His chest felt tight, and each breath was a laborious effort as if he were trying to draw air through a straw. The room seemed to close in on him, the walls pressing closer and closer until he could almost feel them against his skin. He squeezed his eyes shut, but that only intensified the whirlpool of thoughts spinning in his mind.

He began to see his father and brother shaking their heads in disgust, like they had been there to witness his time with Thomas. Every night, he replayed the last moments they had together—his father's conversation and his brother's look on his face as he met God. The memories were relentless, echoing in the silent darkness.

His thoughts shifted to Thomas. The mere thought of losing Thomas felt like being stabbed repeatedly; the pain was sharp and unyielding. The idea of navigating this hellish existence alone was unbearable. He couldn't see a future without him, unsure how long he'd make it alone.

Emilio's breathing quickened, his heart pounding furiously against his ribcage. His hands trembled as he clutched the thin blanket, seeking some form of comfort, some grounding in the midst of his body's self-destruction. The room spun, and a dizzying array of shadows and flickering lights filled his mind despite the lights being off. He tried to focus on the rhythmic snores of the men around him and on the faint rustling of the trees outside—anything to calm the storm. But the memories and fears were too powerful, pulling him deeper into his own suffocation.

Finally, the door creaked open, and a familiar shadow slipped into the room. Thomas moved silently, his steps careful and deliberate as he danced in the shadows.

"Emilio," Thomas whispered. "Come."

The tightness in Emilio's chest eased slightly at the sound of Thomas's voice. He turned his head to face him, his eyes searching for Thomas's in the dark.

Emilio stepped carefully in his bare feet around the other cots, careful not to disturb the floorboards with his shifting body weight. As they stepped outside, Emilio and Thomas hid yet again beside the crates. Emilio thought to himself that the chance that Johnson would discover them again was slim, and if he had, this time he'd kill him, thinking about the fact that he himself had nothing to lose.

"Are you okay?" Thomas asked, grabbing Emilio's hands.

"No, I'm so scared."

"Me too. I'm being transferred out of here. This is goodbye, for now." Thomas began to choke on his own saliva. "We will see each other again, Emilio."

"Hope is all I can have," Emilio said as he kissed Thomas.

"This is only goodbye, for now, I promise."

"We don't know that, Thomas. Don't promise anything; we don't know what's to come."

"I'm going to find you after all of this is done, and we are going to build a house in the forest, that I can promise, Emilio."

Emilio shook his head in disbelief. "All we have is right now, Thomas." Emilio took a deep breath, then kissed Thomas's hand. "I love you."

Thomas sighed. "I love you," he said, then reached into his trouser pocket. He handed Emilio a photograph, one they had taken on his arrival at Petawawa. "I want you to have this photograph of me. Keep my picture with you until the end of the war. Once the war ends, we can take one together."

"I'd like that." Emilio smiled through his tears, and then they both embraced each other one last time before Thomas snuck through the shadows back into his chamber for the night.

PART FOUR

23

1942

Leonarda shut the guest bedroom door behind her as she approached the top of the stairs. Maria looked up at her from the foyer, and Leonarda could sense the pity in Maria's eyes. Leonarda ran her fingers through her hair, feeling the knots and frizz tangle around her fingertips. It had been nine months since she lost the pastry shop, its customer base dwindling to a halt as accusations festered among the community.

As she made her way downstairs, the aroma of breakfast greeted her from the kitchen. Maria had been kind enough to prepare a meal for her, as she often did since Leonarda had moved in. Yet, instead of feeling grateful, Leonarda felt a surge of guilt and frustration. She was supposed to be the one taking care of herself.

The deaths of Raffaele and Salvatore were unbearable, and with the subsequent loss of their livelihood, she felt utterly useless as a woman, unable to prepare even the simplest of meals. Maria told her a thousand times that she was glad to have her there, yet Leonarda considered herself a financial burden.

The sight of Maria moving around the kitchen, effortlessly preparing coffee on her new stovetop percolator, only served to highlight Leonarda's shortcomings. She felt like a failure, incapable of fulfilling her role as a mother and a homemaker, the shimmer of the pot taunting her each time she saw it.

Trying to push aside her feelings of inadequacy, Leonarda forced a smile as she sat at the kitchen table. "Thank you, Maria," she murmured.

Maria turned to her with a warm smile. "It's no trouble at all, Leonarda. You've been through so much. Let me take care of you."

Leonarda nodded silently, unable to voice the feelings raging inside. Her appetite was nonexistent despite the tantalising aroma of eggs frying in a skillet of butter filling the room. Each bite had to be swallowed with force, almost sticking to the walls of her throat.

As they ate in silence, Leonarda's mind drifted back to the events that had led her to this point, as they did each day. Losing the pastry shop had been devastating, not only because it was her only way of making an income but also because it had been her dream. The accusations of collusion with Mussolini had tarnished their reputation beyond repair, leaving her ostracised by their own community. She refused to walk down the streets during the day because, as soon as her face was spotted, she risked being pelted by rotten fruits. The second time it happened, she vowed to be a recluse until the sun had gone down.

With no income, Leonarda had been forced to give up their apartment and seek shelter with Maria. Leonarda was grateful for Maria's generosity, but she couldn't shake the feeling of shame that accompanied their dependence on her.

After breakfast, Leonarda retreated to the small guest bedroom that contained her things. Her entire life was reduced to five small crates. She sank onto the edge of the bed, her eyes drawn to the stack of letters sitting on the bedside table. Emilio's censored letter and the death notices sat on top of the pile, Leonarda unable to stow them away since they arrived. Although she couldn't read the letters, she had circled the English words that Maria had verified with her.

As her hands shook, Leonarda picked up one of the letters and unfolded it. Her eyes scanned the familiar words, but they refused to focus. Tears blurred her vision as she reached the bottom of the page, where two different names were circled in red ink: Raffaele and Salvatore.

Her heart constricted with pain as she traced the circles with her fingertips. They were gone, taken from her for reasons she hated God for. Leonarda awaited the third letter daily, internally screaming as she saw the mail carrier each day. She told God each day as the carrier arrived that if the letter arrived that day, she would commit the sin of all sins.

Closing her eyes, Leonarda clutched the letters to her chest, the weight of them pressing on her breasts. Each day, she contemplated burning the letters, wondering if that would undo their contents and reverse everything. As she began to drift into the darkness around her, she asked God to take her pain away.

Floria's life was a disastrous mess in her own mind. Maria was determined to ensure that Floria's reputation and future were secure, even if it meant resorting to deception. When Emilio was abruptly taken away, Maria saw an opportunity to reshape Floria's future. She concocted a plan to have Floria marry Joseph Carswell, the only suitable bachelor who hadn't been able to fight. For Floria, this arrangement was nothing short of a nightmare. She had been coerced by her mother into a relationship she did not desire.

Maria had convinced her that lying with Joseph after Emilio's departure was necessary to maintain her dignity. Floria obliged, crying the entire time they did.

To convince Joseph's father to agree to the union, Maria persuaded Mr Carswell that Joseph had impregnated Floria, painting a picture of a young couple caught in a moment of passion, with marriage being the only honourable solution. Mr Carswell, concerned about his family's reputation and Joseph's future, reluctantly agreed to the marriage.

*

Two months after Emilio's arrest, Floria married Joseph Carswell. The reception was at the Carswell Manor, with only a few guests attending. The distant Carswell relatives were disgusted by the marriage, reminding Joseph, through the many letters they sent convincing him to annul the marriage, that his children would be half-breeds. Joseph didn't pay any mind to their insults, as Floria had been his only love since childhood.

The marriage was devoid of the love and warmth she had once known with Emilio, yet the image portrayed brought her comfort. Their first child was born a few months later, and his appearance was a constant reminder of her past. The child had a distinct birthmark that Leonarda found unsettling. Leonarda's aversion to the child was so intense that Floria avoided visiting her mother's house, preferring the relative peace of her and Joseph's small cottage in Burlington.

The house stood by the serene waters of the lake. Its white exterior gleamed in the sunlight that shone across the water. Surrounded by lush greenery and fragrant blooms, it was Floria's haven on the surface. Nestled amidst tall trees and colourful gardens, the cottage was charming, with its cosy wooden porch and quaint shutters echoing that. Inside, each room was filled with the scent of fresh flowers and the gentle hum of life most days, but on some nights, the walls absorbed the sounds of violent fits from Joseph's drinking. He had never laid a hand on his wife, yet he didn't need to. His voice hit her so hard that sometimes she'd prefer if it was a belt.

Joseph was deemed unfit to serve the armed forces after his car crash that nearly claimed his life, despite trying to convince the enlistment office seven times. His brother, Donald, had vanished at sea after a German U-boat sank his ship in the Atlantic.

Although Joseph was spared from slaughter abroad, he didn't see it that way. Joseph blamed Floria for his inability to fight despite knowing she had nothing to do with it. The only cure for his emasculated spirits was whisky, copious amounts to boot.

Floria mentally referred to herself as Ms Savoia, only using Mrs Carswell in social settings and formalities. Each time her new surname mixed with her first name in a sentence, she shivered, holding the vomit in her stomach.

Their son bore the surname Carswell and the first name Michael after his grandfather. Michael was a curious boy, always testing his limits with Floria. Michael, with his messy brown hair and warm brown eyes, was an intelligent toddler, full of curiosity and boundless energy. His chubby cheeks and infectious giggles brought the only sliver of joy to Floria in her new home, where every corner seemed to hold a new adventure for the young boy.

From exploring the colourful flower garden with its vibrant blooms to chasing after butterflies in the back gardens, Michael's world was one of wonder and discovery. Floria watched over him constantly, marvelling at him. With each new day, Michael's presence brought light into the darkness of her soul, a soul longing for connection.

One afternoon, Michael and Floria lay in the shade under the large silver maple in the backyard, Floria sipping on a pot of Earl Grey she had been trying to force herself to like. Joseph had informed her that ladies had to drink Earl Grey if they ever wanted to fit in among the other socialites, so she tried each day to warm up to its citrus aromas.

Michael crawled into her arms, rested his head down, and dozed off into a trance. Each time that she had a moment of silence, she thought of Emilio, and each time she thought of Emilio, she wept endlessly. Floria could still smell him, the scent in her brain bringing a smirk to her face as she reminisced. She often pondered if the police had been right and if Emilio truly was a fascist. She couldn't buy the notion no matter how hard she tried and no matter how much, if it were true, it might ease some of the longing in her heart, replacing it with disgust for him. Floria brushed Michael's hair with the back of her hands, then kissed his forehead gently.

"One day, you will meet him. One day," she whispered to her son.

Joseph arrived home from his father's law firm, where he had been working since dropping out of university.

Since he bypassed law school, he had taken Salvatore's old job, yet his father was never as satisfied with Joseph's performance, unable to speak with the Italian clients like his predecessor.

"Floria?" Joseph shouted into the backyard. "Where are you?"

"Out here, Joseph," she replied. "Please keep your voice down; Michael is asleep."

"The boy will learn one day that the world doesn't bend for his needs. Give him to me; I haven't spent time with him all week!"

"Please, Joseph, he's asleep," Floria pleaded, gently picking up her son from their blanket on the grass.

"It's nearly half past five. Why is there nothing on the stove?" Joseph grunted. "We have discussed this!"

"Good lord, I lost track of the time. I can pick us something up instead if you would prefer." Floria dusted her dress off.

"I want a home-cooked meal. If I'm coming home after a long day, the last thing I need is some hamburger or hot dog in a paper bag from some diner." Joseph shook his head. "You have to do your part."

Floria smiled despite wanting to scream. "I apologise. Please, let me cook something quick."

"It better be."

*

Leonarda walked past the building where Pasticceria Bucci used to be. The sign on the front was for a tailor's shop that specialised in gentlemen's clothing. The windows, which once held her many treats, now displayed shiny leather oxford shoes on the bottom and neckties hanging from a rack above, each a vibrant colour with intricate patterns. She couldn't see far into the store in the darkness, yet she no longer recognised the parts she could. The facade, which had been vandalised, had been stuccoed over, the front appearing brand new as if the building had been built no more than six months ago.

Walking past her old apartment, she looked up at the window and nodded at her husband's silhouette. He waved at her as she stopped, but the more Leonarda blinked, the more he faded. The window to Raffaele's bedroom was closed. Leonarda wondered if it would be possible to see the apartment one last time but never mustered up the courage to climb the stairs and knock.

As she returned to Maria's, Leonarda closed the bedroom door, sat on her bed, and sobbed. The room seemed to consume her, the dim light casting long shadows that stretched and warped, giving her a sense of being trapped. She thought about the past, about how everything had changed so quickly and how the life she had known had been ripped away.

The pastry shop had been her life and her passion, and without it, she felt hollow. Her mind wandered to the days when she would wake up before dawn, the smell of freshly baked bread filling the air, the sound of customers chatting and laughing as they enjoyed her creations. It had been a place of warmth and love, a place where she felt she belonged. Now, it was just a distant memory, replaced by accusations.

Leonarda lay back on the bed, staring at the ceiling. The emptiness inside her grew, consuming her thoughts. She wondered what the point of it all was—why she had worked so hard only to end up alone and forgotten. The room was silent, except for the sound of her own breathing, each breath feeling heavier than the last.

She reached over to the nightstand and picked up the photograph of her and Salvatore on their wedding day outside of the chapel in Agrigento. They looked so happy, so full of hope for the future. His face was not that of a soldier who had seen war but rather of a man with a will to survive. She traced her finger over his face, remembering the day they met. But he was gone now, as was the pastry shop, and she was left with nothing but memories.

She felt a premonition that Emilio's letter was to come next week, and the thought of waiting around for it was too much to bear. She never wanted to see it. Leonarda's gaze shifted to the bottle of pills on the nightstand. They were supposed to help her sleep and calm her mind, but they felt like a reminder of her despair. She wondered how many it would take to silence the pain and make everything go away.

The thought lingered in her mind—a dark temptation that seemed plausible. She closed her eyes, trying to push the thoughts away, but they kept returning stronger each time. She thought about Emilio and how he would want her to keep going and find a way to move forward. But it was so hard, and she was so tired. The weight of her grief was suffocating her, making it difficult to breathe.

"Lio," she whimpered. "We will meet again."

She picked up the pill bottle and held it in her hands, staring at it for what felt like an eternity. The silence in the room was deafening, and the shadows on the walls were growing darker. She thought about the life she had lost and the future that had been stolen from her. And in that moment, the pain became too much. The sounds playing in her mind at one hundred decibels—nothing she did could make them stop.

Leonarda opened the bottle and poured the pills into her hand. They felt cold and smooth, like tiny pebbles. She looked at them, her mind still. The weight of them in her hand began to turn down the sounds, but not enough.

Shaking, she raised the pills to her mouth and swallowed them, one by one, until the bottle was empty. She lay back on the bed, her mind going blank and the darkness closing in. The world around her began to fade, the shadows merging into a single, overwhelming void. And as she drifted into unconsciousness, the last thought that crossed her mind was of Emilio holding her hand and telling her that he understood. She reached out to kiss his hand, yet he faded just before she did.

The room was silent once more; the only sound was the gentle rustle of the curtains as the wind blew through the open window. The photograph of Leonarda and Salvatore stood on the nightstand, then the wind knocked it over onto the floor, shattering the glass.

24

In the summer, Emilio had not been as fortunate as some of the other men. While some were sent home, Emilio was to be transferred to Camp Fredericton. The colonel looked excited as he informed Emilio, making himself out to be a hero to the nation for keeping Emilio contained.

Life at Petawawa before the departure was a blur of dull routines and hollow interactions. The vibrant memories he cherished of Thomas appeared at every corner, gutting him each time they did. Each morning, the roll call would rouse him from his sleep, the shrill sound piercing through the thin walls of the barracks, pulling him into days that felt increasingly void of purpose.

The mess hall, once a place of lively conversation and laughter, now seemed like a cave of echoes, the clatter of plates and light conversations failing to fill the emptiness he felt inside. Work that had once been invigorating now felt like mere motions, his body moving through his commanded work while his mind drifted elsewhere.

The brotherhood among the guards had dulled; the new recruits were strangers with whom he shared no history, their faces blurring together in his mind. Even Private Johnson had been moved, one of the only things Emilio felt grateful for.

The gaping void left by Thomas's absence and his brother and father's deaths drained Emilio of his entire personality. He had no idea who he had become, yet he knew he didn't like the man. The cots once occupied by Raffaele and his father had been filled by two younger men from Calabria. He knew these men had, in fact, been fascists. They hummed *Giovinezza* when they thought nobody could hear them late at night, but Emilio did. Emilio's cot had become a place of torment, where memories of Thomas haunted him, making sleep an unattainable dream.

He felt like a ghost haunting the camp, a shadow of his former self. The impending transfer to Camp Fredericton was both a relief and a new source of dread. He hoped that a change of scenery might help him escape the memories that haunted him, but he also feared that the new camp would bring its own set of heartaches.

As the day of his departure approached, Emilio found himself standing at the edge of the compound, looking out over the camp that had been his home for so long. The colonel's smug expression as he orchestrated Emilio's transfer only added to his sense of alienation. He knew that the colonel saw him as a problem to be managed, a threat to be contained, rather than a man struggling with loss.

Emilio packed his few belongings, making sure to keep the only relics of his brother's tucked away: his sketchbook and cross necklace.

The expedition to Camp Fredericton was long and silent, the landscape passing by in a blur as Emilio stared out the window, lost in thought. He couldn't shake the feeling that he was leaving a part of himself behind—a part that he might never reclaim.

After a week, Emilio found the camp to be a stark contrast in comparison to Petawawa. While every corner reminded him he was, in fact, an internee, the camp had a different aura to it. There was a garden, which men, mostly

Germans and Italians, maintained. In it, they grew tomatoes, cabbage, beans, and lettuce. Emilio had helped a few times, as he remembered watching Leonarda tend to her tomatoes as a boy. She would always tell him to trim the leaves closest to the ground and to shake the yellow flowers as they opened to stimulate the plant for more tomatoes.

As he did, he would hear her voice as if she had been at the camp with him, standing over his shoulder and watching in admiration. A few of the Germans also helped him garden, one of whom he knew to be a Nazi. The man, a perfect Aryan statue, stood a foot taller than Emilio and talked almost never. His piercing blue eyes terrified him. Some of the other Italians had told Emilio that the man in the gardens they nicknamed Manfred, whose real name they did not know, was a captured German sailor.

The stories they told about him seemed to check out with Emilio, as he could sense the lust for blood in his eyes. Andrea, one of the men in Emilio's barracks, told a story that he had heard about Manfred. He recalled each detail exactly as he had heard through the grapevine. Manfred had apparently survived his ship being sunk by a British submarine, and he had been picked up by a Canadian destroyer, bobbing like a cork in the middle of the sea. The rumour stated that he choked a Canadian sailor out when he was rescued, killing the man who assisted in his rescue. Emilio believed the stories as the guards paid particular attention to Manfred.

One evening, Emilio had been flipping through Raffaele's sketchbook; each page left him more in shock than the last at his brother's talent. The final page was a sketch of himself, one he had no idea Raffaele had made. In the drawing, Emilio was standing at the foot of his cot in the barracks of Petawawa. He didn't recognise the man in the drawing; that man was fatter, stronger, and still possessed a sliver of hope.

"What are you looking at?" asked Andrea as he sat on his own cot across from Emilio.

"Nothing important."

"Well, can I see it?" Andrea said as he played with his brown, curly hair.

"No!"

"Why not, Bucci?" he smiled. "Is it your girl back home?"

"Girl?" Emilio laughed. "I doubt she waited around for me." He shook his head.

Andrea smirked as he took off his shirt and put a clean one on. "Mine either. She probably ran off with my brother."

Emilio's eyes widened. "You have a brother?"

"Yes, do you?"

"He passed away." Emilio's complexion became glum. "It was actually at the last camp I was at."

"He was at the camp with you?"

"Yes, and my father, who also passed."

"Jesus Christ, Bucci. If you ever want to talk about it, I'm an open ear," said Andrea, his eyes still wide open as he sat back down. "May I ask what happened?"

"Long story, my friend. Long story."

"You think I got somewhere else to be? Look around."

Emilio stared at Andrea and laughed hysterically. "Mentally, I'm on a beach somewhere with a drink in my hand. Physically, I'm somewhere in eastern Canada in a cage with a bunch of Nazis and a few stupid Italians." Emilio shook his head and grinned.

"What did you do to end up here?" Andrea said, staring at Emilio intently. "Because for me, I was in one of those Italian clubs with my friends from school. There was this book we all had to sign to join. Well, you see, I didn't really pay attention to the first few pages, and I just signed the stupid thing. Turns out there was some bullshit about pledging allegiance to the Duce." Andrea took a deep breath in. "I joined this stupid club for the food and to play cards with my friends. I don't know a single thing about politics."

"Make sure you always read the fine print," Emilio said, then smirked.

"Funny one, you are," Andrea returned, then smiled. "No, but seriously, what did you do?"

"Nothing, personally. My stupid brother yelled, 'Long live the Duce' in the middle of a diner."

"The hell did he do that for?"

"Because he had a thick skull. He didn't know a single thing about the Duce either."

"I will tell you one thing. If I meet this Duce fellow, I'm going to kill him," said Andrea. "Bastard took my youth away."

"Mine too. Much more than that."

"Bucci." Andrea took another deep breath, appearing nervous to Emilio. "What do you feel about all this?"

"The camp?" Emilio shrugged. "Some people should be here. Folks like me, and you shouldn't." Emilio fluffed his pillow, then laid out on his cot. "How do they confirm who should and who shouldn't be here?"

"Do you hate them?"

"Them?" Emilio repeated, a look of confusion on his face.

Andrea waited a few seconds to speak, then nervously said, "The Canadians."

"No."

"I think I do. I mean, my father pays taxes in this country, running one of the best fruit markets in the city. My mother learned English so well that she could practically teach it, and my brother was going to enlist before he got struck by a car and left with a permanent limp. I used to love Canadians, but now I'm not so sure. I think I hate them for all of this, but to be honest, I'm not sure how to feel."

"I don't hate Canadians. I mean, I hate it here, in this cage, but outside of the cage, there's a world of beauty, and the people aren't so bad. My father used to tell me that hatred comes out of a place of hurt, usually when something or someone you love hurts you. I think you and I are just hurting, Andrea."

Andrea wiped away the tears budding in his eyes. "Maybe he's right."

"I hate to admit it, but I think he is," Emilio sighed.

Andrea and Emilio lay on their cots until dinner. The food at Fredericton was slightly more bearable as a few of the other Italians helped prepare the menu. Some of the meals reminded Emilio of home, while others were watered-down versions of the food he once loved.

*

The following week, Emilio had been asked to participate in a language class for the other Italians who could not speak English. He became a bridge for them, piecing together the two languages. The classroom was a room the size of one of the barracks, yet it had no beds. Emilio sat in the centre of the circle of men in each class, assisting each man with conversational skills in English. The faces around him were a mixture of curiosity and frustration. Teaching ignited a spark within him that had long been dormant.

Each morning, Emilio would arrive early, arranging the sparse furniture and preparing simple lessons. The men trickled in, their eyes brightening with the prospect of learning. As he greeted them, he found a sliver of purpose. The men were from different parts of Italy, their dialects and accents reflecting the diverse regions they came from. A few of the men came from Aragona, a town near Agrigento. Emilio and them bonding, discussing their home with fond memories. One of the men claimed to have known his mother, yet he wasn't sure if it had been true. Emilio played along despite his uncertainty.

Emilio began each session with basic phrases, teaching them to navigate their new reality. "Good morning," he would say, gesturing broadly. "Buongiorno," they would echo, some voices confident, others tentative. He would then move on to practical vocabulary—words for food, for clothing, for everyday interactions with the guards. He used gestures, drawings, and sometimes even acted-out scenarios, eliciting laughter and easing the tension in the room. In those moments, Emilio felt a connection to the men.

One of the men he swore could have been related to him. Each time the man spoke, Emilio saw his father's eyes. As they stumbled over English words, he encouraged them with patience, reminding them that progress took time, a resource they had plenty of.

Outside the classroom, Emilio's duties at the camp remained unchanged, but his outlook began to shift. He found himself looking forward to the language classes, to the friendship, and to the sense of achievement he felt when one of his students managed to string together a coherent English sentence. He became more than just an internee; he became a mentor.

As weeks turned into months, Emilio's class grew in both size and spirit. More men joined, hearing of the progress made by their friends, and the once quiet room now buzzed with activity. They practised speaking to each other in English, correcting and encouraging, and forming bonds that transcended the barbed wire of the camp.

Emilio saw in their eyes the flicker of something he thought he had lost—hope.

25

1945

The war ended in September, and soon after, the men were released. On the day of his departure from the camp, Emilio vowed to Andrea to keep in touch, with Andrea doing the same, yet Emilio didn't expect either of them to follow through. His life had become a revolving door, and he knew Andrea's time spinning was coming to a halt. 1945 marked the end of an era, yet for Emilio and Andrea, it signified more than just their freedom.

It was a juncture where their paths split, and secretly, they wished to never see each other again as the mere image of each other's faces would remind them of darker times. As Emilio bid farewell to the confines of the camp, he carried with him nothing but Raffaele's things and a change of clothing. The contents of his small leather satchel under his arm were all that he possessed.

As he boarded the train, he sat alone in the last car. The train stumbled into motion, and Emilio settled into his seat, gazing out the window at the passing landscape, a blur of fields and forests rushing by. His thoughts drifted back to Petawawa, imagining this day as a bit different. The empty seats beside him stabbed him violently each time he looked over at them.

Lost in contemplation, he barely noticed the man who took the seat across the aisle from him until the stranger extended a weathered hand, offering an apple from the small bag slung over his shoulder. Emilio hesitated, his gaze meeting the man's, whose eyes held a silent plea. Understanding dawned in Emilio's mind as he recognised the language barrier between them. With a small nod, he declined the offer, a faint smile at the corners of his lips. The stranger returned the smile.

The clatter of the train on the tracks became a soothing backdrop to Emilio's thoughts. Memories flooded his mind, each one a vivid snapshot of the war-torn landscape he had left behind. He remembered the smell of the barracks, the air stale with the scent of sweaty men. For some reason, the scent made him gag in his seat, as if he were still there.

*

As the hours passed, Emilio and the stranger settled into a comfortable silence, each lost in his own thoughts. The sun set, and he took his brother's necklace from the bag, clasping it around his neck. Emilio felt a sense of liberation wash over him, a feeling of freedom he had not experienced in years, yet he still felt chained at the same time.

Hamilton looked as he remembered it. The air was thick with the scent of the factories, and the people were moving about in their busy ways. Hearing and seeing so much life felt foreign to Emilio now. He had to stop and pause for a moment to take it all in. He found it all quite overstimulating. The cars rushing by, the people lining the sidewalks, the stores and restaurants all booming with life—sights he had forgotten about in the woods.

He knocked on his apartment door, hearing the patter of footsteps moving inside, yet nobody answered. He knocked again, and the door creaked open cautiously.

"Hello, sir, may I help you?"

Emilio looked up at the man who had greeted him. He was a black man who stood about a foot taller than he did, with Emilio estimating he was about fifty.

"Yes, I'm not sure we have met, sir." Emilio smiled. "You must be a friend of my mother's. Is she home at the moment?"

"Your mother? Son, I think there is some kind of mistake." The man stood with his arms crossed and a puzzled face.

"Leonarda Bucci, an Italian woman, lives here," said Emilio confidently. He double-checked the apartment number.

"Son, what is your name?"

"Emilio, sir. Emilio Bucci." Emilio began to scan the man's face to see if he could detect a joke hiding in the corner of his eyes. Yet there was no such look on his face.

"Emilio, I'm David, Mr David Walters. I have been living here for a while now. I did hear from the other neighbours that an Italian family used to live here, but that's all I know, son."

Emilio took a step back and shook his head. "My mother moved?"

"I don't know, son. Do you have somebody you can call? I can throw on a pot of coffee."

"No, that will be fine. Don't bother; I will be on my way. Thank you."

"Best of luck, son." David shut the door, then locked it.

Confused, Emilio clutched his bag under his arm and began walking to the Savoia house. When he reached it, the house looked exactly the same. It was as if he had entered a different year like the war had not ever begun.

He knocked on the door with three loud bangs. Maria stood in front of him, then screamed, dropping the wine glass in her hand. It shattered as it hit the ground, throwing shards of glass and drops of red everywhere, splashing up the wall and covering both of them below the knees.

"Emili-Em-Emilio!" Maria shrieked. "Welcome home," she said as she stepped over the glass pile and wrapped her arms around him. "Please come in."

"How have you been?" said Emilio. He carefully paced around the shards. "Should I get a broom?"

"I've been as well as I can be." Maria shook her head. "I will clean it; pay it no mind."

Maria put on the kettle and set up two tea cups in the sitting room. Emilio threw himself onto the green settee, the fabric caressing his legs as he smiled. A few minutes later, Maria entered with a pot of English Breakfast.

"I hope tea and biscuits are alright. I ran out of coffee this morning, and I have to go out to get some more."

"Tea is perfect; thank you." He smiled.

"How have you been?"

Emilio took a deep breath. "I'm sure you have heard about my brother and father."

Maria nodded with a sombre face. "I did. I'm so sorry, Emilio. Terrible thing that happened to you boys. I'll never understand it. You were just a couple of kids, and your father was a good man. He was never the things they made him out to be."

"That's for sure."

"Emilio, I need to talk to you about Floria. She's—"

"Married, I suppose," Emilio said abruptly, cutting off Maria. "I didn't expect her to wait all this time for me. I hope he's a good man."

Maria nodded. "He is. Mr Joseph Carswell."

"My God! That's madness. Joseph?" Emilio smiled, then his face went flat. "What would she want with him?"

"Emilio, she's happy. And for that, you must be happy for her. She has two children—two sons, in fact. Michael is a couple years older than little Donald, or Donnie, as we call him."

"Could they not have been more original in naming them?" Emilio smirked. "Well, I guess I can play the part. I will be nothing but content to her face."

"I understand this is hard. I know how much you both loved each other, but you must know this is for the best. None of us knew when you would be returning, and she had no choice."

Emilio swallowed the saliva that had built up in his throat. "Where has my mother moved to? I went by the apartment this morning, and there was a man living there. An older black man, a nice fellow, but not my mother."

"How do you like your tea? Lemon? Milk?"

"Lemon, please." Emilio sighed. "But it doesn't make sense." Emilio grabbed the blue floral cup as Maria handed it to him. The saucer was mismatched, with gold accents and pink roses.

"What was it all like? Do you want to talk about it?" Maria stirred the milk into her tea. "If you need to talk about it, Emilio, I am here."

Emilio took a deep breath. "Did she say where she was going? I was going to go to the pastry shop next if you aren't sure. I thought for sure she would have told you where she moved to."

"Emilio." Maria paused. "It's gone. The pastry shop is gone."

Emilio nearly spit his tea across the room, but at the last second, he pressed his lips together, the tea dripping down his throat. "What do you mean, gone?"

"Well, after you were all picked up, the customers, well, they stopped coming. Your mother couldn't pay the rent any longer, so she had no choice, Emilio. Last time I heard, it's some type of clothing shop, but I haven't seen it for myself. I never go down that street anymore."

"What does she do for work? How can she afford to eat if the shop is just gone?" Emilo sank into the settee and began to feel dizzy. He hated the look on Maria's face, yet he didn't feel confident enough to call it out.

"Was the journey back home long? I hope you didn't have too many troubles during your travels." Maria placed her tea cup down as she stood up from her arm chair, then sat on the settee beside Emilio.

"It doesn't make sense. Where could she have gone?"

"Emilio, son." Maria grabbed his teacup and gently placed it on the table in front of them. "Your mother loved you very much. She was in a lot of pain. Pain I could not even—"

"No! Stop this right now!"

"Emilio, she truly did." Maria began to weep. "Emilio, she's no longer with us. A couple years ago, she passed away. The pain was too much; she was hurting, Emilio."

Maria wrapped her arms around Emilio as he sat still like a statue. "You can stay here as long as you like." Maria sniffled.

Emilio sank all the way back into the settee and stared at the ceiling. The cracks in the plaster became fuzzy, and he shut his eyes for a moment. When he opened them, tears began streaming down his face.

"What did I do to God?" he mumbled. "Surely, I must've done something."

Maria held him for ten minutes as he cried. He then lay on the settee and stared at the wall for four hours. Maria brought him water and even tried to feed him dinner, yet the steaming clam pasta became room temperature, never moving around his plate once.

*

After a week of lying in the guest bedroom, Emilio mustered up the courage to see Floria in the flesh. With Emilio's permission, Maria had invited her to afternoon tea at the Savoia house, informing her of Emilio's return on the phone.

As she stood in the doorway with her two sons hiding behind her legs, Floria's face appeared red and sweaty. She looked across the foyer to see Emilio holding onto the frame of the doorway that separated the dining room from the foyer with a smile on his face.

"Mrs Carswell. Never in a million years did I think that would be your name." Emilio grinned. "How have you been?"

Floria stuck out her hand for him to shake, but he swatted it away and hugged her. "Emilio, how have you been?" Floria said awkwardly as they embraced.

"You don't want to know. It will dampen the mood." He shook his head. "I'm staying alive. All I can do."

"Yes, please do." Floria grinned. "This is my youngest son, Donald." She turned her attention to Donald. "Donnie, say hello to Uncle Emilio. He's one of the best men you will ever get the chance to meet." She smiled.

"Uncle?" He bent down to greet the child. "I like the sound of that, Uncle. Nice to meet you, Master Donald." He shook the boy's hand, then patted his head.

"This is my oldest, Michael." Floria gently placed a hand on Michael's back and pushed him towards Emilio.

Emilio looked at the child and nearly fainted. He looked at what his father called 'the mark of the beast,' Aldo's mark and his stomach dropped.

"Hello, Uncle. I'm Michael. My friends call me Mikey, though." Michael rushed to Emilio and hugged him, yet Emilio froze.

"Do you like Mikey, or should I call you Michael?" Emilio choked as he embraced the boy.

"I like Mikey." Mikey smiled. "Are you my mother's brother? You are my uncle, right?"

Emilio laughed. "No, Mikey. We grew up together. We both come from the same place in Sicily. Would you ever like to go one day?"

"Depends. Do they have hamburgers in Sicily? Hamburgers are my favourite food."

"No, but we could make hamburgers in Sicily. Maybe we could make them famous there." Emilio smiled.

"No, if there's no hamburgers then I can't go. That's all I eat." Mikey shook his head, then grabbed Emilio's hand. "Come on, my mother said that grandma baked cookies for all of us!"

Emilio looked back at Floria, her eyes filled with tears, and nodded at her with a smirk.

Afternoon tea was rather awkward. The only sounds that filled the room were the clinking of spoons swirling milk into the tea and the boys chewing on the lemon taralli. Floria dared to ask Emilio about his time away, but he shut each conversation down, changing the subject each time. After tea, Maria took Michael and Donald out to the backyard while Floria dried the teaware.

"Are you ever going to tell me what happened?" said Floria as she placed the teapot upside down on a towel.

"Never."

"Emilio! You can't keep what happened inside. Please, when you're ready, I would love to talk about it." Floria shook her head. "You know that I will always be your friend despite everything that has happened."

"Are you happy?" Emilio blurted. "Truly happy?"

Floria dropped the saucer she was washing, and it broke in half in the sink. She wiped the tear from her eye, then turned to him. "Of course. This is my life now."

"Does it have to be?" Emilio took a step towards her. "We could leave all this behind. Take the boys and build that hotel."

"Emilio!"

"I know he's mine, Floria; I'm neither blind nor stupid."

"Emilio!" Floria cried. "You will never say those words to me again!" Floria violently tossed the teacup in her hands onto the counter, then stormed to the back door. "Boys, we need to leave. Say goodbye to Grandma, then Uncle Emilio. We mustn't be late for dinner; your father gets home from work in an hour."

"Floria, please, I'm sorry," Emilio whimpered.

The boys both hugged Emilio and then Floria led them out the front door. She started the engine in her black Ford Super Deluxe, then waved Emilio goodbye. As they drove away, Michael looked out the back window and grinned. Emilio watched his little face grow smaller, then his sobs echoed through the quietness of the street as their car disappeared. The weight of it all bore down on him, making his knees buckle.

He sank to the ground, clutching his chest as if he were trying to hold himself together. Floria's words cut deeper than expected, reminding him of the life he couldn't have. Michael's innocent grin played on repeat in his mind. Emilio knew he had asked too much of Floria, yet he wanted everything he asked for.

Sitting there, tears streaming, Emilio wondered what the point of it all was.

26

1946

Emilio picked up the tomatoes laid out on the table. Their soft skin caressed his hand, fighting the urge to squish one in his palm. The street smelled of the slight aroma of urine and flowers from the vendor a quarter block down the street, wafting in the wind. Emilio paid for three tomatoes and placed them in his bag, carefully placing them on top so they didn't get crushed. A boy rode by him on a bicycle, nearly running over his toes despite having plenty of room, yet Emilio just laughed. He thought for a split second that he would curse, yet he remembered his youth and the joys of misbehaving.

Walking down the busy street, Emilio felt a mixture of nostalgia and melancholy. The city had changed so much since before the war, and yet, in many ways, it remained the same. The familiar sounds of the vendors selling their goods, the chatter of people in animated conversations, and the car engines humming as they passed all brought back memories of simpler times.

He stopped at the diner that replaced Pete's; its interior was exactly the same, yet the only thing that changed was the sign out front. Martha's Diner still had Pete's menus displayed, but the walls were painted a light pink. Deciding to sit for a moment and collect his thoughts, he ordered a coffee and took a seat at one of the small booths.

As he sipped his coffee, his mind wandered back to Floria's words, the pain in her voice still echoing in his ears. It had been nearly a year, yet in his mind, it could have been yesterday. None of his letters were responded to, nor were his phone calls either.

Emilio looked out at the people passing by, each engrossed in their own lives and their own worlds. He wondered how many of them carried burdens like his, hidden beneath the surface of everyday routines. The war had left its mark on everyone in ways both visible and invisible. Emilio's own scars, though invisible to the average person, were ever-present.

As he finished his coffee, Emilio placed a few coins on the table and walked out. He couldn't bear to look down the alleyway; it still stung.

Emilio turned down the block and began making his way back to Maria's house. She wanted him to stay with her until he met a woman. His work at the steel plant, though painstaking, paid him enough to move out, but Maria refused to let that happen. Emilio sensed that she felt responsible for him like he was the son she never had with Giovanni.

"My God!"

Emilio turned around and dropped his bag, the tomatoes splattering as they rolled around.

"Emilio Bucci. How the hell have you been?" Thomas said, then opened his arms, motioning for Emilio to hug him.

"What are you doing here?" Emilio's face became ghostly white as he stood frozen. "I don't believe my eyes. Is that really you?"

Thomas couldn't wait any longer for Emilio to approach him, so he took the initiative and wrapped his arms around him. "You smell nice. I mean, better than your natural musk from chopping wood all day in the bush." Thomas grinned as he placed his head on Emilio's shoulder. "I missed you," he whispered into Emilio's ear.

"I missed you too," Emilio choked. "How have you been?"

"Can't really complain. My father sent me on a train to pick up shoes he had made last month. The man only likes these specific Oxfords he can only get at a shop on King Street. I've learned to not ask questions anymore; he just commands, and I do what he says. He has me staying at the Connaught; it's not too shabby."

"Those must be some shoes." Emilio smiled.

"Tell me about it. I'm also headed to dinner tonight with a few of my friends who live around here. Please be my plus one. They will all have their wives and girlfriends."

"I'll be there!" Emilio exclaimed.

"Well, you don't even know where it is," Thomas said, then laughed. "How about I pick you up at a quarter to six from your house? Then, I can come in for a drink before we leave, and maybe, if you're up to it, we can go back to my hotel."

Emilio blushed, then looked down. "Private Ramsey, that would be breaking the law."

"I never said anything was going to happen. Unless that is, you want it to." Thomas smirked.

Emilio laughed, then said, "I'm not afraid of prison anyway."

"Good boy." Thomas smirked. "Write down your address on this," he said as he handed Emilio a small piece of paper from his bag.

*

That evening, Thomas arrived in a charcoal suit with polished black Derby shoes. The light of the foyer reflected off of his shoes and hit Emilio in the eyes as he looked down. Maria turned the corner to greet Emilio's guest, catching Thomas off guard.

"And this must be the lovely Mrs Bucci," said Thomas as he handed Maria a bouquet of light pink carnations. "It's a pleasure to meet you, ma'am. My name is Mr Ramsey; I met your son back in school, but I moved away years ago," Thomas asserted, then winked at Emilio.

"No, Thomas, this is Mrs Savoia. She's a family friend," said Emilio, his eyes widening.

Maria stood in shock, unable to speak for a moment. She stared at Thomas in confusion, then turned to Emilio.

"Thomas, my mother actually passed away while I was gone." He dabbed his red eyes, then took a deep breath. "I'm sorry I didn't get a chance to tell you."

Thomas's face turned a dark scarlet, and his stomach was tied into a knot. "I'm so sorry, Emilio. I-I did-didn't know."

"Well, shall we have a drink?" said Emilio, cutting the tension in the foyer. "What can I make you?"

"Whisky is fine for me," Thomas mumbled. "Unless you have the ingredients to make a martini because, in that case, a martini."

"One martini, coming up!" Emilio led Thomas into the sitting room, instructing him to sit on the green settee. "Make yourself at home."

Maria took the flowers and put them in a crystal vase. She thanked Thomas for them, then retired upstairs.

"Emilio, I can't believe I did that."

"It's my fault, how would you have known?" Emilio assured. "She—she. Well, you see, she took her own life." Emilio began to cry then Thomas hugged him.

"I'm so sorry," whispered Thomas as he placed his martini down. "Life has been the most unkind to you."

"Very."

"We can stay in tonight. We don't have to go to this fancy dinner. I can pick us up some food, and we can go back to my hotel room, and nothing has to happen. I just want to hold you and talk."

"No, we must go. You look too handsome to just get undressed. What a waste that would be," said Emilio, smiling through his tears.

After the boys had their drink, Thomas peered around the corner, grabbed Emilio's neck, and kissed him. The green velvet brushed his suit jacket, leaving microparticles of green fabric on its surface.

"I've been waiting years to do that," said Thomas, then he bit his lip. "Better than I remember."

"You're a little rusty. Must not have had any practice since," Emilio said.

"Perhaps not."

They entered the restaurant, the exact French restaurant that Emilio had taken Floria to many years prior. The aroma of butter and garlic remained, and the elegant interior was exactly as Emilio had remembered it. Around a large round table, there were two soldiers in army dress and two women on either side of them. The soldier with the slicked chestnut hair, the younger one, caught Thomas's eye at the door and flagged him down.

"You look dapper, Ramsey. I almost didn't recognise you in a gentleman's suit," said the younger soldier.

"You can take the uniform off; Hitler is defeated," Thomas replied, then he grinned. "Emilio, I have known these men for years, friends of my father's. This is Private Davidson, but to me, he's Henry. Henry here was on the front lines in France," said Thomas as Davidson brushed him off humbly. "This is Captain Lawson. I would call him Captain Lawson if I were you; he doesn't take well to his first name. He was with Henry over there."

"Oh, nonsense! Call me Robert. Robert is just fine," he said, then smiled.

"That's the captain's wife, Mrs Lawson," Thomas said as she nodded at Emilio. "Everybody, this is Emilio. We went to school together when we were just boys. Today I was walking through the market, and I spotted him and thought it would be a good idea to have a reunion over some fine French cuisine."

Emilio shook each hand and took a seat beside Thomas.

"Now, Emilio. I don't believe I caught your full name," said Lawson as he placed a bread roll on his plate.

"Bucci, sir. Emilio Bucci."

"Italian. I love Italians, great people."

"Yes, sir." Emilio smiled.

"You don't have to call me sir. Like I said, Robert is my preference," he said. "Tommy boy, pass me the butter," he commanded. "So, Emilio, did you serve?"

"Well, you see—"

"He was stationed in England, working at a base. Although he's humble, Emilio has a brilliant mind. He was decoding top-secret German codes," Thomas interjected.

"Is that so?" said Robert. "Well, it's a pleasure to be in the presence of such a brilliant man. Thank you for all that you did."

Emilio swallowed the saliva in his throat, then looked up at Thomas nervously. Thomas winked as their eyes met. "Thank you, Robert. It was tough work, but I'm glad I did it. You boys fought one hell of a fight across the channel," said Emilio.

"That we did," added Henry. "I thank God every day that I'm still alive. Too many didn't come home with us."

The table sat in silence for a minute; the sound of scraping spoons on their soup bowls was the only noise.

"I think I'm going to have the filet mignon. I had it last time I was here with a few of my friends from Ottawa who were visiting, and it was superb. They finish it with a slice of garlic butter and some fresh rosemary," said Henry to break the silence.

"I'll do the same," Thomas added. "Emilio, anything sticking out to you? Dinner is on the captain." He laughed.

"That cheap bastard wouldn't dare to—sorry, ladies. I seem to have forgotten my manners." Henry shook his head in self-disgust.

"The duck breast sounds divine," Emilio replied. He noticed the duck breast was significantly cheaper than the filet, his sole reason for choosing it. He could still hear his father's voice telling him it was impolite to choose the most expensive item when being treated to dinner.

"Yes, it is true. I am treating." Robert smiled. "Please, order what you like."

"That's very kind of you, Robert," announced Emilio. "Thank you very much."

Robert nodded at Emilio then called a toast.

Amidst the lively chatter and easy laughter, Emilio felt a sense of belonging with his dinner companions. He thought about Andrea's question and finally had an answer. He didn't hate Canadians. These men in front of him were not to blame.

The men traded stories of their wartime experiences, exchanged jokes, and caught up on old times. Despite the seriousness of their stories, there was a lightheartedness to their conversation, as if they were not discussing the horrors of war.

After dinner, the table cleared out slowly as both Emilio and Thomas wished both Robert and Henry a good night. Thomas waited for Robert to exit the restaurant, then sighed deeply.

"I'm sorry for lying. I couldn't tell them the truth," explained Thomas. "I hope you're not upset with me."

"Upset? Imagine what they would have said if I had accidentally told the truth. Dinner would have been ruined. You saved me, Thomas."

"I did, didn't I?" Thomas smiled, then placed a hand on Emilio's knee under the tablecloth. "What do you say we skip going out for another drink? Let's get another bottle of wine at a shop and go back to the hotel."

"I'd love that," Emilio said. "Let's get out of here."

As they left the restaurant and returned to Thomas's hotel room, Emilio felt tension building between them. The wine they had had at dinner had already begun to stir something within him, igniting a feeling in his veins he couldn't describe entirely. He'd imagined that the feeling was similar to that of snorting cocaine; his blood flow maximised around his body.

Inside the dimly lit room, Thomas poured them each a glass of wine, his movements deliberate and sensual yet with an undertone of nervousness. He nearly dropped the wine bottle into Emilio's glass, surpassing a normal fill. The soft glow of the lamp cast a warm hue over Thomas's features, highlighting the desire that flickered in his eyes as he approached Emilio.

Their lips met as Thomas hovered over Emilio on the bed, the taste of wine lingering on their tongues as they explored each other with intense urgency. Emilio's hands roamed over Thomas's body, tracing the lines of his muscles beneath the fabric of his shirt while Thomas's fingers tangled in Emilio's hair, pulling him closer with every kiss.

With a breathless sigh, Thomas began to undress Emilio, his touch sending shivers down Emilio's spine as he revealed the smooth expanse of his skin. Emilio arched into his touch, a soft moan escaping his lips as Thomas's lips trailed down his neck and chest. Emilio slid his trousers off and threw them on the armchair across the room. Thomas smirked as they slipped off the chair and onto the floor.

Their bodies moved together, with Thomas lying over top of Emilio. With a gentle nod, Emilio gave Thomas permission to connect each of them by flesh, with Thomas kissing him as he did.

"I love you, Thomas."

Thomas bit Emilio's ear gently, then whispered, "Good boy." He then inhaled deeply and said, "I love you too."

*

As they lay exhausted and entwined in each other's arms, Emilio felt at peace for the first time in years. His body was one with Thomas's.

"I still have your photograph. I have it framed in my bedroom," Emilio blurted. "I never had the heart to put it in storage."

Thomas sat up and stared at the wall intently. He swigged the entire wine glass and then began to hyperventilate, with tears rolling down his eyes.

Confused, Emilio wrapped his naked legs around Thomas and kissed his neck. "What's the matter?" He brushed Thomas's hair with his fingers.

"I love this. I never want any of this to end."

"It never has to," assured Emilio. "I'm never going anywhere."

Thomas took a deep breath, and then more tears filled his eyes. "Emilio," he whimpered.

"Yes, my love." Emilio squeezed Thomas's hand.

"I need to tell you something, but before I do, you have to promise me you will never leave me," Thomas sighed. "Please, promise me."

"I promise."

"My father is making me get married," Thomas whispered, tears continuing down his red cheeks. "I have only met the woman twice."

Emilio pushed Thomas off of him and then jumped out of bed. "What?"

"Emilio, I don't want this. I'm not like other men. I have never been like other men. When I look at a woman, no matter how beautiful she may be, I feel nothing down there. I feel nothing in my chest either."

"Thomas!"

"The wedding is next month. Help me escape this nightmare. I can't go through with it!"

"Thomas!" Emilio shouted, tears running down his face. "How could you be married and continue this with me?"

"Please, I beg of you. She doesn't know me. My father has been my puppet master my entire life. I can't go through with this."

Emilio shook his head, then put his trousers over his naked body. "You have to tell her that. Thomas, did you just commit adultery with me?"

"Oh, spare me the religious doctrine bullshit, Emilio. We both committed a far worse sin just five minutes ago! Please, you must help me get out of this union. It is a complete mistake to marry her, Ms Baxter." Thomas tossed the pillows off the bed. "Emilio, please don't leave; stay with me."

Emilio shook his head; his face was completely white. "I don't know what to feel, Thomas."

"Emilio, wait!"

"Goodbye, Thomas." Emilio shut the door to the hotel room behind him.

Thomas emerged fully nude, shouting Emilio's name down the long corridor, yet it was too late. By the time he reached the door, Emilio had made his way to the stairwell.

27

The dimly lit guest bedroom sat empty as Emilio had packed his belongings. The only thing in the room was a striped mattress and a desk with a flickering lamp. Floria had declined to see Emilio off despite Maria's many pleas over the telephone.

Emilio stood in the doorway, glancing around the room one last time. It felt surreal, leaving the place he had called home for so many years, especially under such strained circumstances. He sighed, the flickering lamp casting shadows across the walls. He wondered if he had made the right choice and if leaving was truly the best option for him. He tried one last time to convince himself to stay, yet his reasons were nonexistent. The thought of Floria, stubborn and unyielding, refusing to say goodbye was deplorable in his eyes. He thought about the sliver of hope that maybe, just maybe, she would change her mind and that she'd join him with their son.

The sound of footsteps in the hallway broke his daydreaming. Maria appeared, her face a mixture of concern and sadness. "Emilio, are you sure about this?" she asked softly, her eyes searching for any hint of hesitation.

He nodded, forcing a smile. "I have to, Maria. Staying here is just too much for me. You have Floria, but now I have nothing."

Maria bit her lip, nodding slowly. "I wish things were different. I wish she would talk to you."

Emilio shrugged, trying to appear indifferent. "Floria has made her choice."

"Emilio, she has a husband now. She made her choice long before you returned." Maria reached into her pocket and pulled out a small, tarnished key. "Before you go, there's something I want you to have," she said, placing the key in Emilio's hand. "It's the key to the olive grove."

Emilio stared at the key, memories flooding back of his life long before they sailed here, running through the olive trees, the sun warm on their faces. "The olive grove," he murmured, turning the key over in his hand. "It can't still be empty after all of these years."

Maria nodded, her eyes red. "Nobody moves to Sicily, Emilio. They move away. But maybe you can change that. Maybe you can find what you're looking for there."

He looked at her and shook his head in disbelief. "Thank you, Maria. For everything."

She smiled, though her face appeared defeated. "Take care of yourself. And write to me. Let me know how you're doing."

"I will," he promised, pulling her into a tight embrace. "Take care of yourself too."

With a final glance around the room, Emilio picked up his suitcase and walked out, the door closing behind him with a soft click.

As Emilio stepped into the cool evening air, he took a deep breath, trying to steady his racing heart. The street was quiet; the only sound was the distant hum of traffic. He started walking, each step taking him further from the house that held so many memories, both good and bad. His mind wandered back to the days when he and Floria were inseparable. He couldn't shake the feeling that he had been robbed and taken for everything he had in the secular world.

He thought of his mother and father, thinking they would be heartbroken to see him undo all that they had done. His stomach was tied into a knot as he pondered what it had all been for. An alternate future played in his head like a film roll, one where nobody had to die, one where they never left the island of love and sunshine. Emilio shook his head, trying to dispel the melancholy thoughts.

*

Several blocks away, he reached the train station, its grand facade lit up against the evening sky. He entered, the sounds of travellers and the faint scent of coffee greeting him. Emilio purchased his ticket and found a bench, setting his suitcase down beside him.

"There were four, now just one," he mumbled to himself.

As he waited for his train, he couldn't help but replay Thomas's declaration on repeat; the scene he felt was worse each time it played. He glanced at the people around him—families saying goodbye, friends chatting excitedly about their trips. He envied their companionship and their sense of belonging. He never belonged in this land, not once.

The train arrived, and Emilio boarded, finding an empty seat by the window. As the train pulled out of the station, he watched the city lights blur into streaks of colour. He leaned back, closing his eyes, the sound of the tracks putting him into a deep sleep. The journey was long, the train winding through the countryside, passing through towns and cities, each stop bringing him closer to his destination. Emilio spent the time reflecting on his life in Canada, on the choices he had made, and on the uncertainty of what was to come.

Crossing the Atlantic brought back memories he wished he'd forgotten. While he had avoided the below decks of third class, the ship was anything but glamorous. The ship had been used during the war to transport the injured, with the grey paint still covering the exterior and the hallways still carrying the energies of the souls departed in each room.

A while later, Emilio found himself on a ferry crossing the Mediterranean. The sea was calm, and the sky was a brilliant blue. He stood on the deck, the wind ruffling his hair, and watched as the silhouette of Sicily came into view. The island was bathed in golden light, and its rolling hills and rugged coastline were a stark contrast to the urban landscape of Hamilton he had left behind.

As the ferry docked, Emilio felt a surge of life re-enter his body, a feeling he was nearly foreign to. He disembarked, and the cobblestone streets of Palermo were alive. He found a small inn and checked in, eager to rest before making the journey home.

*

Emilio walked into the grove and tossed his bags on the overgrown patio. The trees had been consumed by nature, some of which had died and fallen into piles of sticks. The windows, still boarded, appeared more decrepit than the grove, with the boards appearing to be holding the windows in place. He feared that if he removed them, the panes would come with them. The house was rummaged, its walls still black from the fire. Emilio walked through the charred rooms, memories flooding back. He could almost hear the laughter of his childhood, the voices of Giovanni and Maria, and the rustle of olive branches in the breeze.

He went outside and sat under an ancient olive tree, the branches providing shade from the midday sun. Emilio closed his eyes. The gentle rustle of the leaves and the distant hum of bees created a soothing symphony. He felt a connection to this place that he hadn't felt in years.

*

As the days turned into weeks, Emilio settled into a new routine. He cut down the dead olive trees, worked on repairing the house, and slowly, the estate began to come back to life. He made new friends in the town as everyone he knew was either dead or had emigrated, the locals welcoming him with open arms. They shared stories, meals, and laughter, and Emilio felt a sense of belonging that he hadn't felt in a long time.

One evening, as he sat on the porch, watching the sunset in hues of orange and pink, he thought of Maria. He pulled out a piece of paper and began to write, describing the beauty of his home, the kindness of Agrigento, and the peace he had found. He ended the letter with a request for her to visit soon, yet he knew she had no desire to step foot on the island again.

Emilio sealed the letter and walked to the post office. As he handed it to the postmaster, a hand tapped his back.

"I thought I recognised you, Mr Bucci," said the voice. "You look like your father back when we enlisted."

Emilio turned around quickly. "Fabrizio?"

"I thought I would never see the day. How have you been?" Fabrizio pinched Emilio's cheeks.

"I'm as well as I can be." Emilio took a deep breath. "I moved back. I'm home again."

"That's splendid news! Where are you living? Your old house was burned down by a few mischievous boys. Such a shame."

"I heard. When I arrived, I saw the town had knocked down the walls. All that was left was that cellar out back." Emilio smiled. "Better that way, I suppose. I'm living at the old Savioa estate. Maria gifted me the keys."

"Gifted? Why on earth would she gift you an entire house?" Fabrizio grabbed onto the counter to support his ageing spine.

"She will never return." Emilio placed his hand on Fabrizio's shoulder. "I have big plans, you will see. Agrigento is going to get its first luxury hotel. One that even Americans will come to see."

Fabrizio laughed, then adjusted his cap. "You missed it; there were plenty of Americans in Sicily not too long ago."

"Not those types of Americans, tourists," said Emilio, then he smirked. "Ones that pay too."

"A real shame about Mr Savoia; Giovanni was a good man."

"What do you mean?"

"You didn't hear?"

"Hear what?" asked Emilio as he scanned Fabrizio's face. "He ran away from his family. Not a good man, in my opinion."

"No, Emilio, that is not true," Fabrizio said. "He was a socialist; many didn't know. He was working for a group there and was taken into custody. In his prison cell, another inmate stabbed him."

"How do you know this?" Emilio cried. "That can't be; he was a businessman. Giovanni Savoia was not a socialist."

"He was, Emilio. One of my cousins in Milan after the war had told me about a man who was arrested there who came from Agrigento and asked if I knew him. Whether or not he was involved, it doesn't matter. He didn't abandon his family, though," Fabrizio explained.

"I must write to Maria and Floria."

"No!" cried Fabrizio. "They put their worries to rest long ago; the truth won't bring him back. Why cause them more pain?"

"More pain? Do they not deserve the truth?" scolded Emilio.

"One day, you will understand, Emilio."

Emilio shook his head, then looked at the floor. "I don't know about that."

"Is your family joining you, or are they staying in Canada?" said Fabrizio as Emilio's joyful complexion vanished.

"Fabrizio." Emilio swallowed the saliva in his throat. "The war took them all."

"My God!" Fabrizio's knees buckled, and then Emilio caught him. "You-You mean, you mean to say that your father, mother, and brother are all gone?"

Emilio fought his tears. "Yes."

Fabrizio wrapped his arms around Emilio and then kissed his forehead. "You haven't lost everyone. I made a vow to your father at the Piave and he did to me. Should anything happen to either of us up there, the other would be the man of the other's household. I understand you are now a man yourself, but Emilio, you are and always will be family."

Emilio sobbed as he buried his head into Fabrizio's shoulder. "Thank you. You don't know how much that means."

Fabrizio patted Emilio on the back and invited him over for dinner.

*

The day after, Emilio sat in the sun, basking in the heat of Agrigento. The breeze wafted over him, carrying the faint scent of the sea up the hillside and into his nostrils. He had spent the day clearing debris from the yard and cleaning up the brush, and the stone property walls were once again visible from the house.

A sparrow swooped over his head, nearly colliding with him. Emilio watched the bird dart away, its energetic movements, unlike his own stiffness. He leaned back against the ancient stone wall, its rough surface warm from the sun, and closed his eyes, allowing himself a moment of rest. The rustling of leaves from distant fields and the distant hum of insects were just as he remembered.

Memories of his childhood flooded back—the days spent running through these very fields, the laughter of Floria, the simple joys of life on the island. It was hard to believe that so many years had passed and that so much had changed.

As the first stars began to appear in the twilight sky, Emilio felt alone. The night air grew cooler, and Emilio stood, stretching his tired muscles. He looked out over the landscape, the fields stretching out under the darkening sky, their contours gentle and familiar. He took a deep breath, then yawned.

Emilio lit a candle in the dining room and took out a piece of paper. In his mind, Fabrizio's foolishness was caused by his ageing brain. He drafted his letter for Maria, his hands shaking as the pen glided across the page, unravelling years of lies. He thought back to his father and knew that protecting Giovanni's name was not only his duty but an honour. Even in death, Giovanni deserved his name back. Death did not change such a notion.

Emilio then sealed each letter with the melted candle wax in front of him and pressed the wax with his thumbprint. He placed the letters by the back door, then returned to the kitchen and snuffed the flame. The entire room went pitch black.

28

Everyone marvelled at the sight of a car in the countryside. While few people had cars, most of them were American tourists, ones with money. The tyres tracked along the gravel roads, popping small rocks out behind them as the small Fiat Topolino carried on. Its polished pastel blue paint reflected the Agrigento sun, blinding those who stared too long.

Although petite, the roaring engine cut through the silence of the countryside. The car's arrival was an event in itself, drawing the attention of local farmers and children alike. They paused in their daily routines, shading their eyes with calloused hands, to catch a glimpse of the sleek machine as it whizzed by.

Dust clouds formed in its wake, settling slowly back onto the road and fields, marking its passage. The car seemed almost out of place amidst the rustic beauty of the landscape, a touch of modernity against the backdrop of ancient trees and weathered homes. The aroma of wildflowers and freshly turned earth mingled with the faint scent of gasoline, creating an unusual blend that lingered in the air long after the car had disappeared from sight.

In the distance, the sound of the Fiat's engine could be heard fading away, leaving behind stillness. The subtle yet undeniable shift in the pace of life since the war was on display for all to see.

Emilio had been in the yard with Fabrizio, explaining his grand plans for the property. He stood beside Fabrizio, drawing different shapes with his fingers of where he intended to put a swimming pool, painting a picture of its expansive turquoise waters—the biggest pool in all of Sicily. Fabrizio just nodded, amazed by his visions.

The car pulled down the road and came to a squeaking halt in front of the house. As the door popped open, Emilio began to approach, with Fabrizio behind him.

Thomas stepped out of the car and placed a large briefcase on the ground beside him. He wiped his sweat on his navy wool jacket, then shut the door behind himself. "It appears I have found the right place, Mr Bucci."

Emilio nearly fainted, his knees buckling as Thomas rushed towards him.

"Emilio," said Fabrizio. "I didn't know you had been expecting a guest."

Emilio shook Thomas's hand, both their palms sweaty. "This is Mr Ramsey. He is a friend from Canada."

"A pleasure," said Fabrizio as he extended his hand to Thomas. "I'm Fabrizio. I apologise if my English is hard to understand. It has been a long time."

"Please, sir, call me Thomas. Mr Ramsey is so daft." Thomas smirked. "Your English is flawless, sir."

"How did you—what did—" said Emilio, his face a deep red.

"Well, you see, I had spoken with Maria about your whereabouts when I returned to her house after the last time we had that meeting with our clients at that French restaurant, and she informed me of your new venture out here. I thought to myself that it would be impossible for one of your greatest business partners to not get in on the action out here. Of course, we can talk numbers later, but I would love to get involved in this project." Thomas's eyes sparkled as he grinned at Emilio. "That is, if you would be willing to take me on as a partner?"

"He needs all the help he can get, Thomas. You seem like a good man to have around when there's something that needs doing," said Fabrizio, then he smiled. "Come on Emilio, take the help. You can't build this hotel of yours by yourself. I'm only getting older. Soon, I will be the town's old man, smoking my cigarettes and drinking under a tree. I won't be able to help you for long."

"You are a long way away," Emilio said, then smirked. "Shall we grab a drink inside, gentlemen?"

Thomas and Fabrizio nodded, then trailed Emilio into the house. After a few hours of drinking, laughing, and telling stories, Fabrizio excused himself. On the way out, he shook Thomas's hand once again and informed him how happy he was that Emilio finally had some company.

As the door shut behind him, Thomas walked to the kitchen and sat down at the table, shooting back the wine in his glass. Emilio reluctantly paced behind him and shut the blinds.

"I can explain." Thomas took a deep breath in and out.

"You just show up here after months of nothing? Thomas, what is going on?"

"Emilio."

"Thomas, you can't just show up unannounced; it's very rude and quite frankly—"

"Emilio."

"To my house? Across the other side of the world? This is insane, Thomas!"

"Emilio!" Thomas shouted, then took another deep breath. "I never went through with it. I didn't marry her. It never happened."

"Oh, Thomas, how foolish!"

"I will never marry a woman; it's not for me. I had never even kissed her, and yet I was going to spend the rest of my life locked in a prison cell to keep my father satisfied, a man who never once loved me." Thomas began to cry. "It was never going to happen. The wife, the kids, the house in the suburbs, never!"

Emilio took a seat beside Thomas and grabbed his hand. "You came all this way for me?"

"I made a promise, didn't I?" Thomas smiled through the tears on his face. "I never meant to hurt you, but hurt you, I did. You deserved the truth that night, and yet I thought maybe, just maybe, I would have been able to convince you then to run away with me before it all happened, that I would never have to tell you about the wedding or the intricate life my father had laid at my feet. I wanted none of it. I only wanted you. I love you."

Emilio sat in silence for a moment of self-reflection. "How will this work? We aren't safe anywhere, Thomas. There's no place on this planet that will let us be who we are. We could be arrested almost everywhere, or worse, killed. I want this to work; I really do, but it's not safe."

"I'd rather live an unsafe life with you than live unsafely in my own mind," said Thomas as he squeezed Emilio's hand.

"Unsafely in your mind?"

"Living in a nonstop string of lies. Living with a woman while secretly wishing that I was dead. The thought of having some woman lay beside me for eternity was enough to have me fantasising about placing my father's revolver in my mouth and pulling the trigger. At least then, it would be over quickly."

"Thomas! Emilio shrieked. "Don't you ever say that in front of me again. How could you say such a thing?" Emilio's eyes began to welt.

"It's the truth. I was almost there."

"Stop!"

"Emilio, a life where I must pretend to be your business partner in public, but your lover in private is far better than being her façade of a lover in public but detesting her in my own home."

Emilio rested his head on Thomas's shoulder. "I love you," he murmured.

"When I said that one day I would give you my entire heart, I meant it. No woman could ever get that from me because that person is you, Emilio."

"Thomas, what about your father?" asked Emilio as he played with Thomas's hair. "How did he react to you cancelling your wedding?"

"I've been a disappointment to him my entire life. This was no different. Even when I told him I was going to Italy and I wasn't sure if I was ever returning, he patted me on the back and said, 'I failed you.' I think he knows about me in terms of me being a homosexual, yet he could never muster the courage to call it what it is."

"I'm sure he will come around." Emilio kissed Thomas's cheek. "And if he doesn't, then you will always have me."

"Will I?"

"Always," asserted Emilio. "Besides, I could get used to you being around here."

"You won't grow tired of me?" Thomas grinned, then took a sip from his wine glass.

"Married couples who grow old together always get tired of each other. That's the beauty of being married," Emilio said, then poured another glass for each of them from the wine bottle.

"Married? How would we ever get married? It will never be allowed in the eyes of the law."

"The law?" Emilio smiled. "We aren't particular subscribers to such notions anyway."

"Good boy." Thomas began to laugh, inciting Emilio as well.

The two of them sat for another hour and began to plan the future. For the first time in his life, Emilio felt as if he had one at all. They discussed the hotel; Emilio even talked of building an addition to the manor, yet Thomas could only see the cost. The wine bottle emptied, and the stars above shone brightly, the light penetrating the manor's darkest rooms. Emilio and Thomas, filled with purpose, vowed at that table a life of unity. Their future was no longer a distant concept but a vibrant, living plan that they would bring to life together. As they finally retired for the night, the manor seemed to hold a promise, whispering of the many days yet to come.

*

The next morning, a letter arrived from Maria. Thomas had yet to awaken, but Emilio sat in the dining room, sipping on his morning coffee. He grabbed a fruit knife and dug it into the envelope.

Dear Emilio,
I hope all is well in Agrigento. I miss you dearly. The contents of your last letter did not surprise me; however, I intend to keep Floria unaware of such matters. The news had reached me long before your letter, but I will never disclose that to Floria. You may think me cruel, but knowing the truth would do her more harm than good. I hope you understand why I fled so urgently many years ago. These matters were never discussed, not even with your mother, and I wish to leave them in Sicily.
My late husband was involved with groups I did not agree with, yet the end he met was unjust. I know this truth would only tear Floria apart. The glimmer of hope in her heart that he is still alive is better than her knowing the truth.
I hope one day she visits you, and if she does, I ask you not to disclose your findings.

Love,
Maria

Emilio closed the letter and then stuck the edge into the flame of a candle on the table. The ash and black smoke drifted away, leaving only their scent behind.

29

2005

The Savoia Hotel took nearly twenty years to finish. Emilio and Thomas oversaw each detail, down to the photographs on each wall. In the lobby, a photograph of Emilio and Thomas as young men hung above the mantle of the fireplace. The lobby itself was a blend of modern luxury and Sicilian charm. Marble floors twinkled under crystal chandeliers, while traditional ceramics added a splash of colour. Outside the doors were elegant seating areas that invited guests to relax, surrounded by potted lemon trees and fragrant lavender that filled the air with a subtle, sweet aroma.

As one moved through the hotel, the attention to detail was evident everywhere. The walls were filled with photographs capturing the beauty of Sicily and its people—vineyards, ancient ruins, bustling markets, and serene beaches.

The hotel's centrepiece was its expansive garden, where olive trees once stood. Now, a carefully manicured landscape stretched out, featuring a variety of Mediterranean flowers. Pathways meandered through the garden, leading to secluded benches and small, shaded groves where guests could escape the sun and enjoy a moment of peace.

At the heart of this garden lay the hotel's jewel—a massive pool, bigger than Emilio had once imagined. The Savoia Hotel quickly gained a reputation for luxury and became a destination for tourists from around the world.

Guests came from as far as America, Japan, and Australia, seeking a slice of paradise.

In the mornings, you could hear a blend of languages—Italian, English, French, German, and Japanese—as guests gathered in the breakfast hall. The hall itself was a marvel, with large windows that offered stunning views of the countryside and the Mediterranean Sea beyond. It had been a part of the addition that Emilio had made decades ago. Breakfasts were a feast featuring fresh local produce—juicy oranges, figs, and grapes—along with breads, cheeses, and cured meats.

Thomas lived on the property until about two years ago, when he died of colon cancer. His passing left a profound void, yet his spirit seemed to linger in every corner of the Savoia Hotel. Emilio, though heartbroken, found comfort in the legacy they had built together. The hotel continued to thrive, a tribute to their love and dedication for one another. Guests, unaware of the personal history behind the property, often remarked on the unique warmth and welcoming atmosphere that seemed to emanate from its very walls. Emilio, now the sole steward of their dream, poured his heart into every aspect of the hotel, ensuring that every guest experienced the magic of Sicily just as he and Thomas had envisioned.

His age began to wear on Emilio, yet his spirit remained in its twenties. As his father had instructed, he kept his imagination well nourished, and his youthfulness never faded. His tired knees struggled to walk the property like he did as a boy, yet he still worked as much as his body allowed.

One afternoon, Emilio had been in the lobby while a family from California had been staring at the photograph of him and Thomas.

"Who are those men, Mommy?" said the girl, her face no older than five.

"They started this hotel," said the mother, and then she smiled. "The plaque says that below."

"Are they friends?" replied the girl.

"The best of friends," Emilio chimed in. "That's me and my best friend, Mr Ramsey. He and I were business partners and built this very hotel."

"That's not you; that man has hair!"

"Abigail!" shouted the mother, then she turned to Emilio. "I'm terribly sorry, sir. We are still teaching her manners; she means nothing by it." Her face was red as she grabbed her daughter's hand.

Emilio smiled. "I did, yes. I used to be a good-looking man, I would say."

"Where's the other guy?" asked Abigail intently.

"Well, you see—"

"I am so sorry. She doesn't know when to stop," said the mother, her tone radiating her embarrassment.

"No, it's quite alright. I hung that photograph up because I like to talk about these sorts of things," Emilio said calmly.

"Well, is he here?" said Abigail.

"Oh, he is here. He is always around," replied Emilio, then he smirked.

"Who is that guy?" Abigail pointed to another frame.

"My brother, Raffaele. He is here sometimes."

"Why only sometimes?" Abigail said.

Emilio laughed. "I wish I knew the answer to that," he said.

"We must be on our way. Please say goodbye to the man."

Abigail cracked a smile, then waved Emilio goodbye.

Emilio grabbed his cane and made his way to the front desk. As he approached, Daniele, the man who worked the afternoon shift checking in guests, pulled Emilio aside.

"Mr Bucci, good afternoon."

"Good afternoon, Daniele. I hope it hasn't been too busy for you." Emilio smiled.

"Very steady, sir, but manageable. Mr Bucci, there were two missed calls from Dr Tabone. He wanted you to call him back. He claimed he called your cell phone twice and your line at the house, yet he never got a response."

"I haven't charged my cell phone in weeks. Useless thing it is," said Emilio. "I will call him tonight; thank you, Daniele."

"My pleasure, sir."

*

After his afternoon nap, Emilio ordered room service to his bedroom, like he had done for the past ten years. In his old age, cooking became a task he couldn't do anymore. His favourite meal was the Mikey Burger, one of his many creations and a hit with the guests.

On the phone, Dr Tabone's tone was serious. He had instructed Emilio to come to his office in the morning, refusing to discuss any further details. He had been feeling increasingly fatigued lately, and the lingering pain in his chest had not subsided. Though he felt not an ounce of fear.

Savouring each bite of the hamburger, Emilio tried to focus on the present. The taste brought back memories of Thomas, who had always enjoyed their late-night kitchen experiments. After finishing his meal, Emilio took a deep breath and resolved to face whatever news awaited him with the same strength that had carried him through so much of his life. As he looked out at the setting sun, he whispered a silent prayer and drifted into a deep sleep.

Dr Tabone clicked his pen nervously and made notes on Emilio's charts in his hands. He shut the door behind him, then sat on the chair beside Emilio.

"Mr Bucci, you have high cholesterol, your diabetes is unmanaged, and your iron levels are low."

"I'm old, Doctor." Emilio grinned.

"Mr Bucci, you know that is not why I called you in. Sir, there's an issue with your lungs."

"Six months? Seven? Two?" Emilio laughed. "How many more months before I get to see my family?"

"Mr Bucci! This is no laughing matter. After you complained to me of chest pains on your last visit, I was very concerned. Your previous scan showed abnormalities in your lungs."

"Okay."

"Sir, this is serious; we must act fast. You need to consider all the options we present to you. There—"

"How far along?"

"Mr Bucci. We have not diagnosed anything yet. You need to get a biopsy done to confirm anything."

"No need."

"Mr Bucci. You will be having a biopsy done to confirm your diagnosis. Your appointment is in two weeks. You will need to be there," Dr Tabone asserted.

"Don't waste your time or fancy electrical equipment on an old man like me. I have lived my life now; let me end it in peace." Emilio smiled, then stood up from the bed.

"Mr Bucci, I cannot let you skip your biopsy."

"Thank you for your time, Dr Tabone." Emilio opened the door and shut it behind him.

The door cracked open, and Dr Tabone poked his head into the corridor. "Sir, please, you must go."

Emilio shook his hand then closed the door to the doctor's office, stepped onto the sidewalk, and smiled. With each breath, Emilio felt a sense of peace settle within him, a quiet acceptance even. He turned his face towards the sky, the warmth of the sun kissing his weathered skin.

30

2006

As the echo of the knock reverberated through the foyer of the Carswell Manor, James darted towards the door, but the mysterious visitor had vanished, leaving behind only a solitary parcel resting on the stone steps.

James retrieved the parcel, its weight substantial in his hands, and carried it to where his father and grandmother, Floria, were nestled over a table set with delicate china and steaming pots of tea. Setting it down with care, James looked at his father.

"What is it, dear?" asked Floria as James sat beside her.

"A parcel from a hotel was sent by a Mr Emilio Bucci. The Savoia Hotel. Grandma, isn't that your maiden name?" asked James curiously.

At the mention of the Savoia Hotel, Floria's composure faltered. "The Savoia Hotel?" Floria choked. "What would they be sending us?"

Michael held onto the parcel, then reached into his pockets for his car keys to slice the packing tape.

"Daddy, Marcus spit on me again!"

"Marcus!" called James. "Leave Charlotte alone!"

"Sorry, Daddy!" yelled Marcus from the kitchen.

"Well, what is it?" barked Floria, then she placed a scone on her plate.

"A set of keys and a letter," said Michael, his voice muddled. Michael began to read out loud as he handed the keys to James. "Dear Mikey, I am unsure of how to begin such a letter, but by the time you read this, I will have gone to see the rest of our family. In this box are the keys to a place very special to you; you just don't know it yet. The home that your mother grew up in—the one where I first met her many years ago—became a place where I built an empire, now your empire. I spent years of my life building a place for you and your children and your children's children to call home, even if you cannot live here all the time with your life rooted in Canada."

Floria screamed, then clutched her chest. "That is nothing but lies, all of it!"

Michael shook his head, then continued on, "The keys to the hotel are now yours. I understand that such a business may be impossible for you to manage, but fear not, as I have the best staff already in control of everything. All I ask of you is to show your handsome face every once in a while. Love, Dad."

"Nonsense!" Floria cried.

Michael took a deep breath, then stared at his mother. "Nonna Maria told me a long time ago before she died. It turns out her mind forgot our names, yet never her secrets. Besides, how would he have known that I lived here if I had no contact with him?"

"Grandma, I already knew as well," said James with a smirk.

Floria gasped, then fainted, knocking her teacup to the ground. It shattered, and tea and porcelain splashed over the entire room.

About the Author

Giustino Andrea Scibetta-Lawson comes from Burlington, Ontario, a suburban city in the Toronto area. He is deeply invested in the worlds of political science and history, which he is currently studying.

His first novel, *The Stronger Brother*, made quite a strong debut when it was featured in Kirkus Magazine's October 2023 edition in New York City. Now, he is diving into his second novel, *Petawawa*.

When he is not crafting stories, Giustino loves to travel and uncover the richness of various cultures and histories. It is these adventures that fuel his imagination and inspire his future work. His many trips to his grandfather's home town, Racalmuto, inspired *Petawawa*.

www.gascibetta.com

About the Author

Giustino Andrea Schietta-Lawson comes from Burlington, Ontario, a suburban city in the Toronto area. He is deeply invested in the worlds of political science and history, which he is currently studying.

His first novel, The Scroungers Brothers, made quite a strong debut when it was featured in Kirkus Magazine's October 2023 edition in New York City. Now, he is diving into his second novel Penumbra.

When he is not creating stories, Giustino loves to travel and uncover the richness of various cultures and histories. It is these adventures that fuel his imagination and inspire his future work. His many trips to his grandfather's home town Racalmuto inspired Penumbra.

www.gschietta.com